STONE'S HOMEFRONT

Book Two of Agent Morgan Stone

Adrian J. Smith

Supposed Crimes LLC • Matthews, North Carolina

Published in the United States.

ISBN: 978-1-952150-31-9

www.supposedcrimes.com

This book is typeset in Goudy Old Style.

STONE'S HOMEFRONT

CHAPTER ONE

THE ICE cold can of Bud slammed onto the plastic table with a resounding echo. The garage door was open, the chill air coming inside as Ian went to grab another can. He dolled them out to the guys joining him that night, finally slumping down onto the cooler as he popped the tab on his own can and chugged half of it in two large swallows.

The old radio played in the corner on one of the local stations, but they barely paid attention to it at all. Ian hunched his shoulders, the cold cement under his shoes a reminder of the nasty world they lived in. He couldn't even make his rent payment that month since all the jobs had been taken up by people who didn't even belong in his country. Ian clenched his teeth together at just the thought of them.

Listening in on the conversation, he finished his beer and went to grab another one. Within minutes, he had half that one drank as well. He let out a slow breath, his lips buzzing together until he sat back on the cooler he'd claimed as his and stared up at his buddies. They didn't know anything that wasn't good for them. Snorting, he finished his fourth beer of the night and got up to the fridge Tim kept out there and grabbed another. They would easily go through three cases between the five of them.

Once a month they did this, sometimes in the in between, but this was their time to shoot the shit and get down to business. Ian popped the top on the beer and leaned against the fridge. "You see those filthy dogs moving in the other day?"

"Where at?" Tim asked, his chin jerking up in curiosity. His scruffy barely-there red beard always made Ian laugh. He tried so hard, but he in no way was he man enough to grow an actual beard.

Ian skimmed his gaze to the other three sitting around the garage. "Over by my place, you know, where they all end up."

Tim snorted. "Great, more of them to take our jobs."

Ian couldn't agree more with him. He'd been out of work for months and couldn't find a job anywhere because there were none. Unemployment only went so far, but he wasn't about to rely on the government for anything. They couldn't even keep them in their own damn country, just let them waltz right into the greatest country in the world so they could ruin it.

Scoffing in disgust, Ian chugged some of his beer to distract himself. The city he'd grown up in was ruined, no doubt of it. Nothing about it rang true to what it had been when he'd grown up. The streets had changed, getting darker by the years.

"We need to get some new people in the government who will make some actual changes," Ray grumbled from the back corner of the garage, a smoke between his fingers.

Ian rolled his eyes. "That isn't going to help."

"What do you mean?" Ray took a sip from his beer.

Ian's head spun from the alcohol already running through his system, but he wasn't going to let up any time soon. Sobriety be damned. He needed and deserved to let loose with his buds. "We've had people up there, in the big house, in the courts—whatever. They don't do anything."

Ray's eyes widened, but he did nod his agreement. Ian closed his eyes on a huff. Ray was always the weak link in their little group. He'd talk to them one way, then go back home and talk to his wife, and come back to them like a little puss. Ray crossed one ankle over his knee as he sat at the singular card table in the center of the garage, the one they put up and took down every time they got together so as not to tick off the missus.

"I think it's time we do something about it," Ian muttered.

Ray and Pat turned on him with wide eyes. Ian shrugged. Maybe they weren't as ready for that conversation as he thought they were. Their monthly meetings were far too low key for Ian's taste.

One more beer down, and Ian was ready to go. If they weren't ready yet, he'd have to get them ready. Smashing the can into the floor, he threw it into the trashcan and grabbed another one from the fridge.

"We got to do something about this."

"About what?" Pat asked, his eyes wide.

Ian scrunched his nose and then shook his head with a scoff. "These leeches are taking over. If we don't do something about it, there won't be anything left for us. We deserve jobs. I shouldn't have to fight for a job with some leach who doesn't even belong here. They need to go back where they came from."

All of them nodded their heads in response. Ian swallowed a good swig of his beer. Belching, he snorted again.

"So what are we gonna do?"

"What more can we do?" Ray stated. "We already tell them to go home. We are working to get the government to send them back by reporting them. What else can we do?"

Ian gave Ray a hard stare. Then each one of them there. What he was about to say wasn't something they hadn't heard before, but they'd never taken that final step. Popping his lower lip from his mouth, Ian grunted. "There's more we can do."

"Like what?" Ray asked.

Ray. So innocent. Ian had questioned his loyalty to their cause more than once, but the others had let him stay, who knew for what reason, it all seemed a waste of space for him. If Ray wasn't truly committed then there was no reason he should be there. He would only be a hindrance.

"We could do something big," Tim nearly whispered.

Ian cocked his head to the side as he gave Tim a long and studious look. At least one of them was on the same page as he was. "If they don't have any place to live, then they won't be living here, will they?"

Ray's eyes widened. Tim nodded enthusiastically, slapping his hand on his thigh. "That's it!"

Ian smirked. He and Tim had talked on and off about doing something big to scare them off, to reclaim their land and take it back. It wouldn't be that hard to do, really. He'd even started to look some of it up.

"We can get the stuff."

"Get what stuff?" Spencer asked.

"The stuff we need," Ian answered, trying to keep his answers vague. He still wasn't sure he could trust Ray at all, so he didn't want to give away all of his plans. "I've already got some of it."

Ray wisely kept his trap shut for the next while, his gaze bouncing from one to the other as they finally got into their plans. Ian pulled out his phone and opened up a map of Chicago. It was perfect. They knew exactly where the Muslims all chose to live, where the immigrants clumped together. They could take out a bunch of them at once and maybe even scare the rest of them into running.

"Here." He pulled it up and handed his phone to Tim. "It's perfect."

Tim stared down at the device and nodded before passing it around. "Yeah, but where."

Ian shrugged. "Ray, where would hit them the hardest?"

"Where they live, I suppose."

Tim stood up and got himself another beer, handing Ian his phone back as he walked. Ian set his drink on the plastic table and shook his head. "Yeah, but where?"

"I don't know," Ray answered. "Spence, you know?"

Spencer shook his head but he did give a sufficient response. "There's this complex off Pulaski Road that might be good. A bunch of them live there, and they're talking about making a mosque."

"A mosque?" The word was like a curse coming from Ian's lips. "What do they think this is *their* country? They can't just come in here and do whatever the fuck they want."

Spencer scrunched his nose. "Isn't that what they all do?"

"True that." Ian took another large swallow of his beer. He was finally feeling a little buzzed, though it could just be the high from finally getting to the point of doing something about their Somali problem.

Spencer tossed his can in the trash and sat back down with a new one. "So what are we going to do?"

The smile that lit on Ian's face was bigger than he had expected. They were right where he needed them to be. They were finally with him in ways no one else ever had been. Together they could do it, they could scare off the dogs, send them back where they came from, and he could find a job and get on with his life. "Let's figure out where we're going to scare them that hurts the most."

They rattled off a lot of different places, schools, churches, doctors' offices that saw those kind of patients, but Ian kept thinking about that complex Spencer had mentioned. It seemed to be the perfect option, but they'd have to get more of a picture of what it looked like. Where they could put certain things, like bombs, and still be able to conceal them.

"I can drive by there on my way home," Tim suggested. "Maybe take some pictures."

"Good." Ian liked how their plan was forming. This could get interesting fast. They could do this. They would do this.

"Who is in? Because we're not going to discuss this anymore until I know who is in and who is out." He stared down each and every one of them, giving them a cold look to determine whether they were truly with him or not. He needed to know he had their support.

"I'm in," Tim said first.

Ian knew he would. That wasn't a surprise at all. Tim was his best friend going back years. They'd had these discussions before. They'd talked about what they would do if they stopped holding back on all the stupidity they knew was going on in their country, in their city. No, it was time they took back what was rightfully theirs.

Giving Spencer a hard look, Ian stared unrelenting. "You in?"

Spencer nodded slowly, hesitating in the slightest.

"Ray?" Ian asked, not moving his gaze from Spencer. He wanted to be sure Spencer wasn't going to back out now that he had given his word.

Ray drew in a deep breath and let it out on a sigh. "No, I think I'm out. I'm too old for that kind of shit. Let you young kids do it."

Ian snorted but didn't answer. Tim lightly ribbed Ray a new one, teasing him about being a chicken and a pussy. They could easily do this with or without Ray. He wasn't going to make a lick of difference. He was too stupid to even know how to put a bomb together anyway. Pat declined, too, which also wasn't a surprise.

"That makes three of us, then." Finally breaking his gaze from Spencer, Ian nodded toward Tim. The last of their group wasn't there, but Ian would talk to him about it all soon. He wouldn't be left out simply because he did have a job and have to work. That was what they all wanted anyway.

Ian clenched his jaw, determined not to say anything again so long as Ray was around them. He'd talk to Spencer and Tim about it when he had them alone. Until then, he stood up and went to the fridge, grabbing another few beers. Tossing one to Ray, he popped the top on his own. He was ready to get good and drunk and let off some steam.

A few hours later, a gentle mist of rain floated down outside as the sky darkened in the late spring evening. He was done sitting on his ass and his hands doing nothing. Something had to happen to make a damn lick of difference, and he and Tim, and now Spencer, were going to be the ones to make that happen. They were going to be the ones to get rid of the leeches and maybe even some damn libtards while they were at it.

No one needed precious snowflakes around. They were worth nothing except more weight on the welfare and costing him more money. Grunting, he squatted down on the cooler. He had most of the supplies to make one bomb. He'd been toying with it for months but with no real reason to keep it going and finish it out. Now he had that reason. He had every reason. They had taken everything from him. They were taking over his city, his country, they were changing everything to his disadvantage. They were all a bunch of selfish immigrants who didn't know left from right.

Lost in his thoughts, Ian almost missed it when Ray—tipsy as could be— nearly slipped from his chair and onto the cement floor. Shaking his head in pity and disgust, Ian took a long sip from his beer. This was perfect. They could get done with everything they wanted and needed. So what if he ended up in jail by the end of it so long as he made a difference for someone else, someone like Tim's kids could go to school and not have to worry about the illegals they were stuck in class with.

They would make everything better than it had been. They would make the city what it once was. They would take back their right to jobs, to health, to doctors, to everything they deserved and more. Ian was ready, so was Tim. Spencer—he'd come along as they made plans, Ian was sure of it. Not one doubt echoed back at him this time. They were going to go through with all their plans, whether they were caught or not. They would take down the insurgents into their country and take it back what was rightfully theirs.

Ian waited until it was dark before he headed home for the night. Tim texted him and Spencer some photos in the middle of the night, but they weren't very good, didn't tell Ian much of anything about the complex.

Gritting his teeth, Ian knew they'd have to go back in the daylight to figure out what they might do. It could wait a day or two first though, but he didn't want to lose the momentum they had built up.

Turning on his side as he laid in the bed in the basement of his brother's house, Ian closed his eyes. A sense of peace surrounded him, calmed him, washed over him, and struck him as the best feeling he'd had in a long time. He wasn't stressed anymore. Whatever happened would happen for the better. Whatever happened would make a difference and an impact.

He texted the two of them back and gritted his teeth. They had to only do this verbally. No more trails to who they were.

With a date set up for when they'd meet again, Ian put his plan into motion. He'd figure out exactly what supplies they needed, how to make the bombs, and together they'd find a place and a time to set them.

CHAPTER TWO

MORGAN NEARLY spilled her way-too-full cup of coffee as she attempted to walk from the small kitchenette off the side of her office building to her desk. She stopped short when some idiot decided they could walk right in front of her. She checked the coffee to make sure nothing had slipped over the rim of the mug and then the file folders in her hand. Coffee was definitely more important than a bunch of papers.

With a steady hand, she walked much more carefully back to her desk and set the coffee down. Slipping into her chair, she bent over the files as she opened them up. It had been a long year into their investigation, and she was no closer to figuring out the connection between Mr. Jimmy and all the other lowlifes they had arrested already.

They'd taken out a good chunk of them too, but each and every time she tried to get one of them to flip, they balked at the idea and never spoke to her again. Whoever he was, he must have a great deal of power and sway over everyone. Rolling her eyes, Morgan immediately nixed that idea. No one had that much power.

Pax snorted at her. "I saw your mishap."

"My what?" Morgan stared at her partner, his big square shoulders, his dark skin, and eyes that held every single care in the world in them. He was the perfect best friend.

"Your mishap. Almost lost that precious shit that runs through your veins."

Morgan's upper lip curled into a sneer. "I did not spill a drop."

"Only by sheer luck."

"Shut up. Did you get the file?"

"I did, but I don't know what it's going to do to help you."

Morgan held her hand out for it, but Pax didn't put anything into her palm. When she finally turned to him, moving her attention from her computer to her coffee to him, she glowered. "What?"

"You're chasing nothing."

"I'm chasing a lead."

"There isn't anything in this." He held the file with his other hand. "I promise you."

"You don't know that. I'm the profiler. Give me the damn file so I can read it."

"Not yet."

Morgan tried to calm her heart that was about to race with her anger. Pax teased her, that was fine. He chided her and joked with her, that was fine. Him purposely withholding information she had requested was not okay. "Give it to me."

"Not yet. Hear me out."

Pursing her lips, Morgan pushed away from her desk and crossed her legs and her arms. She raised one thin eyebrow at him and stared him down like she was scolding a little kid for making the world's stupidest mistake. They had known each other for over twenty years, and while she trusted Pax with her life, he was pushing it that day.

"You going to listen."

"I'm staring at you, aren't I?"

"Yeah, but Mel gives me that look, and she doesn't listen when she gives it me."

Letting out a snort, Morgan forcibly relaxed her form and tried to look more open to listening to whatever he was going to tell her. She was pretty sure she either wasn't going to like it or that it would be completely pointless and useless to her, but if she had to listen to him in order to get the information she needed, then she'd do it, albeit not happily.

"Mel doesn't work with you and can't file complaints. Get on with it already, I don't have all day to sit here while you skirt around what you came to say."

Pax narrowed his eyes at her. "There is nothing in this file that will help you."

"Did you even look at it?"

"Yes."

"Did you read all of it?"

Pax's jaw clenched, and she knew she had him.

"So how do you know then there's nothing in there that I don't want?" Morgan raised an eyebrow at him in a dare.

"You're chasing dreams."

"I'm chasing leads. This is a two year case already. It needs to end, preferably sooner rather than later. Give it." Morgan held her hand out again, snapping her fingers to get his attention.

Pax shook his head. "No. Hear me out."

"Then speak, man. I don't have all day."

"Chill out, Stone. You're way too wired, maybe you should switch to decaf."

"Shut up. What's in the file?"

"Nothing. That's my point."

"But you haven't read it."

"I know what's in it."

"Says who?"

"Says your best friend down at Chicago PD. She says there is nothing in the file that will help you."

Morgan's shoulders tensed. She knew exactly who Pax was talking about. She had kissed Detective Fiona Wexford exactly once and had dreamed of it even more times than she dared to count. Last December had been a fit of insanity on Morgan's part, and she strongly wanted to ignore the fact any of it had happened.

"What does she know? I'm the expert."

He snorted. "You trust her."

"Some days. Others no. Give me the file."

"Fine." He shoved it in her direction, knocking it into her coffee cup, which earned him a glare.

Finally having the folder in front of her, Morgan flipped it open to the first page. It was a simple divorce decree, but she'd wanted to read every word of it for a month now as long as it had taken her to get hold of a copy of it. She'd had to twist some arms, fill out a million pounds of paperwork, but there it was right in front of her. The divorce decree of one Jonathon Lockland aka Mr. Jimmy. She knew it was him, though their initial findings that they were one in the same seemed to have faded and there were others now second-guessing that decision and working toward finding alternative suspects. Morgan had no such doubts.

"You going to ignore me now?" Pax's voice broke through her reverie.

"Yes," she muttered as she flipped through the next sheet of paper.

Everything looked perfectly in place from the outside. She'd been through her own divorce years before and remembered how painstaking it was to finalize everything even if the divorce was mutual. No doubt Jonathon had gone through the same, as had his wife. They had one child, currently ten years old.

"Earth to Morgan."

"What?" She smacked her hand down on the desk and turned the best glare she could muster at him. Pax's look of surprise should have been her first warning, but she missed it. "What could you possibly want two seconds after just speaking to me? I've got work to do, Pax."

The clearing throat startled her. Morgan turned and looked up, meeting her supervisor's amused gaze. Rolling her eyes, Morgan pouted out her lip.

"Sorry, boss."

"By all means, take him down another notch or two."

With a deep breath, she turned to look up at Taylor. "Did you need me?"

"Yeah. My office."

"Great," Morgan muttered, abandoning her coffee, her desk, and the file she had waited forever for and then had to wrangle from Pax without even getting a chance to look at it. She wanted to read it, in its entirety before she made a judgement call whether there was something in there or not.

As soon as she got to Taylor's office, she let out a huff. He moved around to the other side of his desk and sat down.

"Shut the door."

Fuck, Morgan thought. If he was having her shut the door, then whatever he was going to talk to her about was not going to be good. Morgan bit the inside of her lip as she shut the door, giving Pax one more glare because she could, even though he didn't see it since his back was turned.

"You're off restrictions."

Her shoulders tensed. "I'm what?"

"You're off restrictions."

Morgan shook her head, not quite believing it. "Really?"

"Yes, but I swear, Stone, if you ever pull something like that again, you won't be working in this unit any longer even if you're lucky to work at the FBI."

She clenched her jaw, wanting to bounce up and down at the giddy feeling taking over. Shaking her head at him with a smile tugging at her lips, she wasn't quite sure what to say. It was a week earlier than she had expected, since the evaluation wasn't due for another week. She'd known she'd fucked up in Seattle and had spent the last four months beating the shit out of herself and staying firmly in the lines.

"Thanks, Taylor."

"Don't thank me, yet. I'm still keeping a pretty close eye on you. What happened... that can't happen again."

"I know." Morgan gave him a sincere look. "I know it can't. I didn't even know what was happening at the time."

"I get your personal life is yours, but when it affects the case—"

"I get it." Morgan stared at him directly. "Trust me, I get it. I have that conversation with myself every day. Why do you think I haven't been on a date since then? If I can't trust my own judgement, who can I trust?"

"Your partner," Taylor answered.

Morgan turned to look out the window at Pax who still sat at his desk. "Perhaps. He didn't know anything."

"I know. It was all on you."

"No, sir." Morgan swallowed. "I may have known Pax for the better part of two decades, but he didn't know I dated women until then."

"Oh."

Morgan knocked her chin up. "I never...we never...it never came up, so I just let it slide."

"But Barbie..."

"Don't ask me how he never figured that one out. Sometimes he is just dense about things, especially things you don't want to see in your best friends. But he didn't know until Seattle."

Taylor picked up a pen and ran it from end to end between his fingers. "You have to trust someone, Stone. If not him, then who?"

"I don't know, sir," she muttered.

"Figure it out, but for now, you are off restrictions and can return to full active duty. You still need to make sure to report everything to me, though, understand?"

"Yes, sir." Morgan shoved her hands into the pockets of her slacks. She couldn't wait to tell Pax. They had both been waiting for that day for months, and she was finally back to working without feeling like someone was watching over her shoulder.

"What do you have on the trafficking case?"

Morgan groaned. "Not much. We're testing other theories as to who Mr. Jimmy might be. Pax is looking up a James Halverty out of Saint Paul. We're pretty sure our suspect is located in this area of the country based on where the lines of trafficking stem from. We've got surveillance going on under the radar and some that's a little more overt. If Halverty is our guy, hopefully we'll spook him a bit into doing something different."

"And if he's not?"

"We're also looking at a James Carrigan from here. We've got the work on him almost done, and I'll start on the profile as soon as they finish getting me the information I need."

"Lockland?"

"I still think it's him, sir. I've never seen someone so calculated in everything they do before. Call it intuition, instinct, gut feeling, whatever. I still think it's him."

Taylor gave her a long look, and she couldn't tell what he was thinking, but Morgan knew he was judging her. "Make sure your preference doesn't cloud your understanding on what you are seeing out there."

"Absolutely, sir."

"Anything else?"

"The Topeka office and Kansas City office are working together to set up another raid, but we're pretty sure Mr. Jimmy isn't there. They should have their plans to us by Friday so we can look them over. I wasn't sure...since I'm off restrictions..."

"No, Stone. I think you need to stick close to home for now."

Disappointment settled in the pit of her belly. "Yes, sir."

"Let me know if you come up with anything else."

"Right." Dismissed, Morgan stepped away from his desk and out the door. Once she was settled in her chair, she sipped her coffee, wincing when it wasn't scalding hot anymore. She'd have to suffer through the only semi-hot coffee until she could make some more.

Pax leaned over. "What did he want?"

"To see if you're still useful to him," Morgan muttered, opening the file again so she could actually read through it this time.

"No, really, what did he want?"

"What's it to you?"

"Did he say something about me?"

"No." Morgan's eyes went wide, and she turned on him. "Why? Did you do something?"

"No."

Morgan wasn't quite sure whether to believe him or not, his words she trusted, but his tone of voice told her something else entirely. Having pity on him, she finally spilled the beans. "I'm off restrictions."

"Seriously?"

"Yes."

"Just like that?"

"What? Did you think I'd have to retake exams or something? Sign away my life in blood?"

"No, I just...I figured you'd get lectured again."

"Well, sorry to disappoint." She clenched her jaw as her phone buzzed on her desk. Grabbing it, she hoped for a distraction, but when she saw her mother's name flash across it, she sent the call to voicemail. She did not have the brain power to deal with that. "I'm going to work now, should you, you know, have your own shit to do."

Pax put his hands up in the air like she had slapped him. She was being particularly mean that day, but something wasn't sitting right with her. If she was truly off restrictions, then she should be able to go to the raid and join in without a problem. All it told her was Taylor still didn't quite trust her yet. Sighing, she flipped open the file and started to read.

Every detail was in place. Her gaze slipped over the words, over the decree, the custody arrangement, the alimony. Then she went back through and looked for what wasn't there. They had records of Jonathon Lockland's financial. Every once in a while, there was money that they couldn't quite account for, but it was never a large sum of it. Even in the financials of the divorce, nothing seemed amiss or outside of what they had already found. Everything seemed to match up.

Morgan was going to have to figure out something, something that stood out for him against the others. She wanted to prove she was right as much as she wanted to find Mr. Jimmy and take him down. He ran, easily, the biggest trafficking ring she had ever seen, and he targeted the least of the least, the ones no one cared about. He'd moved from taking kids off the street when their parents weren't looking to enticing foster care kids, kids who were permanently at risk, into his line of work. She couldn't take it anymore.

Her phone buzzed again, and once more she sent her mother's call to voicemail. The woman had no boundaries and no understanding that Morgan had a job, and even though it wasn't a regular nine-to-five, she needed to respect that Morgan worked for a living, unlike her. Morgan took another long sip from her coffee and finished reading the divorce decree. She slipped it into the file with the rest of the information she'd collected on Jonathon Lockland.

They had a conference meeting about it Thursday afternoon, where all the findings were to be presented and they'd then debate who they thought Mr. Jimmy might actually be. They would no doubt come to no answer and stick more surveillance on all of them. That was how it normally seemed to go any time she tried to prove her point. It wasn't an actual meeting to figure out who had done it. It was yet another bureaucratic meeting to discuss what they were all doing and come to no useful conclusion.

Sighing, Morgan rubbed her temple and finished her coffee before pulling out the files for the other two and getting to work on finishing out the basic profiles for each. She couldn't—like Taylor said—spend all her time on Lockland and ignore everyone else. Spending the rest of her day lost in the probable brain space of a crime boss was exactly what Morgan needed to take her own mind off the fact she wasn't really off restrictions, no matter what Taylor tried to tell her.

CHAPTER THREE

MORGAN SLIPPED through the glass door at her favorite pizzeria just down from headquarters. Frankie was already behind the counter, eyeing her up and down. She'd thought about it once, very briefly, and then had nixed that idea so fast she wasn't sure where it had come from.

"Table for two?"

Narrowing her gaze at him, Morgan nodded. "Yes. Is she here?"

"No, just you, my ever-happy agent."

Smirking, Morgan nodded her head toward the back of the restaurant. "I'll seat myself."

"Fine."

She walked around the corner and down to the back of the building. It was her preferred booth, gave her the best view of everything happening outside through the large front glass windows, and she had nothing behind her except the bathrooms. Ideally, it was the perfect place for her to hunker down, enjoy some grub, and maybe some company.

They had been meeting on a fairly regular basis since December when Morgan had returned from her stint out west catching a serial killer who was both delusional and ever-hopeful. She wasn't quite sure what category to put her in, insane or Pollyanna. Though, the killing part pretty much tipped that scale.

It had been a long few months. She'd been allowed to go back on the case with Pax watching every move and doing everything with her in order to close it out, but she had received a formal reprimand in her file for sleeping with a suspect. Except, she hadn't known she was a suspect when she'd done it, not until the bugger had turned on her and tried to kill her in the middle of trying to fuck her.

Rubbing the bridge of her nose and then her temples, Morgan unclenched her jaw as she tried her best to relax. Lollie was in jail awaiting sentencing since she'd pretty much confessed to everything, but that still didn't mean Morgan wasn't on edge any time she felt herself slipping closer into a relationship with someone else, like Fiona Wexford, who still confused the crap out of her.

Frankie came around the corner, his tan pants belted tightly across his hips, white washrag over his shoulder, pencil behind his ear tucked in with his long brown hair. She had watched him grow up in the last six years since she'd transferred to Chicago. She'd found the little pizzeria one of her first weeks on the job, and there was no going back, she loved it. Frankie's father, Frank Senior—*so original*—had been running the joint then, teaching Frankie the ropes. Over the course of four years, he had slowly given up more and more control so Frankie could take over. It worked out exactly as it should have.

"What'll you be having? The usual?"

Morgan pursed her lips as she crossed her arms and stared directly up at him. He was easily a foot taller than her when she was standing, so sitting, she really had to crane her neck at him. "She's not even here yet."

"I'm busy."

Morgan's lips parted. "Frankie, there is no one in this place except me. I'm after the rush. What are you even going on about?"

The flush in his cheeks was surprising. He slid across from her in the booth, his knees no doubt touching the top of the table. "I got to study."

"Study? Study for what?"

"I'm taking classes again."

"Really? For what?"

"Business."

"Why? You run your own business. It's going well enough, isn't it?"

He gave a nonchalant shrug, and Morgan focused her gaze on him. He wasn't telling her something, that was for sure, but it also wasn't the norm. They may have been friends inside the pizzeria, but they never spoke outside of it except the one time she had caught him accidentally at the pharmacy.

Frankie sighed. "Dad thinks I need a degree."

"Did he have one?"

"No."

Morgan pulled her lower lip between her teeth. "So he wants you to do better than he did?"

Frankie shrugged.

"Look, don't go to school just for him. You'll flunk out like all the other times. If you want to go to school, then go, but don't do it for anyone but you. You don't need a degree to run this place."

Nodding, Frankie let out a sharp breath. "I want it."

"Good. Then don't fucking fail, or I'll be after you."

"Don't want that." Frankie winked.

"Nope." Morgan's eyes lit up when she saw Fiona step through the doorway and into the restaurant. She gave a little wave, which alerted Frankie that someone was there. He scooted out of the seat and waited until Fiona was settled in the booth across from Morgan.

"The usual?"

"For me, yes." Morgan nodded at Fiona. "You?"

"Uh...yeah. I'll just have what she's having."

"Got it. Order coming up! Oh, and Morgan."

"Yeah?" She turned to look at him.

He nodded his head at her. "Thanks."

"Any time. And hey, if you need help with any classes, Fiona here is brilliant. Don't ask me for help, though."

Frankie snorted, the smile tugging at his lips again that she missed so much. He waved them both off and went into the kitchen.

"What was that about?"

"Nothing really. Just giving him a rough time like normal."

Fiona nodded and pushed her light brown hair behind her ear. Her gaze moved down to the table, and Morgan wondered for a second if it was a flirtatious move or if Fiona even knew what she was doing. They hadn't talked about the kiss since Morgan had taken over Lollie's case from Fiona and went off to find the serial killer. They hadn't even talked about Morgan's supposed crush on Fiona since she flew back to Chicago and she'd given Fiona a call to tell her Lollie had been caught. They had both strategically avoided that conversation every single time they had gotten together since.

"So...how's work going? Any good cases I can steal?"

Fiona scrunched her nose at Morgan. "No. I think I'll keep them all, thank you."

Morgan smirked as she grabbed her fork and fiddled with it. Her fingers did not want to sit still when Fiona was around as much as she begged them to. Fiona grabbed her hands, her palm covering both of Morgan's. She gave a squeeze and left her hands there, and Morgan didn't remove them. She didn't want to.

"You got anything interesting going on at work?"

"No," Morgan nearly whispered. Her heart skittered. She'd given her normal answer because there wasn't really anything she could talk to Fiona about when it came to work, and Fiona knew that, but it was still a courtesy to ask. Drawing in a breath, Morgan shifted her hands from the top of the table into her lap. She hated that at fifty years old, Fiona was still able to make her feel like a teenager who needed to sneak around.

"How's your mom?"

Morgan rolled her eyes. "Annoying as ever. She's determined to beat some sense into Clyde, so I had hoped that would take some of the heat off me for a while, but nope, she's still harping on me."

"Harping on you for what?"

"Uh..." Morgan smiled when Frankie came over with waters for both and coffee for Morgan. "Thank you."

Thinking she had gotten out of answering that one, Morgan sipped her steaming coffee. She knew Frankie had made it just like she liked it, dark, black, and with a touch of sugar. When she glanced into Fiona's dark eyes, she nearly choked on the sip she was about to swallow.

"What?"

"You didn't answer me." Fiona raised an eyebrow, humor playing at her lips.

Morgan swallowed around the lump that had formed. "She wants me to get married. Have kids. You know, that shit people think we're supposed to do in life."

"And you don't?"

"Been there, done that. No, thank you."

"But dating...you'd be interested in dating?" Fiona stared directly into her soul.

Morgan couldn't figure out exactly where the conversation was going, but she knew she had to get out of it. They'd traveled down this road once or twice before and it had never gone well. But it had been months since either of them had brought it up, and so she figured they were in the clear finally. "I date."

"Do you?" Fiona looked unconvinced.

"Yes."

"Since Lollie?"

"Yes, since Lollie. Why?"

"You never mentioned it. That's all." Fiona took a long sip from her water with no ice and a lemon slice.

Morgan's heart was in her throat, and she had no idea what to say or how to act. She was always clumsy with these things when it came to Fiona. Anyone else and she had her head on straight, but Fiona stumped her up every time. "A-are you dating still?"

"Sort of."

"Then the conversation is done."

She glanced up in time to see Frankie come around the corner with the food. She uttered a praise of thanks to God for his timing and grinned up at him as he set their plates on the table. Morgan immediately dug into hers like she hadn't eaten in weeks while Fiona slowly ate her ziti.

"I meant to thank you for getting me that file. It's been interesting to read through it."

"Looked dull to me," Fiona commented before shoving another piece of pasta between her lips.

Morgan lifted one shoulder in a shrug. "Boring is sometimes the perfect place to hide the mysterious."

Fiona gave her an odd look. "I envy you, sometimes."

"Envy me what? Trust me, my life is a mess. There is nothing to envy here."

Chuckling, Fiona narrowed her gaze. "No, your mind. Ever since I took that profiling class, lecture, whatever it was, and met you, I've been amazed by how you think. It never ceases to amaze me, actually."

Heat tinged at Morgan's cheeks. She didn't want to be complimented, really ever, but especially by Fiona when it came to her work, especially considering how much she had screwed up last winter and Fiona knew just about everything there was to it. It had all come out whether Morgan had wanted it to or not. The pitying looks had been unbearable.

"I'm serious."

"What?" Morgan glanced up, her train of thought broken.

"You're able to see details no one else is when it comes to personality."

"Everyone else gives me a whole lot of information in order to see those details. It's not without work, and it's not without having a ton of files at my fingertips to compare."

Fiona cocked her head to the side. "Perhaps. Still, profiling, is not my strong suit."

"You profile all the time in Homicide." Morgan took another bite, not wanting her food to get cold before they left. "You just do it differently than I do. You typically know who your suspect is, so you have more to work off. I don't usually know anything of who they are, just what they do, and my cases aren't typical of the norm."

"True." Fiona's gaze drilled straight into Morgan's heart. "You're teaching again, though, right?"

"Next week. How'd you know about that?"

"Little birdie." Fiona smirked. "I thought about attending."

"It's almost the same thing as before."

"Yes, but a refresher course is always welcome. Maybe it'll help me out with my current case."

"Why? Have another female serial killer on the loose in Chicago? I thought you said you didn't have any cases for me to take over."

Fiona paled. "Your lecture is on female serial killers?"

"Yes, using Lollie as the prime topic."

Fiona let out a breath. "Are you ready for that?"

Morgan shrugged again and pushed her food around her plate suddenly not quite as hungry as she had been before. "Probably won't ever be fully ready, to be fair, but I think I am. She confessed to everything. The conviction for her second murder was flipped since the suspect was wrongly convicted, which started a whole new investigation in Lollie's connections. Glad I wasn't on that one. Anyway, she's in prison. It's been months since we've caught her, and I'm finally off restrictions."

"I—wait, what? You're off restrictions?"

Morgan nodded, the smile tugging at her lips. She had meant to slip that into the conversation like it wasn't a huge deal, and she had secretly hoped Fiona would sense otherwise.

"That's fantastic. Congratulations!" There was no amount of sympathy or pity in her tone. Everything Fiona said rang true, like she meant every word of it. Morgan had missed that with everyone else.

"Thanks." The flush she'd had earlier reentered her cheeks. "Really. I'm glad to finally be back on full duty, whatever that means. I still think they're watching me."

"You're either crazy or too into the conspiracy that your job makes you deal with. No one is watching you, Morgan, not if you've been cleared."

"I was cleared months ago during the investigation. Yet, for some reason, I was still restricted from travel and independent investigations."

"Maybe they just wanted to make sure you were healed."

Morgan didn't answer. Pax had said the exact same thing, almost verbatim, but her doctor's note should have been enough proof that she was healed up and didn't need to be on any kind of physical restrictions, and the fact Taylor still wasn't letting her leave set her back up. Something was going on, and it was bigger than she had the ability to think about over lunch.

"So...if I'm not going to your lecture, give me the highlights."

Morgan smiled. That she could do. Leave it to Fiona to switch back to work talk to help put her at ease. Sometimes she was pretty sure Fiona was much better at reading her than she gave her credit for.

"Not much to tell you. You know it all."

"Morgan."

"Fine. I'm talking about profiling, obviously, but I'm using Lollie as a case study as to look for what doesn't fit in a normal serial killer profile. She didn't fit the norm in several ways, one because she is a woman, two because she is gay—"

"Did they determine that?"

"Yes. Three because she wasn't really killing for a compulsion or a need for power, she was killing because she wasn't getting what she thought she wanted or needed. So that messed up a lot of the other profiles we had for the case in the beginning and confused local PD, you excluded, but all the other locals."

"I remember that."

"Right, so that's it in essence. Nothing big or unusual."

"I'd love to see your notes."

"Sure." Morgan finally took another bite of her lunch. "I can email them over to you."

"Perfect." Fiona gave her a wide smile. "I look forward to reading it."

"Hmm." Morgan focused on her lunch, sure they had found their steady place again. No more questions about dating and life and romance. She wanted friendship with Fiona and friendship alone. Kind of. She wanted more, but Morgan was only willing to give friendship until Fiona finished whatever relationship she was in. Morgan had done that before. She'd been the other woman, she'd been the side girlfriend, the random fuck, and she'd been in a poly relationship that had lasted two months, the longest relationship she'd ever been in aside from her random and accidental marriage to Barbie, which managed to make it to a year. Either way, she wanted complete honesty when going into anything with someone else, and she wasn't willing to compromise on that again, especially after what happened in Seattle with Lollie.

They finished their lunch, Frankie coming over to check on them multiple times and each time Morgan sent him away to go study more. Together they walked out of the pizzeria. Morgan buttoned her jacket closed as she turned to walk to her office. They were much closer to her building they were to Fiona's, who no doubt had driven. Fiona surprised her by walking next to her toward the bureau.

When they got to end of the block, Morgan managed to finally catch sight of Fiona's government issued car. "I'll see you next week?"

"Can't next week," Fiona answered. "Got something else going on. But the one after, assuming nothing comes up."

"Yeah." Disappointment echoed in Morgan's chest, but she ignored it. She enjoyed spending time with Fiona immensely. "That's fine. I'm sure I'll have a break in my case by then anyway."

"Still working trafficking."

Morgan let out a grunt as she hunched her shoulders against the chilly spring air that seemed to be clinging. Usually they were out of the chill by then and into the warm of spring. "You know it."

"I hope you figure it out soon."

"Me too. Then I can tell you all about it."

"Really?"

"No." Morgan laughed, her eyes scrunching in the corners. "Not a chance. Maybe in a lecture in a few years from now once all the trials have happened, because I have no doubt this one will have plenty of trials and convictions to go through."

"Maybe then." Fiona gave her a sad smile. "See you around, Morgan."

"Wexford." Morgan brought it back to rank, hoping it would snap herself into reality.

Fiona headed down the block toward her car while Morgan pushed against the wind and walked to her office. As soon as she was at her desk, she stared at the three files in front of her. Jonathon Lockland still seemed like the prime suspect they were all looking for despite the fact his name wasn't "Jimmy" or any variation of such.

With a hot cup of coffee next to her, she looked through the divorce decree. Something about it seemed off. For a couple that had a kid together, there was a severe lack of arguing about when and where the kid would go, and she had won primary and full custody. He had visitation rights. Curious, Morgan wondered if he ever visited or if there was some other kind of silent agreement not shown on paper. She scribbled down her question on a sticky note and slapped it onto the top sheet of the papers.

Everything about Jonathon was clean, but in Morgan's experience, no one was that clean, especially someone who owned a multi-billion dollar business. There was always something dirty going on somewhere. She just hadn't been able to find it yet. Her phone buzzed with a text, and she realized she'd been bent over her desk for hours. Fiona's name popped up with a message, "Don't forget to send me the lecture notes."

Rolling her eyes, Morgan sent off the email and responded to the text. "There. Have at."

"Thank you!" was the only response she received before she dropped her phone. She had a blissful two-day weekend before the start of the next insanity. She could only hope there was a break in the case to give her something to do for it.

Chapter Four

IAN THOUGHT he had everything set and ready to go. He triple checked the calculations he'd pulled off the Internet, made sure to check out his storage of all the chemicals. He'd done a small batch test in the backyard at his brother's house, and it had worked perfectly. His brother hadn't even suspected a thing.

The explosion had been small, but it'd sent a thrill down Ian's spine and into his chest, a thrill like he hadn't experienced before. It had taken everything in him not to call up Tim and Spencer and tell them how it went. Nope, that had to wait until they could talk in person again. When he'd called them to set up the time, he could barely contain his excitement.

Finally they were situated in the basement, beers in hand as was their norm, and he was completely jittery. It was like he'd taken a drug or something. "So when are we doing it?"

"I don't think we should do the complex first," Spencer answered.

Confused, Ian's brows drew together. "Why not? Get the most bang for our buck. It'll be harder once they figure out what we're doing."

"Yeah, but think about it. What if it doesn't work?"

"It'll work! The test run went perfect." Ian glared at Spencer and turned to Tim. "What do you think?"

"I think Spence is right."

Ian rolled his eyes. "You're both chicken. The complex is the perfect choice."

"Not this time."

"What do you mean?"

Tim drew in a sharp breath. "Next time, when we can figure out how to get in and out of there without being seen, but we haven't had proper time to figure all that out yet, including where the mosque they're wanting to build is going. Wait until we know more."

Ian clenched his jaw and his fists. Nothing was going to plan, but at least they would still be able to make an impact, scare some leeches out of their neighborhood. Even if they did start up slow, then maybe it would be to their advantage. It would scare them more and more as the attacks got closer together and bigger. Eventually, he gave Tim a sharp nod.

"Where then?"

"There's a convenience store they all go to. The moms for formula, dads for booze, kids for snacks. It's inundated with them. I suggest we start there, and we know enough about it to get it done."

"Tell me the plan then." They spent the next two hours working through the details. Ian was convinced he had enough supplies for one good bomb, though they'd have to get more in if they were going to keep that up.

When the others left, he ordered some more stuff and then went about searching for more information on the gas station Tim had told him about. In three days. That was their timeline. He had the bomb mostly done. All it needed was some sort of timer, and that would be a piece of cake.

It took them the better part of those three days to finalize all their plans. On one hand, Ian felt completely rushed with what they were doing, and on the other hand, he knew it was beyond time for them to be doing something about the problem. No one else had done anything so far, so it was going to be up to him, Tim, and Spencer to get on with it.

They hadn't spoken to Ray about anything since they'd started their plans. They still met with him during their monthly meetings and during the time they spent after just shooting the shit, but the three of them kept as much silence about their special project as they could. They spoke only in the confines of Ian's house about it, and went individually to check out the area.

Ian ground his teeth together the entire night as he waited out to see what would happen in the morning. They were going to set the bomb early in the morning, sneaking up to the gas station when they were shut down. Stupid filthy animals couldn't even keep the thing open twenty-four-seven like every other gas station.

When his alarm went off, Ian gathered up the supplies and shoved them into the trunk of his car he owed about a million and one payments on. They had everything planned out. As soon as he arrived at the designated meet spot, Tim was already there. Spencer showed up not too long after.

They were three blocks away, and they were not going to walk up to the gas station at the same time. Ian pulled on a black jacket and a baseball cap to hide his face from the cameras. Spencer, who was better at those types of things than he was, had pointed them out during his round of surveillance and figured out where they were pointed—somehow. Ian had no clue how, but he was happy to have that information.

Ian swallowed hard. He sent the timer on the bomb for five hours. It should go off sometime around eight in the morning when there would no doubt be a huge rush of people in and out. It would be perfect.

"Ready?" Ian asked.

Tim nodded. Spencer stared at the backpack and asked, "It's not bigger than that?"

"Nope."

"Eight?"

"Yeah."

"Sure you don't want to do it just before they open? It'll scare them more."

"Nothing like killing me some dogs."

Spencer's jaw clenched, but he nodded nonetheless. Ian still wasn't so sure about him and whether or not he was truly committed to their cause. Deciding to test Spencer's loyalties, Ian stepped right up to him, getting in his face.

"Are you ready for this?"

"Yes."

"You can't back out now."

Spencer paled. "No. I'm ready. There's no other option to get them gone."

"Good." Ian didn't strap the bag to his back. He nodded at Tim and Spencer and then started walking. He was supposed to walk six blocks down, three blocks past the gas station, and then circle around.

It took him the better part of twenty minutes, and by the time he saw the gas station, Tim and Spencer were in place. Tim stood at the corner wall, a cigarette between his lips as he sucked it down, his own ball cap covering his eyes from the cameras. Ian grunted his pleasure at seeing him there.

Spencer was driving circles, checking for cops. When he nodded at Ian through the windshield, Ian knew it was safe to go. He stepped off the curb and into the street. The closer he got, Tim walked off in the opposite direction. Ian's heart pounded. This was it. This was their first stand in a list of many. They were going to scare the hair off some of the dogs around there and they were going to start a war to take back their city, their neighborhood, their country.

His breath came in heavy rasps as he headed to the front door of the gas station. He gripped the handle and jerked, but of course it didn't open. They knew it was going to be locked, but Spencer had said to make it look like he just wanted inside and he was drunk or something. Ian couldn't figure out why, but he did it anyway to satisfy him.

He set his bag down and lit up a cigarette, drawing in the smoke until it filled his lungs. He was so jittery there would be no way he'd be able to go to sleep when he got back to his house. He smoked until the butt was close to finished. Tamping it out on top of the metal black trashcan, Ian pocketed the butt. He then flipped the lid on the trashcan and leaned over it, slipping the backpack into it. He was bent over, covering much of what the cameras could see.

It was the perfect cover. As soon as he had the lid back in place, Ian smoked another cigarette. Eight in the morning could not come soon enough. He finished that smoke, pocketed the butt like he had the other and then he walked off the way he had come. He walked for five blocks before Spencer swung around and picked him up in the middle of a neighborhood where no one would see.

It had worked perfectly. Ian let out a breath. The three of them went back to their houses. Ian was right. He hadn't been able to sleep at all that night. He'd been so full of adrenaline that every time he tried to sit down on the futon he called a couch he'd stood right back up. He'd smoked through an entire pack and drank at least a case of beer.

Stumbling toward his living room after his last smoke break, Ian flipped on the television. It was eight in the morning. He wanted to know, to see, to hear when the news broke about the bombing. He wanted to see what they thought of it, hear the words he knew they'd say. It was done to make everything better, done to turn their neighborhood around, done to scare them. The ones who didn't deserve to be there. The ones who were taking over moment by moment.

When nine rolled around and there was no sign of breaking news, Ian was at his wits end. He scrounged through the basement for another smoke, finally finding one, but he was going to need more. Any time he sat down, his body was exhausted, but he couldn't stop his leg from bouncing or his hands from shaking.

Ten. Still nothing. Tim had called once already. Spencer nothing. Ian snorted. If anything had happened, he was pretty sure Spencer was the one who would have ratted them out, the one who would have given them up, told someone, anyone. Ian swallowed. He needed smokes.

It took him ten minutes to get to the smoke shop where he preferred to buy his stuff, a place that catered to true Americans. He bought plenty to keep him going, charging it to the one card he still had on him that would let transactions go through.

He was shaking when he got back, barely able to get the cig into his mouth and lit. Tim was parked outside, and as soon as Ian showed up, Tim was out of his car, coming straight round for him.

"What the hell happened?"

Ian glanced up at him with a curious look. "What do you mean?"

"I mean, nothing happened. So what the hell happened?'

Clenching his jaw, Ian looked around the neighborhood. His brother lived in one of those stupid suburbs they'd built, far out from the center of town. He'd hated moving there, but he'd had no option. Shaking his head at Tim, Ian said, "Shut up. Let's go inside."

It took them less than a minute to get down into the basement. Ian shut and locked the door behind time. "Have you heard from Spence?"

"No. You?"

"No." Ian sucked down his cigarette, not caring that his brother hated it when he smoked inside the house. He needed it. "I don't know what happened."

"I drove by. Nothing happened."

"Do you think...do you think Spence called it in?"

"I don't know, man." Tim ran a hand through his salt-and-pepper hair, his rounded face from the extra sixty pounds he carried around weighing on him even more. "You don't think he would, do you?"

Ian had to be the sane and rational one. He had to be the one who was calm. "If he did, he'd probably be gone by now."

"True. But he's not answering his fucking phone."

"Nope. I tried him too." It was a lie, but Tim didn't need to know that. Ian hadn't called either of them. Tim had called him, multiple times, and Spencer had been silent on all fronts. "Should we go over there?"

"Maybe." Tim grabbed his phone and put it to his ear, no doubt calling Spencer again. When there was no answer, he cursed and slammed his cellphone onto the coffee table. "What the hell are we going to do?"

"Nothing. There's nothing we can do. We've got to figure out why it didn't work, assuming Spence didn't give us up, and then we'll go from there for the next time."

"Next time?" Tim's eyes were wide with shock. "What do you mean next time?"

"This was never a one and done kind of deal." Ian stared directly at Tim, making sure his meaning was understood.

"It didn't work."

"It will work," Ian said through clenched teeth. "It will work. We just have to figure out what went wrong this time."

Tim let out a sigh. "Let's go find Spence."

"Righteo."

They took Tim's car, since it was nicer and didn't smell so much like smoke. He drove directly to Spencer's small apartment. When they got to his door, Tim pounded his fist on it. Ian stood next to Tim, fidgeting with the cigarettes he had just bought in his pocket. It took Tim knocking two more times before Spencer came to the door, looking wasted off his ass.

"What?" Spencer asked.

Ian shook his head, grabbed Spencer by the shoulder and shoved him inside. Tim followed closely behind, shutting the door behind them. Ian took Spencer to the couch and made him sit down. The apartment reeked of booze and pot. He gripped Spencer's chin and raised it up to stared directly at him.

"Shit."

"What?" Tim asked.

"He's gone to the wind for sure. You anywhere near sober, Spencer?"

"No," he grunted.

Ian shook his head. "When did you start?"

"When I got home." Spencer slurred all his words, everyone taking him three times as long as normal to actually speak them.

"Fuck," muttering, Ian looked around the room again. He grabbed Spencer by the wrist and dragged him to the bathroom and shoved him in to an ice cold shower. "You didn't do anything stupid did you?"

"Drink. And smoke."

"No, stupid like call the cops."

Spencer popped his head out, staring at Ian. "No."

Ian looked over his shoulder at Tim and shrugged. "You trust him?"

"Yeah."

"Then something else went wrong. Sober up, Spence. We've got shit to figure out."

Spencer took a thirty minute shower, and when he came back out to join them, he still wasn't sober, but he was at least more put together than before. They sat around his living room until Spencer's girlfriend came back from her shift. Immediately, Ian had shut up. Spencer was still high as a kite, and she looked none too happy with him.

Standing up, Ian grabbed his pack of cigarettes. "See you tomorrow, Spence."

"Yeah."

As soon as Tim and he were outside, they could hear the shouting inside. She really laid into him. Ian gave Tim a sheepish look. "I fucked it up."

"What do you mean?"

"If Spence didn't call and no one found out, then I'm the one who fucked it up. Come on, let's go to your car." As soon as they were inside and headed back to Ian's house, he laid it all out. "There's no other explanation. We'll see if they found it, but if they didn't, then the bomb didn't go off, meaning I fucked something up along the way so it didn't go off. I'm going to have to go back and look at what I did."

"You wrote it down?"

"Of course I did. There's a lot of numbers in it." Ian shook his head. "It's not exactly put this here and that there and then you're done. No, you have to decide how big of an explosion you want and that is determined by how much you put of one thing in verses another."

"Oh." Tim gripped the steering wheel tightly. "Maybe it's a sign."

"Sign of what?"

"That we shouldn't do this."

Ian clenched his jaw hard. He was done with the whisy-washy bullshit. Tim and Spencer needed to man up and do what needed done in order to take back what was rightfully theirs. He couldn't and wouldn't hold it out for them.

"Are you with me or not?"

Tim stopped. He paled. "I'm with you, Ian."

"Good. Then we need a new plan. Where are we going to hit next and when?"

"You sure?"

Ian sent him a scathing look. "Yes. When Spence sobers up, we'll bring him in. Until then, let's figure out what we're doing."

"Shouldn't we wait to see if we've been had?"

Ian shrugged. "Why? If we wait, we'll never know. Let's plan. Let's take back what is rightfully ours. Let's make it safe for your kids, again. Let's make it so they can find jobs when they graduate. I'm tired of this bullshit, of living in a place where I was born where that doesn't even matter anymore. You said you were too. So are you?"

"Yes."

"Then where next?"

Tim's eyes were wide. "There's that factory we talked about."

"Yes. Perfect."

CHAPTER FIVE

MORGAN WOKE up to her phone shrilly ringing next to her ear. Groaning, she squinted at it as she tried to make out the words. Unable to, she gave up and answered. "What?"

"Bright little thing you are in the morning."

"It's not morning. It's still dark outside." She twisted onto her back, her legs still tangled in the blankets on her bed. She rubbed her eyes as she tried to wake up, but the severe lack of coffee in her bloodstream did not bode well for her functioning. "What time is it?"

"Three."

"What?" Morgan looked at the clock on her nightstand. "Why the hell are you calling at three in the morning, Pax? I don't do booty calls anymore, you know that. And never with you."

"Like I'd ever want your booty."

"Shove it."

He good and truly laughed at her. Pouting, Morgan forced her body into a sitting position on her mattress. She brushed her bangs out of her face and stared down at her messy floor around her in an attempt to locate some kind of clothing to wear as she was no doubt getting called in to work.

"We got floated a case."

"What do you mean floated?"

"From your little friend over at the Chicago PD."

"A murder?"

"Okay, so maybe not your little friend, but from CPD."

Morgan ignored his jovial tone. Catching sight of a pair of slacks that looked halfway decent on the floor near the corner of her bedroom, she stood up and snagged them. "What kind of case?"

"There's some unrest in one of the extremist groups in town."

"They're in perpetual unrest." She shoved one foot into her pant leg and then the other, balancing the phone in the nook between her shoulder and her ear. "You're going to have to give me more."

"Don't know more. I haven't talked to the witness yet."

Sighing, Morgan zipped and buttoned her pants then spun in a circle to try and find a shirt. She hadn't done laundry in near a month, and well, that had obviously been a mistake. "You better have the good stuff."

"Right here sitting next to me."

"How far out are you?"

"Pulling up now."

"Shit." Morgan grabbed whatever shirt was closest to her. "Give me ten."

She didn't wait as she hung up. Shoving her head through the hole in the shirt, she pulled it down over her breasts and belly, tucking it into the slacks. She grabbed her shoulder harness for her weapon, checked her weapon before shoving it into the holster, and grabbed whatever blazer she could find on the floor to cover it up. She looked a mess. She knew she did, but when she was dragged out of bed at three in the morning, whatever witness they were meeting could deal with it.

With the promise of coffee from Pax, Morgan bypassed her own coffee pot and went into her bathroom. A quick brush of her teeth, and an annoyed roll of her eyes at her hair, she shoved water on her hands to try and make it go back down into place. Her short hair was always unruly. She could only ever tame it with a shower, which she definitely did not have time for.

Sliding into the car with Pax, she let out a breath of relief when he immediately handed over the good stuff. She took in a deep whiff and then had that first blissful sip of it. "Thanks."

"Any time." Pax put the SUV into drive and pulled out from the curb of her condo building. "CPD got a call in couple hours ago from a guy, clearly drunk, who keep saying something is going to happen."

"Okay, slow down. Start from the beginning. Who is he?" She stared out the windshield, holding her coffee like it was her lifeline, which it likely was.

Pax let out a breath. "We're not exactly sure. He says he's a member of National Freedom Party, but from our records, that's a pretty low lying group. They don't do much other than talk a bunch of crap."

"Yeah." Morgan closed her eyes and tried to drum up everything in her memory about that group, but she wasn't coming up with much. "Who do they hate again?"

"Who do they not hate? That's kind of the point."

"Oh."

"Yeah. Drink up. I need you not in caffeine withdrawal for this interview."

Morgan huffed. "What made them send it up to us?"

Pax shrugged. "Someone put a memo out for some reason that we were looking for information on them."

"We? As in the bureau?"

"Yup."

"Are we?"

Pax shrugged again. "Who knows, but we got a call, so now we're going to interview."

Morgan sipped even more of her drink, feeling the caffeine hit her system and her brain thinking more clearly. "Taylor knows?"

"Yeah, he said he didn't know what was going on, but since it's a hate group that we should check it out just in case, and if nothing, it'll rebound back to the CPD."

"That's stupid. Waste our overtime hours for this when they don't even know if it's our case or not."

"It could be."

"Only if there's a credible threat."

Pax shifted his gaze to her before looking back out the front window. "He says there is."

"A threat or a credible threat."

"I don't know, Stone. I'm just as frustrated with going as you are. It's Monday. I was supposed to do breakfast with the girls before taking them to school today and now Mel's got to do that and I'm stuck in this damn car with you."

"Real nice." Rolling her eyes again, she pushed back into the seat and focused on her coffee. "You interviewing or am I?"

"You are. You're better at it than I am, besides, if he's anti-Black people, he probably won't even speak to me."

"Yeah, but he's probably anti-queer too." Morgan clenched her jaw. It was the first time she'd really brought it up with Pax in a way that made it obvious she also experienced discrimination, not in the same way, but it was very likely this guy, whoever he was, didn't like either of them.

"You can hide yours for two hours."

"Fuck off." Morgan scrunched her nose, and then swallowed her own anger before brushing her hand over her face. "I'm sorry, that was uncalled for. I'm just...I'm tired."

"We all are."

Determined to keep her mouth shut for the rest of the ride to the station, Morgan made sure to finish her coffee. She missed what she and Pax used to have before the glass had been shattered last Christmas. She missed their banter and their friendship, but she wasn't wrong, something had shifted between the two of them since then. Mel had even mentioned it in a text at one point.

Pulling up at the station, Morgan got out first. Pax slammed his door shut shortly after she closed hers. They were led back into an interview room where the man was waiting for them to arrive. Morgan caught a reflection of herself in one of the large mirror like windows and cringed. She was definitely out of sorts. Laundry first thing before she went to work that morning, that way she could at least have something clean for the next day.

"He says he's been part of NFP for years, but nothing like this has ever happened before."

Morgan stared at him as the detective spoke. "What's his name?"

"Ray Arnold."

Letting out a breath, Morgan nodded. "Okay, you fill Agent Jones in. I'm going to talk to him. You recording?"

"No."

Morgan thinned her lips and sent Pax a look before she pushed open the door and walked into the room. The scent of alcohol was way stronger than she had anticipated, and it hit her like a brick wall as soon as she was four paces inside. She sat across from Ray at the table and tried to keep her nose plugged at the same time.

"Hi, Ray. I'm Agent Morgan Stone. I'm with the FBI. Do you want to tell me what brought you here tonight?"

His jaw trembled. His fingers curled and uncurled several times. He leaned back in the wooden chair and then shook his head at her. "No."

She had hoped since he'd already come forward to talk to the police once that it would be easy for him to talk again, but her assumption had been wrong. Sighing, she started from the beginning. "Can you tell me your full name please?"

"Raymond Arnold." He speech was slurred beyond what she'd first heard when he spoke.

Morgan swallowed and glanced out the window, knowing Pax was right outside and listening in. "All right, Ray, can I call you Ray? Anyway, Ray, the Chicago Police called us in because you mentioned a group you're a part of. What group is that, exactly?"

He shook his head, crossing his arms and staring at the table top.

"You know, Ray, I can have my partner come in here and ask these questions, but he's a pretty big Black man, and was just roused from his bed in the middle of the night to come all the way down here to listen to you talk, and well, he's a bit cranky when he gets woken up in the middle of the night. I'm the much better option to be dealing with, trust me."

Ray looked around the room, his pale blue eyes finally landing on Morgan and he gave a slight nod. "Nothing happened."

"Why don't you start from the beginning, because the Chicago Police detective that called us in here just wants to make sure that nothing is going to happen. That's all I'm here for too, okay?"

"Sure."

"So, let's start again. What group was it that you mentioned you were a part of?"

"National Freedom Party. I've been a member since I was twenty-eight."

"Wow, that's a long time." Morgan noted the name and the year he joined in the notepad Pax had thankfully remembered to bring and shoved in her hand at some point. "What do you do in this group?"

"We don't anything, really. Just meet, get together, talk about politics."

"That's a pretty heavy subject for just a fun gathering of guy-friends."

He shrugged but didn't give her any indication he was going to say something else.

Morgan set her pen down and stared right at him. "So why did you get piss-faced and come down here in the middle of the night to talk to a detective? Tell me your story, Ray. I want to hear it."

He still was barely looking at her, his gaze glued to something on the table top in front of him, something Morgan had no idea was there because she didn't see what was so interesting about an old wooden table.

"Ray?"

He cleared his throat. "Oh right...nothing. Just drunk ramblings."

"Hmmm." Morgan glanced again through the window. Ray was no doubt sobering up, which was going to make her side of the conversation much more difficult if he was suddenly holding back on what he wanted to share. "What would those drunk ramblings be?"

Ray finally looked her dead in the eye. "Nothing you would understand."

"Try me. I'm a pretty understanding person, even my partner says so."

"Your partner?"

"Yeah, Agent Jones. I told you about him earlier." She knew what Ray had meant by his question. It had been exactly what she'd told Pax would happen, but she sidestepped it as best as she could.

Ray pursed his lips together and drew in a long slow breath. "Nothing much to say."

Trying to take a different tact, Morgan switched gears. She'd noticed the simple gold band on his left ring finger and opted to go in that direction. "You married, Ray?"

"Yes."

"How long you been married?"

"Thirty-three years, I think. 1989. June."

Morgan raised her eyebrows at him, writing the information down. "That's a long time to be married."

He shrugged. "We're a good match."

"What's her name?"

"Carla."

"Such a pretty name," Morgan complimented even though she didn't mean it. "You have any kids?"

"Two. What's this got to do with anything?"

"Just trying to get to know you a bit better, see if you'll be more comfortable talking to me then." And more sober, but Morgan didn't add those words out loud. "Are your kids still at home or are they out on their own?"

"They've got families of their own now."

"Oh! So are you a grandparent?"

"I really don't see what the point of this is." His tone had a bite to it.

Morgan wished she had a whole pot of coffee in her system before she had tackled this conversation, not that she hadn't done it before with less sleep and less coffee, but as she got older herself, she found those two things were always on her want list. "The point is, Ray, I want to get to know you. I want to figure out what keeps you interested in this group of friends you've got going on, and what they might be up to, since you came in here saying they were up to something. We take these types of conversations very seriously. I don't want to dismiss them since you were so brave in bringing them forth."

"I told you, there is nothing going on."

"Was there talk about something that might happen?" Morgan made eye contact with him, trying to assess how much he knew and how much he didn't, if there really was a threat or not.

"No." When he hesitated in his answer, she knew she had hers.

"Who are your friends in the group? The ones you see most often?"

Ray clenched his jaw and shook his head. "I'm not telling you that. I'm not getting anyone in trouble."

"Is there something they'd get in trouble for?" Morgan stared down at her notebook, watching him out of the corner of her eye and hoping the less intimidating she made herself the more open he would be.

Her theory didn't work. Morgan spent the next two hours with Ray and got nothing out of him. He went silent. Finally Pax pulled her out of the room. He stood over her with a cross look on his face.

"What? I tried."

"I know you did. I'm still mad about being here at three in the morning."

"To be fair, it was closer to four by the time we got here."

"Don't remind me," he muttered. "They're going to release him, since there's nothing to hold him on."

"I hope following up."

"Yeah, and I'm betting Taylor will want us to do that, too."

"Someone else can, one of the newbs." Morgan's eyes widened. "I'm tired. Why were we on call again? Should we not have to do that at this point, Pax? I mean, we are twenty-year veterans in the FBI, shouldn't they put this kind of hardship on the younger ones, the ones who don't know their ass from their elbow?"

He snorted, which was exactly what she had been going for. Pax nodded his head toward the exit. "Shall we?"

"Don't we have to talk to Detective whatever-his-name-is?"

"I got it covered already."

"Really?"

"Yes, while he were winding up for the sixtieth round of questions on Mr. Arnold in there."

Morgan shook her head. "You get their report."

"They'll send it tomorrow."

"Great. Just something pretty to add to mine."

"You know it. Wanna grab some breakfast?"

"Yes! And coffee."

"Addict."

"Of course," she teased as they walked out of the building. Morgan stopped short when she saw Fiona coming in. She'd almost forgotten that she worked there, that they might see each other if they got stuck there long enough. Morgan had been there before, to see Fiona too, but it had been so long ago, and a memory she wasn't quite sure she wanted to keep around.

Morgan stumbled her step, but Pax caught her arm and held her steady. "You okay?"

"Yeah, just tripped. Clumsy me."

Straightening her back, Morgan bolstered herself for seeing Fiona again. She always had to try and prep herself for it. With a deep breath, she squeezed Pax's arm to let him know she was fine and then stepped away from him as Fiona came closer, finally figuring out who was standing there.

"Agent Stone, Agent Jones, what are you doing here?"

"Detective Wexford," Morgan started. "We landed a case, kind of? Actually, I'm not really sure on that. We landed an interview." Morgan glanced at Pax, and he gave a nod of agreement. When she turned back, Fiona stared directly at Pax, her eyes wide with surprise. "We didn't get much from it, so I doubt you'll be seeing us back here any time soon, not to mention it likely wouldn't be our primary case since we already have one."

"Right," Wexford muttered.

Morgan cocked her head to the side, curious as to what exactly was in Fiona's tone, something about it didn't ring true for everything she had known about her. "You okay?"

"Yeah, late night." Wexford's gaze moved from Pax right to Morgan, staring her down with those telling eyes.

Pax cleared his throat. "We were just going to grab some breakfast before heading to the bureau."

"Right!" Morgan smiled. She wanted to reach out and grab Fiona's hand, but she resisted, knowing the last time they had held hands in that very office, Fiona had done it subtly so no one else would see. "Do you want to join us? Is your shift starting soon?"

"Uh..." Fiona's lips parted. "I can't, Morgan. Not today."

Pax's head swiveled to Morgan, and he gave her an odd look, one Morgan couldn't quite read. "Okay, next time then. I have to get me some coffee before my day begins. Very much necessary."

"I'll see you around." Wexford stepped around them and headed straight into the building.

Odd didn't even begin to cover what had just happened. It was like they were back to being complete and awkward strangers again. The only difference had been someone else was around to witness whatever they talked about, someone in their line of work. Filing that away for the future and to figure it out, Morgan stepped forward to head toward Pax's car. When he didn't move, she asked, "You coming?"

"Yeah." He cleared his throat and then walked with her. "Where are we eating?"

"Good Egg?"

"Sure."

Morgan hopped in the passenger side of the vehicle and waited for Pax to get in and take her right where she wanted. Food and coffee, two things she could in no way live without. It didn't take them long to pick up their food and to head into the office. Morgan was halfway through her meal with Pax excused himself awkwardly. She clenched her teeth when her own phone rang, her mother on the other end of it. With time to spare, she answered.

"Ma, what's up?"

"Just checking in, baby."

Morgan cringed. "What's wrong?"

"It's Clyde. I don't know what to do with him."

"Like I keep telling you and everyone else. You cannot make him sober up. He has to choose to do it. Until that happens, there is nothing to do except support Lauren, especially through this pregnancy."

"I know. I just...I've never had one of my kids mess up this much."

Morgan snorted. If only her mother knew half the stuff her kids had gotten up to. All nine of them had done things she would be appalled with. The only difference was Clyde's were a bit longer lasting than anyone else's, well, that and less acceptable on the awful-scale. Carrie being married three times over was simply another symptom of the problems they all faced.

"He'll be fine, mom. I promise. I've been checking in on him and Lauren every week. That's all we can do for now, and when she's ready to have that baby, feel free to ask her—ask her first—" Morgan made sure to emphasize that part "—if she wants help and then how she wants help. She might not want you there. Clyde says he'll go to rehab when she's given birth, but again, this isn't anything new for him. He's been a drunk for years."

"Morgan!"

"What? Ma, I'm not going to sugar coat it. The kid has had issues for years. This isn't anything new, and every time Lauren gets pregnant, we go through this. So...until he's ready to work his shit out, this is what has to happen, and I swear to God, Ma, if you send them money, send it to Lauren and Lauren alone. Do not give anything to him."

The silence on the other end of the line told her she was already too late on that one. She'd call Lauren and figure it all out when she had a chance, until then, she needed to get back to work. "I've got a big case that just came in, okay?"

"Yeah, okay, sweetie. Are you coming home for Easter?"

"For...what?" Morgan glanced at the calendar on her desk. "That's in two weeks."

"It is."

"No. I'm not coming home. If I was, you'd know about it." But that was a lie. If she was going home, two weeks beforehand was right about when she would tell her mom she was heading to the west coast.

"Okay."

Morgan nodded toward Pax coming back. "I've got to go. I'll call you soon. Love you."

"Love you, too." When she hung up, Pax gave her a questioning look.

"Your mom?"

"The one and only." Morgan turned back to her desk, ready to dive into research about whatever hate group they had just encountered and to remind herself of all the memos that had been sent out about them. It was going to be a long day of slogging through computer crap, but she could get it done, at least now that she had coffee. With her focus on the task in front of her, Morgan started up her report of their interview that morning and went to typing away.

CHAPTER SIX

MORGAN SPENT the better part of the morning at her desk with an endless supply of coffee. She gone over her interview with Ray so many times she knew she had to stop thinking about it. She'd gotten absolutely nowhere with him in two hours. It was rare for her to do so poorly in an interview. Perhaps Pax should have taken lead at some point or gone in first to really irk Ray into talking—that or it would have had the opposite effect and shut him up even more.

Sighing, she took her glasses off and rubbed two fingers hard against her left temple to try and ease the ache she had forming in the front of her head that shot all the way to the back. She needed more coffee. Lack of sleep always gave her a migraine.

She had checked in on all the extremist hate groups that had popped up in Chicago in the last ten years, the ones who the FBI had deemed worthy enough to watch. Nothing. Well, not nothing, but nothing about Ray being involved in them as best as she could tell. Sighing, she rubbed her temple again and downed the last of her coffee.

When Morgan looked around for Pax, she couldn't find him. He was no doubt, somewhere, doing something. Grabbing her mug, Morgan went for a refill. All she'd found in the files she'd been through was hate, hate, and more hate. And a whole lot of anger. It made her head hurt. Frankly, it made it her heart hurt more than anything. She almost couldn't tell if the sex crime of human trafficking she'd been working the better part of two years was better or worse than the blatant hatred of another individual solely based on—well, in her opinion, nothing other than someone was outwardly different.

As she cleaned out her mug and poured more hot liquid into it, she gnawed on her lip. With one added teaspoon of sugar to her coffee, she took a chance. With her life-juice in hand, Morgan left her floor and took the elevator two floors down. As she exited, she drew in a deep breath of freshly brewed coffee somewhere in the nearby vicinity. Good, she could get another cup should she run out.

Morgan walked confidently through the winding halls until she came to the one singular desk she was looking for, and sure enough, her counterpart sat right there. Her hair was drawn back in a tight bun, greying streaks here and there depicting her age and giving her away, although her eyes were young and light. Morgan slipped to lean on the corner of the desk and stared out at the rest of the room, startling her poor friend out of whatever she was working on.

"Morgan." Her voice was cold, ice in each syllable as her gaze slowly rose to Morgan's.

"Adena."

"What brings you down here?"

Morgan smirked as she took a slow sip from her cup. It was a game they played, like they weren't overly familiar with each other, like they hadn't known each other for years, or spent a few drunken nights together between the sheets. "A case."

"Hmmm." Adena squinted at the computer screens she had running in front of her. "What kind of case?"

"Your kind."

Adena gave a little snort. "No doubt."

Morgan gave it. "It's an extremist hate group, kind of. Not one I've ever heard of before."

"Oh?" That had Adena's attention, she turned toward Morgan, her neck stiff so she moved awkwardly like she couldn't bend right. It had always weirded Morgan out a little. "Tell me more."

"It's called National Freedom Party, but they haven't done anything. At least not from what I've found."

"Let me see." Adena pushed up the glasses on her nose then opened new search parameters. She typed quickly, far more quickly than Morgan had ever hoped she could. As she waited for an answer, she sipped her coffee, wishing she had more answers already. "Here we are."

Adena turned and looked up at Morgan, crossing her arms.

"What?"

"There isn't much there."

"Figures." Morgan rolled her eyes. "Is there anything on them?"

"Yes, I just printed it."

"Thank you."

Adena still stared at Morgan, her brown eyes that matched her brown hair both dull and unnerving at the same time with how much they held in them. Morgan could never tell with her what she was thinking, at least not after their little tryst or two, whatever it was. Rolling her shoulders, Morgan started again to try and get some more information.

"Are they violent?"

"No, not historically. They've barely hit our radar."

"Well, I guess that's good."

Adena nodded and focused on her computer screen. "It's more a group of men who get around, drink, and complain about how bad they have it because they're white."

Morgan has to hold back her snort. "Except they blame it all on people of a different race?"

"Specifically immigrants, but yes, people with brown skin, but more typically, those who are Muslim."

"Wonderful." It had been just what Morgan suspected. "Is there any specific group they target or is it a general hatred of all brown-skimmed Muslim immigrants?"

"Basically that." Adena jumped up from her desk and headed for the massive printer-copier in the corner of the room. When she returned, she handed over a few papers to Morgan. "This is everything we have on them."

"It's not much."

"Like I said, they're not very active in terms of violence or deemed a threat to escalate to violence."

Morgan pursed her lips as she skimmed the information. "I had an interview last night with an individual who is part of this group, who said there was some sort of threat of violence."

"Really?"

"Yeah. At least that's what he told CPD. As soon as Pax and I showed up, silence."

"What did he say the threat was?"

"Silence." Morgan gave her a sideways glance. "I'll let you know if I find anything else, but if you could keep your ear to the ground on this group, I'd appreciate it."

"Absolutely."

Pushing off the desk, Morgan headed to her floor and her desk. Pax was back, and when Morgan looked over his shoulder, she saw he was working on the trafficking case and Mr. Jimmy. Morgan slipped into her own chair and handed the file Adena had given her over to Pax.

"Adena?"

"Yeah. Not a whole lot, but something to check out."

Taking the proffered papers, he read them over while Morgan concentrated on their primary case—Mr. Jimmy. He was a headache in and of itself. Dimitri worried her, too. He was their one solid lead on figuring out who Mr. Jimmy was. He'd been a runner for the crime organization, and Mr. Jimmy—unfortunately—took interest in younger, minor, boys. Dimitri had been subject to him on more than one occasion, and thus far, he was the only witness and victim they had who could identify him.

She'd checked in on Dimitri's progress weekly, making sure he was doing well in school, but also that his therapy was going well and effective. She wasn't truly sure the impact of what Dimitri had been subjected to would come full force until he was much older, but she would likely check in on him even after their case was finished—if it was ever finished.

Pax interrupted her thoughts. "It looks to me like an individual from this group has decided to go rogue. Since Ray felt uncomfortable with confessing what he suspects is going on, I think he's not in on it at all."

Morgan turned to him with a smirk. "You sound more like the profiler now. You been holding out on me?"

He wrinkled his nose. "Nope, just been around you long enough to figure some things out."

"Yeah, sure, whatever. You are right, though. Ray does not fit the profile as someone who would take extreme measures from what I saw of him, although I didn't see much of him or hear from him."

"Did Adena say if she thought it was a credible threat?"

Morgan shook her head. "No, because she hasn't looked at our reports yet, but previous to this, they were not deemed a threat. I like your individual idea though, may be worth it to look into the group and see who sticks out as capable, maybe if there's more than one."

"Anyone is capable of violence if pushed."

Morgan gave him an odd and watchful look before slowly turning back to her computer. "Want to do dinner soon? It's been awhile since I was around to just hang out with you, Mel, and the girls."

He nodded. "Yeah. Sounds good. Text Mel."

Snorting, Morgan focused on the hate group she'd been researching. Finding an individual who was heading toward violence was going to be far harder than finding a group heading toward it. Unless someone spoke up, like Ray, they most likely wouldn't find them until it was far too late especially since these groups rarely had membership rosters easily accessed. If only they could crack Ray. One of their counterparts who had a bit more time was headed to CPD to try again. Morgan was eager to see the report.

She was so tired of the racism, of the negativity, but really of hate. The further Morgan dove into the hate groups in Chicago, the more the ache in her chest grew to the point she found herself nearly constantly rubbing between her breasts to try and ease it. There was no logical sense to anything she was seeing. Although, to be fair, nothing was logical about hate.

When the call had come in that the second round of agents had gotten nowhere with Ray, Morgan finished her report and submitted it. Then she sent an email to Adena to see if she was interested or could find anything Morgan had missed. It didn't take Morgan long to go back to the case that was supposed to have the majority of her attention, although in a lot of ways it felt they were no closer to catching Mr. Jimmy than they'd been last Christmas.

She pulled up another interview with Dimitri, one that had been archived from three weeks ago, and put headphones over her ears. Sipping her coffee, she hit play and closed her eyes, listening only to the different tones in his voice.

"I...I don't know who he is." Fear. He felt fear. Dimitri knew something.

"That's okay, Dimtri," the female interviewer comforted. "It's okay if you don't know who he is. We'll figure that out. What did Mr. Jimmy have you do for him?"

Dimitri huffed. "I've told you all before. I'm a runner."

The interviewer drew in a slow breath through her nose. "What did you run for him?"

"Anything he wanted. Mostly money, sometimes, or notes from his pimps." Defensive.

Morgan took another sip of her coffee, keeping her eyes off the screen. She'd watch the next time around when she went through the interview again.

"Do you have a pimp?"

"No! I'm not that kind of runner."

Morgan's heart jumped. She reached up and backed up the video, listening again to Dimitri's voice.

"No! I'm not that kind of runner."

"No! I'm not that kind of runner."

Morgan sighed and let out a sharp breath. "I've never met a runner who also didn't put out on the side, albeit, probably not willingly."

They'd have to go down that line of questioning again. He'd already admitted to them Mr. Jimmy liked boys, younger boys, of which he was one, and Morgan—along with just about every other interviewer involved in the case—was pretty sure Dimitri had been victim to Mr. Jimmy. Getting him to admit that would be a difficult task. Sighing, she focused back on the interview.

"Okay, Dimitri. Do you know any of the other runners who work for Mr. Jimmy?"

"No." Obstinate. The interviewer had forced Dimitri to put up walls, and now she was stuck tearing them down. Morgan wished she'd been in that room with him, but she couldn't be in two places at once.

"Did you ever see anyone who works for Mr. Jimmy?"

"Y-yes." There was a pause before he continued. "I was a runner, so I saw lots of people."

"Do you remember some of their names?"

Dimitri let out a huge sigh. "I told you that already."

"I know." The interviewer's voice softened to make Dimitri more comfortable. "And like I said before, we're going to have to go through this information many times just to make sure we have everything so we can catch Mr. Jimmy."

"You won't catch him," Dimitri muttered.

"I'm sorry, I didn't hear you."

This time, Dimitri near shouted it. "You won't catch him. He's untouchable."

Morgan's stomach twisted, and she popped her eyes open, pausing the video. "He's untouchable."

Mulling that over, Morgan grabbed her notebook and wrote it down. If Mr. Jimmy thought he was himself untouchable, then that added to his profile. However, she couldn't tell if it was Dimitri saying that because he believed it or if Mr. Jimmy had told him as much. Morgan glanced at Pax, who was elbow deep in some kind of work before bending closer and backing up the video a bit to watch the next part.

"You won't catch him. He's untouchable."

"Untouchable?"

Dimitri nodded.

"What does that mean?"

Morgan could have kissed the woman for asking the very question she'd wanted asked. With her pen between her fingers, she prepared to write exactly what Dimitri said.

He shrugged but said nothing.

"What does it mean he's untouchable?"

Dimitri's lips thinned, his gaze did not move up from the table. "You can't touch him."

The interviewer put her hand on the table in front of Dimitri to garner his attention. When he moved his gaze in her direction, but not looking her directly in the eye, she spoke. "Dimitri, you know this is a safe place, okay. You can tell me whatever you want here. I'm here to make sure you are safe and that Mr. Jimmy doesn't find you, but I can't do that until you tell me everything you know."

He nodded. "He doesn't like to be touched."

Morgan's stomach dropped.

"He only likes to touch."

"Touch you?"

Dimitri nodded.

"Where does he touch you?"

Dimitri didn't move. "Everywhere."

"Okay," the interviewer drew in a deep breath. "Okay, where does this happen? In his office? In a bedroom?"

"It's always at the hotel. I only ever see him at the hotel."

"Okay, and this hotel, it's the same one you told us about before?"

Nodding, Dimitri's shoulders drew in as he closed himself off. Morgan closed her eyes, wishing he'd open up a little more, but she could understand why he didn't. He'd been *employed* by Mr. Jimmy since he was born. Born into the life with no hope of ever getting out. He never knew any different to want it.

"Did Mr. Jimmy ever say anything to you about his personal life?"

Dimitri sat in the quiet for a little before he finally whispered, "One time, he told me I was around the same age as his son, year or two older maybe. But he didn't really talk about anything."

Morgan froze. She played that part of the video again before she tapped Pax's arm and handed him the headphone so he could listen in. Pax told her to replay it with a motion of his hand and then pulled the headphones off.

"I'll be damned."

"The only one on our shortlist who has a son around Dimitri's age is Jonathon Lockland." The excitement in every word she spoke was not well concealed. Morgan practically bounced in her chair.

Pax nodded his agreement. "Tell the boss."

Jumping up from her seat, Morgan went to work. By the end of the day, they had surveillance permanently affixed to Jonathon Lockland and Lockland Holdings. Not to mention, Taylor had magically approved an undercover or two to start in on surveying him. Morgan had been sure it was him from near the beginning, but finally everything was coming into place to prove it. Jonathon Lockland fit her profile perfectly.

CHAPTER SEVEN

IAN SAT in his basement bedroom, bent over the makeshift plastic table he had borrowed from Ray. His back ached, but he had to perfect the bomb. He had to make it work this time, unlike last time. He'd spent hours in research, working through where he had gone wrong, what he'd done incorrect, and he was pretty sure he'd figured out the problem.

With the final piece in place, Ian sat back and stared at the bomb. It was perfect. He'd only managed to get enough supplies for one because delivery had been messed up. He'd thrown a minor fit when that had happened but was back to focusing on the task at hand. They needed to do something about the leach problem in their neighborhood. It had become irrefutably clear over the past three years that no one was going to do anything about it.

No one had done anything yet, and their population had continued to grow. They had continued to take jobs that were meant for good American-born people. Ian shook his head at that insanity of it all. He was born there. He deserved to have a job, to be able to go into an interview and not be turned away because he didn't meet *diversity requirements.*

Ian knew he was right. He had waited to make a move, to do something, and he was done waiting. If he didn't take matters into his own hands, no one would. He taped everything down on the bomb so there would be no loose wires. Then he carefully placed it in the backpack he had bought the day before and settled it into the corner of the room.

Cleaning up after himself, Ian made sure to take care with everything. The last thing he wanted was his snowflake of a brother to come down to the basement for whatever reason and ruin his plans. Pausing, Ian put his hands on his hips and surveyed the room. He was ready to do whatever it took in order to make a difference for someone else. If that meant he was a martyr or made one example of, so be it. It would be an example he was proud of.

He had one hour before Spencer and Tim came over. One hour to make sure he had his head on straight and knew what they were going to do. They were going to make a difference for sure, but exactly how they were going to do that was a different answer. An impact. Ian sneered, his upper lip pulling until he laughed. Yes, they were going to make an impact for sure.

Ian put the final touches in his basement, then he went out to grab some beers. If he had his way, which he most likely would. They'd be starting tomorrow with their newest plan. Tim was already doing a lot of the surveillance and checking the place out, counting how many people went in each morning, when they came out for lunch, when they left for home. He'd even put it all on paper in a grid so they'd be able to see.

Two hours later, they sat around in the basement, Ian with a beer can in his hand as he sucked down his third one of the hour. He was going to slow down soon. He needed his wits about him. Ian made sure to observe both Tim and Spencer carefully. Tim he didn't have too many worries over, but Spencer. He was a wild card, and his girlfriend was even wilder. He could never tell with them what each would do to piss off the other.

When they were sufficiently relaxed, Ian leaned forward as he sat on his couch, his elbows on his knees, beer dangling in his fingers. "So what are we going to do next?"

"What?" Spencer asked, his eyes wide.

Tim smirked and took a swig of his own beer.

Ian cocked his head to the side and directly stared at Spencer. "The last time we fucked up. I've worked on the kinks. It'll work this time. So what's next?"

Spencer shook his head. "Maybe we shouldn't."

"You want in or not? You have to be willing to make the sacrifice so others can live. Think about Tim's kids. Don't they deserve the right to work, to have healthcare available to them, to be able to find places to live, places that aren't taken up by *them*."

It took him a minute, but Spencer eventually nodded. "Yeah. They do."

"So...what's next?"

Tim set his beer on the table. "I think we should do the factory next. It's where most of them work. If we destroy where they work, maybe they'll go home since they won't have any source of income."

"Or if they don't go home, maybe they'll just leave here," Ian added. At Tim's nod, he continued, "I think it's a good idea."

"Which factory is this?"

"The food processing place over in Bensonville, or there's the shipping container place, which is closer to here."

Ian rolled his shoulders as he debated. "I think we should stick closer to home. Easier to make a difference for those we care about if we stay around here."

"Agreed."

Spencer was oddly quiet. Ian ignored him.

"Did you look at both?"

"Yes." Tim grabbed an envelope and a pen from the coffee table and started sketching.

Ian turned his head to the side to get a better view of what Tim was drawing, and he realized far enough in, that it was the factory itself. When Tim finished, he turned it around so Spencer and Ian could better see.

"Here is where everyone goes in and out. They have to swipe an identification card to get in and out. Here is where they all take their breaks. It's behind a fence."

"How do we get behind there?" Spencer asked.

Tim shook his head. "We don't. How much of a radius do you think this bomb has?"

"Maybe twenty or thirty feet," Ian answered, already knowing where this was going. "It'll hit the door from the fence."

"Right, so we just have to get it to the fence. There are cameras here and here, so we will have to wear something to cover ourselves because there is no way to avoid it."

"Spencer, you'll do this one."

"What?" Spencer went rigid. "You sure?"

"Yes." Ian grabbed his beer. "When is shift change?"

"Six in the morning."

"We'll set it at three."

This time they drove together in one vehicle to try and avoid being seen. Parking down the road, Ian gritted his teeth as he grabbed the backpack and set the timer on it for three hours. A bubbly feeling in his gut roiled to life as the excitement and anticipation of everything worked its way into reality.

It would work this time. Silently, without speaking, he handed the bag to Spencer, who shook his head with wide eyes like he hadn't slept a wink since their first attempt at making a difference. Ian knew that at least he himself would sleep soundly for the first time in months if their plan actually worked.

"You do it," Spencer whispered. "I'll do the next one."

"I'll need you the next time, and if you back out on me again, I'll know where your loyalties lie." Ian clenched his molars. "I'm half-tempted to say I know where they lie right now."

"They don't, Ian. Really. I'm with you on this, all the way, one-hundred percent."

"Then do it."

"I don't want to mess it up. I don't want to do something and make it not work this time around."

Ian gave him a hard stare, mulling it over in his head. It wouldn't be impossible for them to switch it up this time, but the next time, they would need all three of them to be on their toes. "Fine."

Nodding his head at Tim, Ian pulled the hood of his black jacket over his head. He donned leather gloves and covered as much of his face as he could with a bandana. He was going to make this worth it.

Tim and Spencer stayed in the car, Tim driving and Spencer in the back next to where Ian had been sitting. Ian stepped out into the chilled middle-of-the-night air and let out a huff of breath. This was the right decision. It was the only decision. His heart ramped up its pace. The anticipation for the next three hours might be enough to do him in, but he couldn't wait to see what sort of an impact they made this time around.

His rubber boot splashed into a puddle underneath him. He hadn't counted on the rain, but it shouldn't affect too much. The bomb would be protected in the backpack, ready to go off now that the timer was set.

He had to walk the three blocks by himself, but he knew Tim was driving around the other way to pick him up right where they had designated the meet. He wanted to make sure they were as safe as could be for the next time they did something, which depending on how this one was received would determine their timeline.

Ian adjusted his mask, his steps firm and sure as he moved. He got to the front of the factory. Next time, they'd have to find a better way to get inside and to make the job more worth their effort. Ian knew, without a doubt, that there would be a next time. This was not the last people had heard from him. It would take more than one simple incident to scare off the dogs from their part of the town. He should have done something sooner, way sooner, if he'd wanted to protect what was rightfully his.

As soon as he made it to the fence and the gate where people would enter, he saw his target. The trashcan. Smirking under his mask and disguise, Ian stepped forward and slipped the backpack into the metal trashcan then stepped away from it like he'd done nothing wrong. He shoved his hands into his pockets, hunched his shoulders, and moved on the way he'd originally been heading. If anyone saw him on cameras, it would just look like he had dropped something in the trash like a good citizen. They wouldn't know anything different until it went off.

He made it the four blocks to where Tim was to pick him up and slid into the back of the vehicle next to Spencer. They drove off then headed for Ian's brother's house and the basement where he was staying. As much as he wanted to stay close by and see if his bomb actually worked, if it actually worked this time, he knew it was a risk they couldn't afford. Not if this was only the first step in their plan to take back Chicago.

The beer came out early, although, Ian had never truly stopped drinking it until an hour before they'd gone out to the factory. Spencer was wasted by the time dawn hit. Tim was sipping at his, but he had to go to work and earn to provide for his family. Ian sat on the couch, glued to the news stream, needing to know when it would hit.

Six in the morning came and went. Tim's knee bounced annoyingly, but Ian tried his best to ignore him. He knew they were all on edge, all waiting to see what would happen, how it would happen, what would break first. He flipped through different news stations, all talking about the weather and this or that. He hated the morning news. It was nothing but a bunch of fluff. Chugging another half a beer, he settled on his normal station and waited.

Seven in the morning. Still nothing. Tim begged off to go home and shower and get ready for work. Ian clapped him on the shoulder as he left. Spencer dove into another beer, but he was halfway passed out in his chair. Ian thought about asking Tim to drive Spencer home, but he preferred to keep an eye on him.

By ten in the morning, he'd wondered if the bomb had gone off at all. Spencer was down for the count. Ian stood and walked back and forth in the basement, his energy bubbling like it had the time before. He had to know. He was damn sure it had happened, that it had gone off, that their plan had worked.

He knew he shouldn't have, but Ian grabbed the keys to his car and left the house. He slipped behind the wheel and turned the engine. He had to see for himself. Driving along the way Tim had driven earlier that day, he took it slow. He didn't want to come off as suspicious, but he also needed to come off as sober. It wouldn't do him good to end up in jail.

Brushing hand through the back of his hair, clipped short against his head, he made sure to follow every road sign. When he got closer to the factory, he knew they had succeeded. Police vehicles lined the streets and they were barricaded with firetrucks. He swallowed and pulled to the side, straining his neck to try and see what he could, but he was still at least a block down.

Lights on the tops of the vehicles flashed. That excitement bubbling in his stomach rejuvenated. They had done it. They had managed to take their first stand against the insurrection of immigrants into their country, against them taking jobs from him and people like him. He watched for at least twenty minutes before someone from the fire engine started to come over to his vehicle. Waving them off, Ian turned his car around and headed home.

As soon as he got into the door, he let out a breath of relief. Spencer was still passed out on his couch. Ian grabbed his phone and sent Tim a quick text, telling him all was well and that they'd talk that night. Now all they had to do was wait and see what the fallout would be. How big of an impact did they make?

CHAPTER EIGHT

THE SCENE seemed chaotic from the outside, no doubt, but everything was working just as it should be. She'd slipped her warm jacket on, sending Pax a sidelong look as they stared at the wreckage that was no doubt a bomb.

She'd heard about the explosion within minutes of it happening, but when the Chicago Police Department had called the FBI for assistance, she had landed herself the case. It was the calm before the storm. It ached in her bones. Tents were erected to try and bring in some of the shrapnel that was around, another one for injured who were able to stay on scene. They'd sent five to the hospital already. She kept a running tally in her head, but she knew she was going to have to write it down sooner rather than later so she didn't forget it. Pax gave her a bewildered stare.

"What?"

"A bomb? At a factory? What do you think? Disgruntled former employee?"

"No idea, Pax. You can stop guessing and start asking questions if you want." She raised a brow at him as she sipped from her bio-friendly travel mug she'd insisted on getting herself for Christmas. "Which reminds me, let's start with the managers, see what they have to say. The owner is still out, apparently out of town for whatever reason."

"Who is it?" Pax pulled out his notebook.

Morgan grimaced. She had about a hundred names running through her head and was trying to draw on just one to get her brain moving. "Kelly Roberts."

Pax nodded. "Is she coming back soon?"

"He," Morgan answered pointedly, "had already booked a flight for this afternoon. We can talk to him tomorrow."

"Good."

Morgan took another sip from her drink. "Into the fray?"

"Sure."

She didn't wait as she took her coffee with her. She might get chided over it later, and it might be stupid because writing with one hand while standing and having a coffee in the other was going to be difficult, but she would get it done, somehow.

Morgan started with some of those who were close enough to the explosion to get hit from the burst but not severely injured. The first was a tall, lanky Black man, who sat on the curb of the parking lot. Morgan bent down so she was on even footing with him.

"Hi, I'm Special Agent Stone, I'd like to ask you some questions about this morning."

He shrugged, his dark eyes not moving up to meet her face. She really wished he would, but Morgan could imagine after a morning like he'd had that it would be difficult to focus on anything. "You were outside when the explosion happened, right?"

He nodded.

"Did you see anything? Anyone?"

He shook his head.

She wasn't going to get a great amount of information from him this way. "Would you mind telling me your name?"

"Diric."

"Okay, Diric, what do you do here for work?"

He shrugged. "I'm on the parts line."

Morgan had to draw on what little patience she had. Diric was not super talkative, and she had no doubt that she was going to have some issues with getting him to open up. If everyone was like that, this was going to be a long investigation. "How long have you worked here?"

"Two months."

Morgan wasn't writing anything down after his name. He wasn't telling her pertinent information as of yet. "What time does your shift start?"

"Six."

"So what time do you get to work every morning?"

He did look at her then, his dark, near black eyes boring into her. "Before six."

"All right." Morgan wrote the time down in her notebook. It was what they had already known. The explosion had happened right during the start of a new shift, right when the most people would be injured or even potentially killed. "What days of the week is the factory open?"

"All week."

Morgan sent a glance to Pax, hoping he was having better luck than she was. "Did you see anything odd this morning when you came in to work? Anything out of the ordinary?"

"No."

Morgan took a sip from her coffee. "Would you tell me what happened? What you remember?"

"I got here, like I do every day. I got up to the gate, got inside after being let through, and then I don't remember anything until someone helped me stand up. My ears hurt."

Cocking her head to the side, Morgan checked on his head. She could see some blood on his skin, but he didn't look too injured. "Have the paramedics checked you out yet?"

He nodded.

"Okay, good. It's probably just from a concussion or from the blast of the sound. You'll want to see a doctor for sure." Morgan handed him her card and stood up, her back and thighs aching as she moved. Pax was finishing up whatever interview he was doing. They had so many people to talk to, Morgan had no doubt they'd be there all day if not longer. They'd still be doing interviews the next day.

Taylor had promised to send over some more officers as they freed up schedules, but thus far it was six of them working the scene itself. When she turned to start in on the next interview, she stopped short. The car pulling up to the scene looked very familiar. Her heart raced.

Detective Fiona Wexford stepped out, her shoulder-length brown hair moving in the breeze. Wexford pocketed her keys and rounded her car, nodding at those around her. Then she stopped short. Their gazes locked.

"Fuck," Morgan muttered.

"Fuck what?" Pax asked.

"Shove it." Morgan rolled her eyes at him. "Nothing you need to worry about."

"What's Homicide doing here?"

"I'm betting they're investigating the murders, and we're investigating the explosion."

"You mean bomb."

"Shhh, don't say that too loud, Pax. There are media people everywhere."

"Whatever, Stone." He knocked his much larger shoulder into hers and went on to a new interview while Wexford stepped right up to her.

"Special Agent Stone."

"Detective Wexford." Morgan could barely keep the smile from tugging at her lips. She loved to hear Fiona say her name like that, in that slightly-annoyed but oh-so-superior tone that she did just about every time they met for whatever case or professional function they found themselves at.

"You investigating some murders?"

"One."

"Oh? So the others?"

"Still hanging in there."

Morgan nodded. "You got here late."

"I had a...thing to take care of. Want to fill me in?"

Morgan made sure to trail her gaze up and down the full length of Wexford's body, from her lips, to her chest, to her hips, her toes clad in those ugly brown boots, and then back up. Heat rose in her cheeks, but she wasn't going to give in to it this time, not with being surrounded by all the other officers in the area.

"No. I think you have your own people for that." With a cold shoulder, Morgan walked back to the line of injured employees.

Wexford's lips parted but that was the only sign she was perturbed by Morgan's attitude. Morgan went through three more people to interview before she was out of coffee. She'd have to find a way to get more soon if she had a chance. She was just checking in with Pax when the tap on her shoulder distracted her. Turning, she found Wexford standing stiffly in front of her.

"I think we should talk about media."

"Yeah, that we should. Pax?"

"You're on for that one. You're much better with the media than I am."

Morgan wrinkled her nose. "Not true, and frankly, I think given the nature of where we are and where the attack happened you would be the better option."

Pax narrowed his eyes. "Why?"

"You know why." Morgan put her hand on her hip. "Don't you even dare try to pull this one over on me."

Wexford cleared her throat. "That's all fine. What are we going to tell them?"

"We tell them there was an explosion, nothing more. We don't know anything else until tests come back anyway." Morgan stared directly into Fiona's eyes, wondering what was going through her brain. She did not want to work this case with Fiona if she could avoid it. They had done well finding a balance of friendship, but adding in working together was going to be too much for her feeble brain to keep up with.

Wexford glanced from Morgan to Pax then back to Morgan. "Can we just cut the crap already?"

"What crap?" Morgan shot back.

"That crap." Fiona sent her a daring look. "Whatever *that* is. I'm here to investigate two murders."

"Two?"

Fiona shrugged. "The second one didn't make it through surgery."

"Damn." Morgan raised her eyes to the sky. She'd had hopes casualties would be few and far between. "Fine. But remember, you called us in for help."

Putting her hands out to her sides, Fiona shook her head. "*I* didn't."

"Someone did," Morgan shot right back.

"Why the attitude, seriously?"

Pax snorted, and Morgan spun on him. "Want to weigh in?"

"Uh...no. I'll let you two sort this out." Pax's jaw tightened before it went lax.

Morgan knew she was being pissy, but outside of her initial reaction to Wexford when she'd shown up, she couldn't figure out why. There was something else going on, something she couldn't put her finger on, but it had bugged her any time she, Pax, and Fiona where in the same vicinity.

"All right. Pax will do the press release. Pax, call Taylor, let him know what's going on."

"Yeah, on it." He stepped away, a phone pressed to his ear.

Morgan raised a brow at Fiona. "I'm sorry. I'm just...I'm out of coffee."

The smile that tugged at the edge of Fiona's lips was a warm welcome. Morgan had been a jerk. She seemed to always be making an ass of herself wherever Fiona and work were concerned.

"We don't want mass hysteria, but we are thinking this was intentional. We found evidence of it being a bomb, but until our guys look at it, we're not going to know for sure."

"Do you think there's more?"

Morgan shook her head. "We've had people scouring and looking, and they haven't come up with anything. Based on where it was placed..." Morgan spun in her shoes and turned toward what was the gate and the entrance into the building "...over there, we're betting they couldn't figure out how to get access inside so they just set it outside."

When she glanced back at Wexford, her stomach twisted. All she had to do was keep to business, keep to the work. They could work together again and not end up in a pissing war over who had the case or not. Surely they could manage that at least.

Pax came over. "Taylor says it's a go."

"Good." Morgan stared him in the face. "And he agreed you're doing it."

Pax rolled his eyes. "Yes, but he'll take over from here on out. Just because I'm here today."

Morgan stepped in closer to the two of them. "Plan of action?"

"No b-word," Pax said.

"That can mean multiple things, all of which should be avoided, but do go on." Morgan smirked at him, glad she was finally feeling a little more on her feet.

Pax sighed and shot a nervous look at Wexford. "You know what I meant. Just an explosion that's being investigated to make sure it doesn't happen again. Emphasize safety concerns for the factory workers, don't create panic."

"Good." Morgan punched him lightly on the shoulder. "You've got this. It's almost like you've done it before."

"Shut up," he muttered.

Fiona grinned at the both of them. "Either of you have any luck with talking to the witnesses?"

"They're pretty tight-lipped. Hard to get anything out of them."

"I'm having the same issues," Pax said. "So far they haven't seen much, though. They were coming to work, explosion happened, that's about it. No one they didn't recognize, but they don't know everyone they work with, so that's not too much help. They'll pulling off footage for us so we can check that out."

"I'd like a copy of that," Fiona interjected.

"Of course," Pax answered. "I don't think we're going to get much from witnesses this time around. It'll mostly be our investigation that'll get us the answers we're looking for."

"Right." Morgan's phone buzzed in her pocket. She pulled it out and glanced at it, sending the call to voicemail and shoving it away. "Pax, let's set up the press release, and then we can be done with media for the day."

Wexford walked with them toward the barrage of media vans. She let out a grunt when her phone buzzed again. Grabbing her phone, she answered the call. "Mom, now is really not the time. I'll call you back tonight."

"Morgan, don't you talk to me that way."

"I really can't talk right now. I promise, I'll call tonight."

"I'll hold you to that."

Sighing, Morgan hung up without even saying goodbye and put her phone away again. When Wexford gave her an odd look, she shrugged. "What? I don't have time."

"She's your mom."

"You'd talk to her that way too if you knew her. Trust me." Morgan muttered the last two words and stepped closer to the media fray. They all started to come over to them. Pax took the lead and stood up in front of the two of them, Wexford and Morgan flanking him on either side.

"I'm only going to do this once, so let's all gather around," Pax stated.

They waited a few minutes for the cameras and reports to be in place. Pax let out a breath when he was ready. "We are investigating an explosion that happened here today at about six this morning. We have nothing significant to report at this time. The FBI was called in to assist CPD in this investigation, and we are investigating this together. It has our top priority. For right now, there is nothing to be worried about. We'll have another release for you later tonight."

Bowing out of the release, Pax walked away. Morgan smiled as she followed, glad he hadn't allowed an opportunity for questions to be asked. Some of them still tried, but by the time they'd caught up with the abrupt end to Pax's release, they were already ten feet away and heading back toward the crime scene.

Morgan turned to Wexford. "We've got people taking down names and contact information, so we can follow up with those we miss tomorrow."

Wexford nodded. "Good. You'll also give me a copy of that, yes?"

"Absolutely, Fiona. Whatever we have is yours just as I hope whatever you have is ours."

Fiona gave her an odd look, and when Morgan raised a singular eyebrow in reaction, she finally got a response. "I don't think that's how it works when you liaison with the FBI. I'm pretty sure you are the ones who don't share information."

"Guilty as charged," Morgan smirked. "I will give you all that you have requested thus far, how's that?"

"Better for honesty." Wexford caught sight of something, and when Morgan saw what it was, she noticed another detective beckoning Wexford. "My partner's got something for me."

"Don't forget, Fiona, sharing goes both ways."

"It does." Fiona reached out, her hand touching and then squeezing Morgan's forearm.

Heat seared through her and up her arm and into her chest. Morgan held her breath to keep it at bay. She had hoped after months of building a friendship with Fiona that would have stopped, but it clearly hadn't. She sighed seconds after Fiona left her vicinity. It was going to be a long investigation if they were stuck seeing each other day in and day out. *Professional.* That was the word of the week, apparently. *Keep it professional, Stone. You've got this.*

CHAPTER NINE

BY THE next morning, Morgan knew it was a bomb. She'd seen the message on her phone when she'd creaked her eyes open at o-dark-thirty in the middle of the night. They were still dissecting the fragments, working on its origins and the make up. She'd closed her eyes and had gone back to sleep.

When she woke up next, it was to a pounding on her door. Brushing her bangs out of her eyes, she turned and glared at the door to her bedroom like it was the door to her apartment. Checking her phone, she saw it wasn't even six in the morning yet. Cursing, Morgan pushed her way out of the bed and grabbed her phone. It was riddled with texts and phone calls from Wexford.

Groaning, she had an inkling who was at the door. Either way, Morgan grabbed her gun, holding it tightly in her left hand as she walked barefoot through her definitely way-too-dirty-to-entertain apartment. When she got to the door, the knocking stopped. Glancing through the peephole, she sighed and put her forehead to the cold metal, hoping it would wake her up faster.

"You better have fucking coffee, Wexford. I'm not letting you in without it."

When there was no response, Morgan looked through the peephole again, this time seeing only a coffee cup and Wexford's thin and knobby fingers. One of them was quite crooked, actually, now that Morgan was looking. She'd have to ask about that sometime.

Unlocking the deadbolts, she opened the door and took the coffee before Wexford even came in. Fiona hadn't been to her apartment since December, since Morgan had given in and asked her to stay the night after she'd gotten back from Seattle, after Lollie had tried to kill her in the middle of a really decent fuck.

Ignoring her trail of thoughts, Morgan took a long sip from the coffee and hummed in pleasure. "Jesus, you make the good stuff so good."

Fiona spun around, her dark eyes wide and a blush to her cheeks.

Morgan's face flushed with embarrassment. "That's not what I meant. I swear. I just...shit. I need more of this."

She set her gun on the kitchen counter and moved to the couch, flopping onto it. With the cup in one hand, she took another long sip as she stared at Fiona over the rim.

"Well?" Morgan asked.

"Well what?"

"Do you have a reason for pounding on my door at five in the morning or do you just want me to take a wild guess?"

"It's nearly six."

"It's *not* six."

"Nearly."

"Fiona." There was a warning to Morgan's tone. "Why are you here so early? And thank you for the peace-offering."

Fiona pulled off her jacket and dropped it onto the back of the kitchen chair. She sat next to Morgan, their thighs brushing, and then she rubbed the heels of her palms into both her eyes.

"Jesus, have you slept at all?"

"No," Fiona grumbled. "It was...it's a long story."

"Did you work all night?"

"No." Fiona refused to look at Morgan, her cheeks paling and her shoulders tensing.

"All right, I won't ask." Morgan took another sip of her drink. "Everything okay?"

"You just said you wouldn't ask."

Morgan rolled her eyes. She wanted to get snarky, wanted to have a quick argument. It would certainly rub off some of her anger from being woken up twice that night, not to mention that weekend. She was not getting her week off to a good start.

"Did you call your mom back?" Fiona asked.

"What?" Stunned by the turn of conversation, Morgan narrowed her gaze. "Uh...yeah. Briefly. Why?"

"Just checking. What'd she want?"

"Carrie had her baby."

"Carrie is your...?"

"Middle sister. There's me, then Beth, then Jenessa, then Carrie—she's been married three times, had a baby with each. It's rich. Anyway, then Serena. Always was the quiet kid in the corner that I could never tell if she was going to be the one to randomly kill us all or not."

"Oh my God."

"What? She's not. I swear."

"I can't keep your siblings straight."

"Well, half of us aren't straight, so that might be why."

Fiona snorted. "Who are the rest?"

"Amya is next, she's a police chaplain, used to be a cop. You might like her, actually." Morgan's lips turned up at the thought of her baby sister. She was the one who was making the most of her life thus far, and the one she liked the most. "Then Aisling, and finally Clyde, who is also a screw up and Lauren keeps sticking it out with him for some God awful reason. Oh, and I forgot Lydia, she tends to keep a pretty low key."

"I can't even begin to fathom how you keep up with them all. It's hard enough for me just to keep track of my one brother."

Morgan shrugged. "I'm the oldest, so I've been doing this for fifty years at this point."

When she looked at Fiona, Fiona wasn't looking in her eyes. Her gaze was locked on Morgan's lips. Morgan's breathing quickened, her stomach dancing around. The coffee on her tongue was a stark reminder that they were definitely off-duty, and her thin pajama clothes told her how close her bedroom was. She shifted her own gaze to Fiona's much fuller lips. They pulled up in a smile, one side quirking higher than the other.

"Just checking," Fiona whispered.

"Checking what?" Morgan asked, lost in the sea that was Fiona, fully allowing herself to be swallowed up by the tide of lust she found there.

Fiona inched in closer, her hand on Morgan's knee. "That you still like me."

Morgan could have died. "I do."

"Then why don't you kiss me again."

Morgan's tongue moved unbidden against her lips, wetting them with all the anticipation she could hold back trying to break through the dam. It would be so much better this time. Not awkward. Not rushed. Not unexpected. Definitely appreciated, to its fullest. "Are you single?"

"Not yet. Not by your standards, anyway."

"Then there's nothing to talk about." Morgan focused on her coffee, pulling every ounce of self-restraint she had left into her chest and holding onto it like it was her only lifeline. She would not go down that road. Not again, not ever. And after Lollie, she really wanted her next relationship of whatever sorts it was to be in the free and clear of honesty. "Why'd you come over here? Surely it wasn't for that."

Fiona let out a sorrowful sigh before she shifted away, giving Morgan some much needed space. "No. Did you see the report?"

Morgan had seen a lot of reports since she and Fiona had parted ways at the factory. Wexford could be referencing any number of them, but she had an inkling it was the one that had come in a few hours ago.

"The one about the bomb," Wexford elaborated.

Morgan grimaced. "I skimmed it. I was waiting until daylight to actually look at it. Unlike you, I enjoy sleep."

"I like to sleep." Fiona's lips formed into a slight pout.

Morgan could have kicked herself for causing it. She needed more than a few inches of distance. "I'm going to shower and get dressed for the day, since I'm pretty sure you're not going to let me go back to sleep."

"I'll make coffee."

"You do that." Grabbing the cup Fiona had brought with her, Morgan headed for her small bathroom. Leaning against the counter after shutting and locking the door, she grimaced. "It's never-ending."

They were back at the Chicago Police Department. They were built for interviews in a way the bureau wasn't. Morgan had followed Fiona there and then up to her floor. Just her presence, and Pax who had arrived shortly after them, was enough to raise the tension in the room. Sometimes she hated that her title had that affect on people. Other times it worked quite well to her advantage.

The interviews were divvied up. Morgan took hers and started in on them, once again, landing herself in a room with Diric. She sighed as she walked in, and gave him a small smile as she sat across the table from him.

"How are your ears?"

He nodded at her, his eyes looking much more with it that morning than they had been the day before. "Much better, thank you."

"Good. I'm glad to hear that. I wanted to talk to you a little bit more about yesterday."

He once again nodded at her.

"I just want to know what you saw, what happened."

Diric swallowed. He glanced at the door Morgan had just come through. "I'm here legally."

"Okay, but I'm not asking you that, Diric. Really. You're not in trouble. I just want to know what happened yesterday so that we can hopefully figure out what happened."

He paused. She could tell he wanted to say something, but he was holding back, and she wasn't quite sure why. She tried to make herself as open as possible to him, as non-threatening as she could be for someone in her position and someone in his position. She waited, biding her time, as she watched his mind work. Eventually, he nodded to nothing in particular.

"I think it was the trash."

"I'm sorry?"

"I think it was the trashcan that exploded."

Morgan stared at him. "What makes you think that?"

He shifted in his seat, his long legs moving under the table as his dark eyes locked on hers. "Because that's where Yasir was standing while he waited to be let in. We all stand there until they let us in, but they'd just opened the gates and were checking badges. Yasir is my cousin."

"Okay." Morgan shifted her notebook and wrote everything down. "So he was standing by the trashcan when it exploded, then what?"

"Then nothing. I don't remember anything."

She'd known the explosion hadn't happened from the building itself, already. That was generally clear based on where the most injured were, but having an exact point of impact to look at helped.

"What you've shared is very helpful, Diric. Thank you."

"I just want to go back to work."

She sighed. "I think it's going to be a little bit until they can get the building in working order, but I should think you could be able to go back to work soon. Do you like your job?"

"Oh yes. It's a good job. Perfect for us."

"Do you have a family?"

"Yes, my wife, and three daughters."

Morgan smiled at him. "I'm sure they're adorable. Do you know anyone who you work with or have worked with—I know you haven't worked there long—who isn't happy with the job?"

"No, nothing like that. We all like the work. The pay is good, and there are good hours for us."

"Anyone quit recently that you know of?"

"No, but the day I started someone was fired."

"Do you happen to know who that was?"

"No."

Morgan scribbled a note on her pad to check it out. "Were they angry about being fired?"

"Yes. He was yelling loudly at our supervisor. He had to be escorted off the property."

"That is very helpful, thank you, Diric. I'll check this out for sure."

"You're welcome."

Morgan finished up her interview and headed to find Wexford and Pax. They had some brainstorming to do, and she wanted to know if anyone was interviewing and learned more about this supposed person who was fired two months ago. She grabbed a coffee, downing the contents before filling the Styrofoam cup back up. She hated using Styrofoam, but there was no other option there and she'd conveniently forgotten her travel mug when she'd finally convinced Wexford they had to go to work that morning.

"Need a fix?" Pax whispered in her ear.

Morgan nearly jumped out of her shoes, spilling the coffee all over herself, but she managed to catch it just in time. "Not funny, Pax."

"Sure it was. You're just mad because you almost spilled. You're like a junkie."

"Caffeine is legal. So is coffee for that matter."

He rolled his eyes, but his back stiffened when Wexford wandered closer. "Conference room?"

"Sure."

Once they were all settled, Morgan sipped her coffee. "Anyone hear about some guy who was fired a few months ago and really didn't take too kindly to it?"

The shakes of heads between the other two in the room meant they had a bit more digging to do.

"My guy also says it was in the trashcan."

"Mine too," Fiona added. "Have we gotten anything else back about the bomb?"

Morgan pulled out her phone and checked her messages. Pax did the same. When they were done, they both shook their heads. "It takes time to get this stuff through the right tests. I don't expect to hear anything for another day or two and even then only preliminary results."

"I think this was a hate crime," Fiona whispered.

Morgan straightened her spine. "We don't know that yet."

"The factory is a hub for Somalian immigrants. You can see for yourself with every name we have on our interview lists." Fiona matched her stance to Morgan's. "They go in and out at the same times every day. They would have had to look into it to know that, but the bomb went off exactly when they were letting in the workers for their shift. That's not a coincidence."

"You don't know that it wasn't just a disgruntled employee. Which is the same thing I told this big oaf yesterday. Until we ask the right questions, eliminate theories, we cannot go off on a tangent into one theory that this was a hate crime done by an extremist group."

Fiona leaned against the conference table, her arms crossed, and her body drawn in on itself. "I know. You're right. I know. We have to work the process."

"Because, hate crime or no, Wexford, *you* want this to be just a regular old murder."

"Why?" Fiona shook her head, eyes wide, looking from Morgan to Pax.

Morgan snorted. "Because then you get rid of us."

Grabbing up another file, Morgan headed out for her next interview. Pax caught up with her halfway down the hall, spinning her with a hand on her elbow. "What was that all about?"

"Nothing," Morgan muttered.

"And yesterday, what was that?"

"Nothing, Pax. I told you."

"You're not...you're not *dating* her, are you?"

"God no." Morgan glared. "And keep your damn voice down. I don't want the whole world here to know who I like to date."

Pax lowered his voice. "What is going on?"

"Why won't Taylor let me go to Kansas? It's my case, Pax. I should be working that, not stuck here looking into some pissed-off former employee with a vendetta on their hands. I need to talk to Dimitri, see if I can something else from him. Hell, I need to talk to Reilly. She's been through months of therapy now, surely she remembers something else."

"Morgan, you know why you're still here."

"No. I don't." Morgan glanced around to see who was looking and watching them. "I don't, Pax. That's just the thing. I'm cleared of any wrongdoing. I'm off restrictions. And yet, here I am, investigating nothing I should be investigating."

"This is the job, you know that."

"Yeah, I do know that." Morgan glared at him. "I'm going to finish out my interviews and I'll meet you back at the bureau."

"Morgan, just take a chill, please."

With one more glare, she walked away. If she stayed there any longer, she would no doubt say something she regretted.

She made it to her own desk by late afternoon, and she was glad to have her leave of the CPD offices and Fiona's constant hovering. She poured herself a cup of coffee and settled in. She pulled up the research she had started on hate crimes in Chicago along with hate groups and dug into the mind of who might want to do this if it truly were a hate crime. These were always a special breed of interesting.

Finally, she got some sort of report from their own labs about the bomb. It was a singular bomb, and a simple one at that. It had a small blast radius from start to finish and was never intended to be bigger. It was likely it only took one person to make and set it, which again pointed away from the hate group and toward an individual. It could be an individual acting on their own, but since the dawn of high speed Internet, individuals had come out of the woodwork to create groups to spew their hate with. More backing.

Morgan moved from her desk and headed down two floors, finding herself leaning over Adena's desk. "Hey, curious if you found anything on that file I gave you the other day?"

Adena shook her head. "No, but I haven't had much time to look into it yet."

Tapping her fingers against the edge of Adena's desk, Morgan leaned down. "Anything popping up on your radar at all?"

"No. We keep a pretty close eye on the groups out there. Here." Adena pulled something up on her computer screen and turned the monitor over so Morgan could see.

Morgan squinted. She felt her pockets for her glasses and realized far too late she had left them sitting on her desk. She focused her vision as much as she could, but the words floated over the screen too rapidly for her to keep up. "What is this?"

"It's a forum, essentially. They're speculating that this was not one of theirs, but they wished they'd done it, which tells me it really wasn't any of theirs."

"Who is they?"

Adena turned her chair to face Morgan more fully. "The major race-focused groups we have in the greater Chicago area, the ones who are most likely to participate in violence."

"Hmm." Morgan glanced at the screen again. "None of them are taking credit?"

"None. They're all just as lost as we are."

"We haven't shared it was a bomb. That might affect how they respond?"

Adena shrugged. "I'm not sure it will. They're all assuming it was."

"We gave no indication—"

"Of course you didn't." Adena gave her a small smile. "But this is what these groups train and look for. They are fully aware of what targets they want to hit."

Curious, Morgan squatted down so she could be closer to Adena. "What targets they want. You're saying they've already got some idea of where they would hit."

"Routinely. They may change them up every now and then, and that's when we flag potential dangers."

"Can you give me a list of the current ones we're watching closely?"

"Sure."

"Thanks. Just uh...email it over." Morgan stood up, realizing she was far too close to Adena for comfort. She did not want to give the wrong impression. "This was helpful. Thank you."

When she got to her floor, she knew Pax was back. He had refilled her coffee for her, which made her smile, but he was nowhere to be found. Sitting at her desk, Morgan checked her email, still not having anything from Adena. Instead, she shut down her investigation into the bombing and pulled up her reports on the trafficking case. Surely some of their undercover officers would have something new to report by then. Losing herself in the case she really wanted to be working on, Morgan lost track of time.

CHAPTER TEN

IAN MADE sure to watch the news reels as much as he could. He wanted answers. They had talked, briefly, about an explosion, but that was it. Anger surged in his chest every time he thought about it. If they thought it was just some stupid explosion and not an actual threat, it wouldn't scare anyone. Well, it might, but not enough. They needed to do something bigger, something that would truly make the filthy dogs want to go back where they came from.

It wasn't going to make a lick of difference if they weren't scared. The impact they had made was next to nothing. Spencer had pretty much been drunk since he heard they'd killed three of them. But it was good. It was good they had at least some small impact. Three families scared was better than none scared. He had to get rid of them, get back his job as soon as he good. He deserved it, so did everyone else around him: his brother, Tim, Tim's kids. This was all for them.

Ian picked Tim up, and they drove to the bar. Spencer didn't need any help getting drunk since he was there already. They sat down in one of the corners of the room with their beers in hand. Tim stared at the table, but Ian was still raging mad.

"We need to lay low for a bit," Tim whispered.

"I know," Ian answered. His foot bounced on the rung of the bar stool, his fingers tapped against his glass. He was jittery as hell. And if anything, he was the one who needed to calm down, not Tim and not Spencer. "They didn't take it seriously."

"Who didn't?" Tim asked.

"Anyone," Ian whisper-screamed across the table. "No one took it seriously."

"Yeah." Tim shrugged. "I thought it would be a good place to start out, but maybe I was wrong."

Ian clenched his jaw. It had been a good place to start, to test out what kind of impact they would have, what changes they would need to make. "It was a good place. Next time we just need to go bigger."

"Bigger?" Tim's eyes widened. "You sure?"

"Yes." Ian swallowed down a swig of beer. "Much bigger."

"When?"

"Few weeks from now? You want to figure this out without Spence here?"

Tim leaned back on his stool. "Let's face it, he's not the brains of the operation."

"He's not, but he is useful."

"Some days." Tim took a slow sip of his beer. "Where?"

"Somewhere easier to get to. Don't get me wrong, the factory was a good idea, but we couldn't get close enough to the building to get anything inside. This time, we need to make a good impact."

Tim let out a slow breath. "I'm just tired of it all. It's too hard to keep working with them, too hard to keep up the ruse that I don't see good people losing out on good jobs because they're not the right color to fill diversity requirements. I hate having to pass up someone for a hire so I can do that."

Ian paused, staring up at Tim. "It's not your fault. You know that. It's their fault for not standing up for what this country was built on. The backs of our ancestors. We're the ones who fought for this freedom, who fought for the right to have jobs and to earn money to not have to worry about them raping our daughters."

Tim nodded his agreement. "I know, Ian. It's so hard to watch our neighborhood go to pits."

"Least you still have a neighborhood." The last of it was said into Ian's beer, which he promptly downed the rest. Waving over the waitress, he ordered another one. Leaning in, he kept his voice low. "Two weeks."

"Where?"

"Don't know. We'll figure it out. Until then, let's see what really comes of this factory thing. I'd hate for someone to get the wrong idea about it." Saying the last bit a little louder for those in the back who no doubt hadn't heard him yet or knew what had happened, he shook his head. "It's all just a bunch of shit."

"A big bunch of horse shit."

Snickering, Ian grinned. "Yeah. Horse shit. You think Spence will be up for joining us?"

"I really do," Tim answered. "He may not be with it, Ian, but look at him. He never stood a chance. Unlike you, he didn't grow up when there was a time for people like us to get jobs. He grew up when there were none, when we'd already let them all into this country. He didn't grow up with a family that had a strong backbone or morals. The kid is lost, and he's just that—a kid."

Ian agreed. "He is just a kid. That's why I worry about him. If anyone is going to take up this cause, it should be us, the ones it won't matter to much. We can do this for them, make it better for them. Then his kids, and yours, won't have to deal with it."

"I don't want my kids to have to deal with this. They deserve so much better than what we've been handed."

"That's why we're doing this!" Ian shut up quickly when he saw the waitress coming over with his beer in hand. As soon as she was out of earshot, he repeated himself. "That's why we're doing this."

"I know. I just wish Ray could see that."

Ian snorted. "Ray's an old idiot. He doesn't know his left from his right, and he doesn't know what to do with himself unless his wife tells him to do it. She probably even tells him when to shit and when to piss."

"I guess."

Tim didn't seem too convinced, so Ian dropped it. Ray and him went back far. They worked together for years before Ray had finally retired. "You going to the meeting tomorrow?"

"Yeah. You?"

"Planning on it. I need to be around some like-minded people."

Tim chuckled. "I get that."

"You hear if they have any thoughts on who done it?"

"Nothing. Don't even think they think it was anyone. Why? You hear something?"

"Nothing." His anger was back. This time it wasn't just because of the injustices he was experiencing but it was because of the failure of him to do something about it. Twice now. He had to do something different next time, something he couldn't fail at.

They took a few days to round up ideas. Meeting in Ian's basement, he was ready to get everything moving. The supplies had come in, and he'd begun working on what they would need. He didn't want to wait any longer. Sitting across from Tim, Ian weighed their options.

"You haven't talked to anyone, have you?" Spencer asked Tim.

"Who would I talk to? You talk?"

"No." Spencer's hand fidgeted in his lap. "I keep waiting for the cops to show up and arrest me."

"For what? Chickening out?" Ian sneered. "The cops have no idea what happened. They think a gas pipe burst or something."

"Or something," Tim repeated, raising his eyebrows up and down. "They really don't know what's going on, Spence. They've got nothing to go on, nothing to see, nothing at all. They have no idea who we are or what we did. They really don't. They've got their heads so far up their asses with trying to follow the rules the governments makes them follow that they can't even enforce the laws anymore nonetheless spend the time trying to figure out a crime they don't even think happened."

Spencer nodded. "Okay, yeah. Just checking. What if...what if we hit that street where they all hang out?"

"What street?" Ian asked as he glanced up from the map laid out on the table.

"You know, where the store is. There's a few apartments down there, too, where they all live together like cattle. There's supposed to be some kind of big thing going on there next week. We could hit that."

"Will they be outside?" Ian asked. He wanted to cover all his bases this time.

Spencer nodded. "Should be. They do it every year. How have you guys not seen it?"

"You live right across from it, Spence. We don't. We don't see that kind of stuff."

Spencer nodded, his hands still jittery. Ian had noticed it multiple times, and he was pretty sure Spencer was taking more than just alcohol, but he wasn't going to comment. Like Tim had said at the bar the week before, Spencer had never stood a chance of growing up with a backbone. And that's exactly what Ian believed addiction was, a spineless, cowards act.

"If everyone is out, how are we going to do it?" Tim asked the obvious question.

Ian mulled it over. He did know about the festival. He'd always avoided going out that day if he even remembered when it was. Usually he just tried to avoid that street all together. He rubbed his beard that he hadn't shaved in weeks, and stared down at the map in front of him. Spencer was right—it was the ideal place to hit next.

"Why don't we just drop them where we can and go. Set them to all go off at the same time. That way we know when to leave but no one else does."

"How many?" Tim asked.

"Three. One for each of us."

"We should do six," Spencer added.

Ian turned to him with open eyes. "You sure?"

"You get enough for it?"

Ian glanced at the bedroom where he'd set up his workstation. He'd been working on making the basics for the bombs, had even ordered supplies again. It was going to take some time for them to come in, but he had enough to make five at least.

"Maybe. I'll have to see as I go."

"How many?"

"Four, maybe five."

"Do it. If we want to scare them off, if we want to tell them like we mean it, then we have to mean it," Spencer said.

It was the first time that Ian had thought Spencer was truly with them. One glance at Tim told him he thought the same thing. Spencer was taking the bull by the horns, and he wasn't letting go. It was perfect. Exactly what they needed.

"When's the festival?"

"All day," Spencer answered.

"Saturday?"

"Yeah."

"Let's do it, then. I mean, we aren't getting any younger, and we need to show these lowlifes who's boss. I'm tired of living like this." Ian clenched a fist as he stared down at the map. It really was the perfect plan. They might get caught that time, but it would be worth it. He had to keep reminding himself that. This was all to make their town better, to take it back from the people who had stole it from him, to get lives back on track.

Tim stood up and walked toward the bedroom. "Need help, Ian?"

"Yeah. If we're going to do this in five days, I need all the help I can get."

The three of them wandered into the bedroom. Ian lifted the cloth he had put over the work station and started to set everything up. He took three casings and set one in front of each of them. "I'll tell you what to do, okay?"

"Sounds good." Tim rolled up his sleeves and got ready to work.

Spencer stared from one to the other. "I'm not sure I'm smart enough to figure this out."

"Well, good thing you don't have to and I'm just going to tell you what to do." Ian shot him a glare. "Don't worry. I'll double-check everything to make sure you did it correctly, okay?"

"Yeah, sure."

The three of them worked, simultaneously putting together three bombs. It took them hours, but they were done before dawn. Tim had begged off close to midnight, heading home, but since Spencer had only his sometimes-girlfriend to go back to he remained, and he stayed relatively sober, which was a surprise for Ian.

Ian set the bombs to the side, being careful with them. He calculated how much he had left of everything and readied himself to make the next one. "I think I can make two more, but definitely not three."

"Give me two on Saturday."

Ian glanced up at Spencer. "You sure?"

"Yeah. I need to make up for the last time."

"All right. You asked for it."

CHAPTER ELEVEN

IT WAS ten in the morning when Morgan got the call. She had almost missed it between coffee runs to the small kitchenette in her division. She grabbed her phone and pressed it to her ear. "This is Special Agent Stone."

"Morgan. It's Dana. Something…I don't know…something happened."

Every muscle in Morgan's body tensed with fear. Dana Atwood. She hadn't expected to hear from her pretty much ever until the trial. "What happened?"

Dana sighed. Morgan slipped into her chair at her desk and immediately grabbed a notebook and pen, ready to write everything down exactly as she heard it. When there was silence echoing on the like, Morgan checked her phone to make sure it was still connected.

"Dana?"

"Yeah, sorry. I don't know. Last week Dimitri told his caregiver he saw Mr. Jimmy. She thought it was just another nightmare."

"I assume he has those often?"

"Yeah."

Morgan wrote down the word "nightmares" on her pad. "But this wasn't?"

"No, but it took her another week to figure it out because once again Dimitri told her he saw Mr. Jimmy."

Morgan twisted in her chair to look for Pax. He needed to know exactly what she was hearing, but he was nowhere in sight. "Where?"

"Apparently it's been more than just the twice. He's been seeing him for months."

"You're kidding me."

"No." Dana's voice wavered on that word. "I wish I was."

"Have you looked into it any?"

"Yes." There was a petulant tone to her voice, like Morgan was questioning her abilities when she really was just fishing for information. "We've found nothing, but of course, we don't have a name yet."

Swallowing, Morgan pulled up her files. She was sure it was Jonathon Lockland of Lockland Divisions. He had enough power, grit, mystery, and creepiness about it for it to be true, but they hadn't verified anything. She worried her lip. "Give me the dates Dimitri says he saw him. I'll compare to the dates we have for traveling."

"I did that."

Morgan rubbed the bridge of her nose and grabbed her glasses and plopped them on her nose as she went to check the reports from the under-covers that had been turned in, hoping something in them would give her some sort of information. "And none of it matched?"

"Nothing."

"So either whoever he is he's sneaking under our radar or..."

"Or...we have no idea who Mr. Jimmy is."

"Fuck," Morgan muttered as her shoulders tensed even more. She didn't want to have to start from scratch of figuring out who the hell Mr. Jimmy was. They had spent months in surveillance and searches. They couldn't be that far off the mark, could they? "Where did Dimitri say he saw him?"

"The store, the house, the school."

"Damn it."

"I've moved him already."

"Out of state, I hope."

"Yes. It's in the report, but Morgan, there's something about this guy that doesn't sit right with me."

Morgan stopped at that. She always listened to gut feelings, and she wanted to know what Dana had to say. She wanted to hear someone else's opinion of it. "What do you mean?"

"Why would he come back for some kid? There's no reason for it, not himself. If he wanted another boy he certainly could find one. Why would he come back for Dimitri, who was nothing more than a toy to him and a runner? It's not like Dimitri had a high status in the organization. I can see him sending someone to find him and either take him or kill him, but this? This is weird."

"You're right." Morgan made a few notes. "It doesn't quite fit our profile, but it may help round it out some more."

Dana grunted her agreement. "He's never come back for one of kids he lost before."

"That we know of, anyway."

"Right, but Dimitri...he—"

"I know. He might not have been high in status, but his position was invaluable. How is he handling the transition?"

"Not well."

Morgan rubbed her temple. "What's going on?"

"He's shutting down, Morgan. I don't know what I can do to help him anymore. He's been transferred to another agent anyway, but he was so despondent when I took him."

"You took him?"

"Yes. I wasn't going to trust it with anyone else. I think he needs to go underground."

Morgan would hate to put him underground. It would make him shying away from anyone worse. He would see no one except his caregiver and the agent in charge for months if not years depending on how long trials took, and she had a feeling once they found Mr. Jimmy and finally arrested him that the trial would be years, if not longer with appeals he would no doubt file.

"I'd hate to do that."

"I know. I do, too, but I don't see any other way to keep him safe."

"We could figure out who this asshole is."

Dana sighed. "Yeah, that'd be a start, but I think he has an obsession with this kid, one that goes beyond just a cell."

"Perfect." Morgan wrote down the word on her notepad right next to nightmares.

While the giddiness ran deep in Morgan's chest, the fear for Dimitri was just as equal to it. An obsession with him meant they might more readily find Mr. Jimmy, but it put the kid in far more danger than they had originally thought. She would have to report everything to Taylor as soon as she got off the phone, and she would try her best to head out to wherever Dimitri was and interview him herself, assuming Taylor would let her.

"Keep him above ground for now. Let's see what we can come up with, not just to keep him safe, but also to maybe lure this guy out."

"Morgan, I'm not sure I like the sound of this."

"I don't either, but I'm tired of this case being at a standstill. We have to make a break sooner rather than later. It's been two years already, and months since we had our last major break."

"This doesn't guarantee one."

"I know that." Morgan worried her lip and nodded at Pax as he sat next to her. "But we have to do something."

"Not at the point of risking a kid, or anyone for that matter."

Morgan sighed. "I know. And I wouldn't let it go that far ever, Dana. I think for now we just need more information. I'm going to see when I can head out to interview him. If not, he'll need to be interviewed as soon as possible in order to get the right information from him."

"They're planning on talking to him tomorrow, I think."

"Where's he at?"

"It's in the report. You'll see."

Narrowing her gaze at her computer, Morgan turned fully to Pax. "Okay, thanks for calling."

"Any time, Morgan."

Hanging up, she dropped her phone onto the desktop and leaned over it, rubbing her cheeks wildly. When she finally leaned back, Pax had one thick eyebrow raised at her and a curious look on his face.

"Dimitri got moved."

"Why?"

"Mr. Jimmy showed up. At least three times that we know of."

"You're kidding."

"Nope." Morgan swiveled her chair a bit. "You reckon he's got a thing for this particular kid?"

"Maybe." Pax ran a pen through his fingers, deep in thought. "Where was he moved?"

Tilting her chair, Morgan moved the mouse on her computer and pulled up the report Dana had filed. She skimmed it and focused back on Pax. "Texas."

"I've got a friend down there."

Morgan snorted. "Pax, I think we've both got friends in Texas."

At his blank look, she shook her head slowly.

"We both used to live there."

"Right. We could have Jameson go interview the kid."

Pursing her lips as she thought, Morgan nixed that idea. "He's not exactly gentle when it comes to interviews, and think this kid needs a gentle touch. It takes him a while to warm up and open up."

Pax lifted and dropped on shoulder. "Taylor's not going to let you go."

"Why would you say that?"

"He's not."

"Pax, why would you say that? You don't know that."

"I know."

"Fuck this." Pushing herself a little too forcefully from her chair, Morgan stalked into her supervisor's office. "Got a minute, boss?"

"Yeah."

She swallowed as she pressed her hands to her hips. "On the trafficking case, our witness had to be moved because the suspect found him. Apparently he's been seen three times that we know of, but we all thought it was PTSD, but now the kid is claiming he really saw him."

Taylor's eyes moved up to her. "And?"

"And I want to go interview him."

"Where was he moved?"

"Texas."

"No."

Morgan clenched her jaw. Her hands fisted, nails digging into her palms as she tried to center herself. "Am I off restrictions or not?"

Taylor huffed out a breath. "You are."

"So why can't I go?" She resisted the urge to curse, knowing it would only get her in hotter water.

"I need you here on this case."

"What case?" Morgan wanted to punch something. The trafficking case had been hers from the start. If she had been removed from it, then he better damn well have a good reason why.

"This hate crime one, with the bombing."

"I have a case. I don't need another one."

Taylor nodded toward the door. "Shut it."

Morgan twisted sharply and shut the door a little too hard. Her voice was in her throat. She wanted to scream and rant. She was tired of being held back, of being treated like her mistake months ago was still an issue while they all said it wasn't.

"You were so eager to jump at a new case last December, remember?"

She gave him a sharp nod.

"Why not this one?"

"Because this one isn't my case. I want to focus on the other one."

"Stone, the trafficking case has agents on it from all around the country. It is not *your* case."

"It is. I made the profile. I've been working it since we started it."

Taylor huffed. Morgan was at a loss. Without anything to tell her what to do or why this was all happening, she wanted to just walk away. Surely she could get hired elsewhere, right? Fiona had to have some recommendation of where she could get a job working in law enforcement.

"This isn't a punishment." Taylor's voice was soft and gentle.

"Like hell it's not. Send Pax. He can work the hate crime. Leave me to trafficking."

"No."

"Why the hell not? He's better for it. It's in his wheel well. I profile."

"Then profile this bomber."

Holding in another curse, Morgan rocked up on her toes and then back down. Shoving her hands into the pockets of her pants, she shook her head. "I don't get it. Am I cleared or not, because you all are treating me like I'm still being punished for not knowing I was sleeping with a suspect. If I had fucking known, I wouldn't have done it!" Her voice was near a screech.

Taylor put his hands down flat on the desk. "You need to watch yourself, Agent."

Drawing in a slow breath, Morgan took his advice and calmed herself as best as she could. "Why can't I go."

"I need you here. That's it. End of discussion."

"This is bullshit."

"Feel free to file a complaint if you really think it is, Stone, but I warn you, I have my reasons and they will be backed up."

Grinding her molars, Morgan stormed out of his office. She plopped down at her desk. Pax gave her a sidelong glance but wisely said nothing. Morgan grabbed her phone and opened it up, noting the two missed calls from her mom and a text from Fiona.

Lunch?

Morgan huffed out a breath and wrote back. *Can't.*

Please.

Checking the clock on the wall, Morgan sent Pax another look before she answered. *Can't.*

She had never had Fiona almost beg her to share a meal together. Every nerve in her body was on high alert. She wanted to check in with Dimitri, make sure he was okay and that he knew what was going on. Instead, she was sidelined in Chicago, slammed with absolutely nothing. Months of work she had done, hours of it tossed aside and thrown into someone else's waiting hands. She better get credit for it, some type of recognition when they brought the asshole in.

Her phone buzzing startled her. Fiona had texted again. Reading it, her heart thrummed. *I'll pick you up at seven tonight.*

Not arguing even though she'd try to get out of it later, Morgan tossed her phone onto her desk and closed down the report on her trafficking case. She was nose deep for the next hour in her bombing case, trying to put together some type of profile for Taylor to look at when Pax touched her arm gently.

"You okay?"

She glared.

"Bad question. You want to grab dinner tonight?"

"Got a date," she spit out, not caring her tone was still laced with anger.

"Yeah? Wanna share?"

"No."

She was pouting. She knew it, and she hated it, but for the life of her, Morgan could not get her mood to change. She wanted that case. She didn't want to be saddled with a hate crime. The squickiness of hate crimes were not something she wanted to deal with when she was still in an uproar about the last supposed hate crime which really wasn't because their killer had turned out to be a lesbian.

"Mel said this weekend would be good if you wanted to dinner then."

"Yeah, sure," Morgan grumbled.

Her day had been far too long, and she was tired of it. By the end of it,

Morgan was no closer to figuring out her bombing than she was before. She'd put out requests to other agents to search for people purchasing bomb materials. She'd looked for reports of supposed incidents about to happen, but aside from Ray, who hadn't given her a lick of information, everything had been semi-quiet on that front for months at least.

With a sigh, she grabbed her phone when it buzzed. It was just hitting five, and since she was banned from going to Texas and had a shit day, she was leaving at five. Packing up her bag, she answered the call as she slung her bag over her shoulder and walked away from a quiet Pax.

"Hey, Ma."

"Morgan! Thank God you answered this time."

The worry in her mother's tone set her on edge, but she'd only missed the two calls from earlier. "What's wrong? Did something happen to Dad?"

"No, no, nothing like that."

"Then what is it?"

"It's your sister."

Rolling her eyes as Morgan stepped out of the elevator and into the parking garage, she clenched her jaw. "You have to be more specific. Which sister?"

"Carrie."

"Are the kids okay? The baby?" Worry etched its way into her chest. Morgan hit the button on her key fob to unlock her vehicle and then maneuvered her way into the car, starting the engine.

"They're fine. It's Carrie herself."

"What's wrong?"

"She's got a new boyfriend."

"Is she even divorced yet?"

Her mother hummed. "No, I don't think officially."

"Sweet Jesus," Morgan muttered. "She never takes a break, does she?"

"How awful of you to say."

"What? It's true." Morgan set her phone so she could talk through her car and then pulled out into the road. She had two hours until Fiona was supposed to pick her up, for whatever reason, and she hadn't made her excuses to get out of it yet. All she wanted was a good cup of whiskey and to wallow in her own self-pity. She knew she was still being punished. There was no other explanation for it.

"Morgan?"

"Oh, huh? Yeah? What, Ma?"

"You need to talk to her."

"Oh my God. I am not your errand girl. If you have a problem with the guy she's seeing, you talk to her. I am not sticking my nose in that mess."

"Think of the kids."

"I think of them often, when I send them birthday cards, gifts, and

Christmas stuff. I'm not going to call her up about this."

"You're her sister."

"Yes, and I know enough to stay the hell out of it. Look, Ma, I'm driving and I don't want to hit anyone. I'll talk to you later. Okay?"

"Fine. Call me tomorrow."

"Yeah, sure." Hanging up, Morgan rolled her shoulders and tried to let the tension from the day ease off her. Going toe-to-toe with Taylor had been stupid. If he had been in a bad mood, he could have written her up for the way she talked to him. But she was so frustrated with it all, and all the hard work she had put into Mr. Jimmy's case was down the drain. All for what? Because she'd fucked up once in her entire twenty-year career?

Scoffing, Morgan pulled up outside her high-rise and drove into the parking garage. When she got out, she angrily marched her way up to her apartment and locked the door behind her. Before she even contemplated throwing all of the shit on her floor into a closet before Fiona showed up, she poured herself a triple shot of whiskey and downed it in two gulps. Wiping the back of her hand over her lips, she got to work making her home presentable.

CHAPTER TWELVE

FIONA KNOCKING on her door was still quite a shock, and Morgan was already downing her second triple shot of the night. When she peeked out the peep hole, she sighed. Unlocking and opening the door, she let Fiona come in, but this time she was bearing no gifts of coffee.

"Rough day?" Fiona asked.

Morgan narrowed her gaze at her. "Yeah, kind of. Why?"

"You seem tense."

"You didn't exactly give me an option about tonight."

Fiona's lips pressed together tightly. "I could leave."

"No, you're here."

"Gee, is this what you were like all day? I can see why it was rough then. I feel so welcome."

"Sorry." Morgan put her hands up. "Sorry, really. I'm not mad at you."

"What happened?"

Morgan grabbed the whiskey bottle. "Drink?"

"Are we ordering in? Because I haven't eaten, and seeing as I have to work tomorrow, I don't want to be hungover."

Morgan grunted. "Order what you want."

Pouring them both glasses, Morgan grabbed them and settled onto her couch in her small living room. Fiona made a call, ordering something, she wasn't sure, and she didn't particularly care. When Fiona sat next to her and took the glass, the touch of their fingers sent a shiver into her chest and her nipples hardened. Morgan cursed her body and wished she could control it better.

"What's going on, Morgan?"

"Nothing."

"Tell it to me with what you can."

Morgan sent her a sidelong look, chugged her whiskey and set the glass on the table. "They took my case from me."

"What case?"

She rolled her eyes. "The one I've been working on for forever. I can't say more, you know that."

"Why did they take it?"

"I don't know, honestly. Taylor said he wanted me to stay in town, then he said he wants me on this hate crime race war case thing which I don't even know if it is a full case yet, but he's still not letting me leave town even though he says I'm completely cleared and off restrictions, and he won't give me any more explanation than that."

"The bombing case?"

Morgan nodded.

Fiona took a small, deliberate sip from her cup. "I'm working that case."

Morgan's heart jumped while her stomach dropped. "You're working it? Beyond just the homicide?"

Nodding, Fiona leaned her shoulder into the back of the couch. "Yeah, I'm working with the FBI and with more departments in the CPD on it. I'm not in charge or anything."

"No." Morgan swallowed, wanting to smack herself in the face. "That would likely be me."

"You?" Fiona raised an eyebrow.

"Yeah, if we're forming a task force, that would be me."

The smile tugged at Fiona's lips, one side pulling higher than the other, the small dimple just above the right side of her mouth. Morgan longed to press her mouth there, to run her finger over Fiona's lips, to taste. Pulling her mind back from its wandering, she focused on Fiona's dark eyes.

"They'll likely tell me tomorrow. I left early today."

"You did?"

"Rough day." Morgan turned away from Fiona, trying to give herself some space. They fell into a comfortable silence until their food was delivered. Fiona got up and paid for it, bringing it back to the small coffee table and bypassing the kitchen table that was littered with junk Morgan hadn't put away.

They finished eating, talking randomly about life and the mysteries of the world. Morgan had refilled her cup twice more and had a pleasant buzz going on. She didn't bother to clean up their plates. She'd get to it eventually. She was about to ask Fiona if she wanted another drink but opted not to as she herself could probably do without.

Fiona straightened her back and slid to the edge of the couch. "I should probably get going. It is late."

Morgan glanced at her watch. "It's not too late."

"I have to work early."

"Your task force."

Fiona smirked. "Yes. My first one."

Morgan smiled and heat flashed into her cheeks. She had no idea what possessed her, but it was so much like the first time. At least this time they weren't at a crime scene. Morgan slid her hand behind Fiona's head and pulled her in close, their lips touching. Fiona's lips parted on contact.

Keeping her eyes open, Morgan tangled her fingers in Fiona's shoulder length hair as she moved her tongue along the line of her lips like she had imagined doing dozens of times. Fiona hummed, and the sweet sound set every nerve in Morgan's body on edge. Moving up, Morgan pressed one knee into the cushion on the couch and changed the angle of their kiss so she was above Fiona.

Fiona's fingers dug into Morgan's waist, holding tight. Morgan pushed so Fiona lay against the arm of the couch and she could cover her. Their lips never left each other, tongues dancing and testing. She drew in a sharp breath as she slid a hand down to Fiona's hip, trying desperately to find the edge of her blouse to tug it up. She wanted skin, hot skin, smooth skin, any type of skin she could get hold of.

As soon as the pads of her fingers touched Fiona, Morgan's shoulders relaxed. Fiona cupped her cheek, taking more control of their embrace as Morgan shifted so she could lay more firmly on top of Fiona.

"Morgan." Fiona was breathless.

Morgan moved her hand up higher, wrapping her fingers around Fiona's ribs as she tilted her hips into Fiona's. She wasn't going to give this up because she wasn't going to make this mistake again.

"Morgan, stop."

Sighing, Morgan moved away and pressed her forehead into Fiona's shoulder. Her heart beat so fast it felt like a stampede. Closing her eyes, she tried to catch her breath, catch herself, but it was damn near impossible.

"What's wrong?" she whispered.

"You're drunk," Fiona answered.

"Not the first time I've had sex when drunk. I assure you, I will not regret this."

"I will." Fiona's hand was in the short hair at the back of Morgan's head, kneading the muscles at the base of her neck. "And I'm pretty sure you will."

"I won't."

"Morgan. We can do this some other time, when we're both sober."

Whimpering, Morgan pushed herself up so she hovered over Fiona. "Are you still with someone?"

Fiona paled. Cursing, Morgan shoved the rest of the way off and dragged her hands through her hair and down her face. She should not have done that. Standing up, she walked out the sudden burst of energy that shot through her body.

"I told you, I won't do this while you're with someone else." Morgan's mind spun because it was all her fault. She'd become the one person she'd sworn to herself she never world again.

"I'm not really with someone."

Morgan shot her a glare. "Are you in a relationship with someone? That's what I keep asking. You keep saying yes."

"Morgan, listen to me."

"Are you with someone?"

"Kind of."

Morgan stared with wide eyes. "Get out."

"Morgan."

"Get out, Fiona. I won't do this. I won't be the other woman. I won't put myself in that position ever again. I can't, and I won't."

"Why? I'm not saying it's right or wrong, but why? Why are you so opposed when I'm telling you it's okay."

"It's not okay!" Morgan's voice rose. "I will not be the other woman. I won't."

"Okay." Fiona stood up slowly from the couch, her voice lowering as she stepped closer and grabbed Morgan's hands, holding them firmly. "Okay, I won't push. But you started this."

"I did. And it was wrong. Thank you for stopping me." She refused to look into Fiona's eyes.

"Tell me what's going on inside that head of yours." Fiona's voice was soft.

Morgan wanted to move away and hide. Fiona was being far too nice to her, especially with what she had just pulled. She shook her head and broke away from Fiona's grasp. Refilling her drink, she downed it. Hangover be damned. She was going to regret the morning no matter what.

"I think you should leave."

"Not until you talk. All night I've seen you bottle things in, you need to talk to someone, Morgan. It doesn't have to be me, but you need to talk to someone."

"Who?"

"I don't know. Pax? One of your sisters maybe?"

Snorting, Morgan walked over to her sink and set the empty glass in it. She went back to the living area and started to angrily clean up their dinner. "I can't talk to them about this."

"About what?"

She clenched her jaw, her head hurting from how tight she felt. "About any of this."

"About any of what? Stop skirting around the issue."

"About how it almost ruined everything!" Morgan shouted. Her breaths came in short rasps. "I won't do that to them."

Fiona's lips parted in surprise, her dark eyes widened. She stepped closer, her hand on Morgan's elbow, and she gave a gentle squeeze. "How what almost ruined everything?"

"I'm the oldest, Fiona, you have to realize that I am privy to certain information in our family that my siblings are not, and you must realize that I'm not stupid and I can do math."

"I'm not following."

Morgan's hands were back in her hair, and she collapsed onto the couch. "Serena was barely two, and it got bad. I mean, how could it not with five of us running around and Dad always at work."

Fiona slipped onto the couch next to her and pressed a hand to Morgan's thigh, giving her silent support.

Morgan reached for Fiona's hand and covered it for a brief moment before she rubbed the bridge of her nose. "I remember there were weeks when Dad wouldn't come home at all, and any time he did, they would just yell at each other. Then we'd go to church Sunday morning and wear our stupid frilly dresses Mom made us wear and pretend like life was fine, but it wasn't."

"What happened, Morgan?"

"She was cheating. Two years of it. It didn't even stop after the twins were born, at least, not right away. Dad told her she had to choose, the kids or not. After that, everything was different."

"What do you mean?"

Morgan leaned her head back and stared at the ceiling. "I always tried to give Amya extra attention because Mom didn't really care too much. She coddled the twins, but they were often forgotten. But I was the oldest, and I left the house before they were grown, and well, we can see where that landed Clyde. He's got problems out the wazoo."

The smile slid onto Fiona's lips as she leaned in closer to Morgan. "You did everything you could do, but you can't put keeping a family and marriage together on the kids."

"You don't get it."

"You can't. It's not your responsibility, Morgan."

Shifting to stare directly into Fiona's eyes, Morgan shook her head. "You don't get it. The way we grew up? You didn't get divorced. It would have been the biggest mark on us all if they had. Sometimes I wish they had."

"You can't make decisions for them."

"No, I can't. But I won't make the same mistakes as them."

Fiona nodded. "I get it."

"Do you?"

"Yeah." Fiona squeezed Morgan's leg again before she shifted away and broke the contact. "I won't make you do anything you don't want to."

"I was married once, you know." Morgan changed the topic, hoping to get off the subject of her family's secrets that no one knew she knew.

Fiona's eyes widened. "You were?"

Morgan nodded. "For about a year, technically."

"I never would have guessed that."

Morgan smirked. "We were drunk in Vegas, figured why the hell not. We were best friends for years. Talk about a mistake."

Chuckling, Fiona leaned in closer to Morgan's side. "Have you ever been close to getting married to someone you actually want to marry?"

"No." Her voice was near a whisper. "You?"

"I was engaged once. Right out of college, but he couldn't handle the fact I was a cop."

"Not unheard of." Morgan moved her hand down to Fiona's and folded their fingers together, rubbing her thumb over the topside of Fiona's hand. "Give up on love?"

"For a bit. More just having fun while I can."

"Smart woman." A smile tugged at Morgan's lips. "I do the same, so whenever we do end up together, because I have no doubt that will happen eventually, it will be for the fun."

Fiona's voice was low, her lips right next to Morgan's ear when she spoke. "I like the sound of that."

"Good."

Before Morgan knew what was happening, Fiona's lips were on her ear, sucking her lobe and scraping her teeth over the sensitive skin. She moaned and closed her eyes, digging her fingers into Fiona's hand as she tightened her grasp.

"Fiona, what are you doing?"

"I promise we won't go further tonight. Just give me this."

"Fiona." Morgan opened her eyes, staring directly into Fiona's dark ones. She wasn't sure she could stop again. She hadn't wanted to stop the first time but had been so thankful Fiona had put up the boundary, the one she was now tearing down.

"Just...I promise. Not while you're drunk, but please."

Fiona's fingers against her cheek, turning her head so their lips brushed was her undoing. Morgan reached up, covering Fiona's other hand as their mouths connected, moving together in a gentle embrace, so unlike their first kiss that night.

"No, stop," Morgan whispered. "Stop. I can't do this. I told you that."

"Yeah, yeah, you did. I'm sorry. I overstepped."

Morgan whimpered. She wanted it so bad, wanted so much for Fiona to be unencumbered so they could be together, but until then, it wasn't right. It wouldn't work. With her heart in her throat, she didn't dare look up at Fiona. Morgan closed her eyes. "It's late."

"It is." Fiona let out a sigh as silence permeated the room.

Not daring to say anything else, Morgan kept as much distance as she could without moving. Fiona took her time standing up, and Morgan didn't follow. She watched every move Fiona made as she grabbed her jacket and slipped it over her shoulders, as she checked her pockets for her keys before she gave Morgan a soft and heated look.

"I will tell you sometime."

"Tell me what?" Morgan asked.

"Tell you about my relationship. I think you'll understand. I hope you will, anyway."

"I'll try."

"I'll hold you to that." Fiona gave her a small smile as she reached for the doorknob. With one last look over her shoulder, she left almost without another word. The buzz Morgan had earlier was gone, and she was left with the wobbly feeling of leftover drunk she really didn't want to face. Grabbing water and aspirin, she stripped and willed herself into sleep.

CHAPTER THIRTEEN

MORGAN'S HEAD pounded, more than she had anticipated. Between the alcohol she had consumed before Fiona had shown up and while she was there, she should have guessed she was going to feel like shit that morning. She drank only half the amount of coffee she normally did and the rest of the time stuck to water.

Pax had given her a few wary looks, but she'd sneered and turned back to her computer with her glasses propped on her nose. No way to get out of those that morning. She needed them to keep her eyes from blurring over. Eventually, Pax twisted in his seat and tilted his chin down at her.

"Late night?"

"You could say that," she muttered.

"What's going on, Morgan? Talk to me. It's not like you to shut me out. We've been friends for twenty years."

Sighing, Morgan shifted in her seat and stared directly at him. He was right. Normally she would have shared everything with him by then, her fear about her own abilities, her fear that every decision Taylor was making was just a confirmation about her fear over her own abilities. But she didn't. Something held her back, and she hadn't quite been able to figure it out.

She'd even called Barbie over talking to Pax, trying to explain everything to her through a simple twenty minute phone call had been a disaster, but she had tried. And Fiona had been right, she did need to talk to someone—anyone. "I'm just stressed."

"Okay....what about?"

She shook her head sharply. "Not having my case."

"He didn't take it away from you."

"He's not letting me work it either. Did you know they're making a task force?"

"Who is?"

"CPD."

"For this bombing?"

Morgan gave a sharp nod.

"How'd you know that?"

"Wexford told me." She focused on her computer and pushed her glasses farther up her nose. She was reviewing Adena's report but wasn't finding anything useful. There was no intel about hate groups rousing to action in the recent months, but she had no doubt in her mind the bombing at the factory had been a hate crime.

"Morgan."

"Huh?" She glanced at him again. "What?"

"You didn't answer me."

"Answer you what?"

"Was Wexford your date?"

"No. I didn't have a date last night. Went home and got shit-faced. Regretting that decision." Her stomach roiled at the thought of alcohol, and she tried to forget it. "Do you think it's a group we don't have on our radar?"

"It could be." His voice was firm. "It could be individuals, too. Hard to tell. Aren't you the one working up the profile."

Morgan's jaw clenched. She sent him a death stare and went back to her computer. "I am."

"So what does your profile say?"

"Not a whole lot." Morgan grabbed her glasses off her nose and dropped them onto her desk. "Because I have zero information about who these people are because no one is giving me information. You want the basic profile of a racist bomber? Here you go. They usually want to experience power, achievement, importance, purpose, and they have a knack for dehumanizing whoever they want. Something along those lines."

"Is that what this one wants?" Pax took a pen between his fingers and wrote down what she was saying.

Morgan snorted. "Who knows because no one has given me any kind of information yet."

"What do you need?"

"I need answers. What kind of device was it? Was it singular? Was it small? Was it well-made? I need to know how many people might be involved, which if I could get the report back on the bomb itself, I might know. If CPD would share the video footage from all the cameras in the area they have gathered, I might be able to answer that. If it is one person, that's different. If it is a small group? That's a whole other profile." Anger laced every word she said, frustration ebbing through her voice and out into the open office.

"Morgan," Pax nearly whispered as he leaned in closer and made eye contact. "I love you, but you need to chill the fuck out."

Grunting, she grabbed her mug and stood up to refill her coffee. He might have been right, but that didn't mean she had to like what he was saying. The queasiness in her stomach was not helping as she stepped into the small kitchenette. She knew what she needed. It wasn't to talk or to tell anyone. She needed to get laid. She hadn't had sex since Lollie's crazy ass in Seattle and that was an utter disaster. That had been why she'd nearly jumped Fiona the night before.

With her cup in hand, Morgan figured she could kill two birds with one stone. Heading down two floors, she left the elevator in search of someone she knew who could give her some answers and someone who might just want a quickie that night. Rounding the corner, Morgan plastered a bright smile on her lips as she saw Adena sitting quietly at her desk.

"Adena," she stated, her voice clipped but still warm.

"Morgan."

"Got anything new for me?"

"Nope." Adena barely looked up from her computer.

Morgan sighed, this might be harder than she had anticipated. She sat on the corner of Adena's desk. "No chatter about another attack?"

"Nope."

"No groups claiming ownership?"

"No."

Sighing, Morgan took a sip from her steaming coffee. "Any individuals coming forward so far to tell us their friend of a friend was talking about bombing Somalis?"

Adena looked up at her then, her brown eyes locking on Morgan's. "Isn't that *your* job?"

"Kind of. Did you ever figure out which group that Ray guy was part of?"

Adena did nod then, and Morgan could have jumped for joy. Adena reached into her desk and pulled out a very thin file, handing it over to Morgan. Setting her coffee on the desktop, Morgan opened the file and skimmed it. There were no more than four sheets of paper in it, so it didn't take her long to get through them all.

"This is it?"

"They're not a particularly active group. Pretty low level, hardly a buzz word on them except for one time four years ago when there were talks about an attack."

"Oh?" Morgan's ears perked up at that. "How far did it go?"

"No more than talk."

"What kind of attack?"

"There were no specifics."

"Was there an informant?"

Once again, Adena turned a glare at her. "That's *your* job."

Putting her hand up in the air, Morgan backtracked. "I'll find a report to read. Can I take this?"

"Make a copy."

Morgan headed to the copy machine and slid the papers through, wanting to keep everything in front of her so that she could get to work as fast as she could. The sooner she found out some information about who was behind the factory bombing, the better. She needed and wanted to complete that profile.

Back at Adena's desk, she slid the original document in front of Adena's line of sight. Leaning down so her lips were pressed close to Adena's ear, Morgan whispered, "Thanks. Dinner?"

"When?"

"Tonight."

"What are we eating?"

"Everything." Morgan said the word with all the hope she could muster.

"Seven?"

"My place."

"See you then."

Not taking another chance someone might overhear them, Morgan grabbed her coffee and slipped from the room. She headed back up two flights of stairs and sat at her desk, fully reading the file Adena had given her. Pax gave her a curious glance as she moved so he could read with her. She needed to build up a basic profile. That much was clear. Even Pax didn't have the profile for a hate crime memorized. That would be easy enough, but then she would make individual sub-profiles based on whether or not their racist was involved in a group or acting on their own.

She wanted to avoid it a little longer in case the full report on the bomb came back. When Pax had finished with the paper, he handed it back to her and said, "I think we need to talk to Ray again."

"He wasn't very talkative the first time."

"Did CPD have any better luck with him?"

Morgan shrugged. "I have no idea."

"Didn't you ask Wexford?"

"No. Why would I ask her about that?"

"Because she's the liaison."

"She's the what?"

"You didn't hear?"

"Hear what?"

"They're making a task force."

"I know that. I told you that."

"Right." He leaned in closer so only Morgan would hear. "Wexford is their liaison."

"To who?"

"To you."

"Fuck." Morgan's shoulders tensed. After everything that had happened the night before, being stuck working closely with Fiona was going to be an absolute disaster. "Wait, when did you hear about this?"

"A few minutes ago while you were with Adena."

Guilt settled into the pit of Morgan's stomach. Good old Catholic guilt her mother had saddled her with. Sighing and rubbing her temple, she downed the rest of her coffee. "Why, was there a threat we somehow missed?"

"No." Pax's dark eyes went wide. "I think they're just preparing."

"It's not like the CPD to be on top of these things. Usually we're the ones pushing them to do it."

Pax shrugged. "Maybe Wexford really wants to add liaison to the FBI onto her resume."

"What? Why would she do that?"

Shrugging again, he turned to his computer effectively ending the conversation. Morgan sighed and checked her phone. She had no messages, no texts, no missed calls, and no emails from Wexford. She strongly suspected she wouldn't hear from her for weeks or more after whatever the fuck the night before had been and the disaster it had turned into.

Pushing Fiona out of the forefront of her mind, she focused on the task at hand. She needed to finish out her profile, but first, she needed more information about the bomb. With her metal canteen of water in hand, Morgan left her desk and took the elevator down. This time she went to the basement where their crime scene gurus were located.

Knocking on the door to the laboratory, Morgan waited until she had someone's attention before just walking in. The young man sitting at the desk had the brightest blue eyes. His hair was curly against his head, but left long enough that should could probably twist her fingers around it twice before tugging. Grunting at the inappropriate thought, Morgan knew she had been right in her assessment earlier when she'd asked Adena over.

"I'm Stone. Do you have an update on the bombing investigation?"

"You mean Operation Time Lord."

Morgan raised an eyebrow at him, trying to keep the smirk off her lips and the chuckle out of her throat. "The what?"

"Operation Time Lord." He gave her a funny look. "Isn't that the name of the case?"

"Uh...no. But yes, the bombing at the factory."

His cheeks turned bright red. "I'm so sorry. I'm...I'm new here. The guys must have been playing."

Morgan put her hand out to calm him down. She didn't need some upset newbie on the lab squad to be so embarrassed he couldn't tell her anything. "If you're new, what's your name?"

"Kenny King, ma'am."

Letting a sweet smile grace her lips, Morgan leaned onto the desk he was at. "No need to call me ma'am. You can call me Stone or Morgan. Your choice."

He nodded at her.

"So my case?"

"Right." He clicked a few things on the computer and pulled up an analysis, then moved his hand, indicating Morgan should look at it. Having forgotten her glasses upstairs, she wasn't much help in seeing the screen itself, but even then, she wasn't sure she could interpret what it was saying anyway. She was just about to ask him a question, when a door opened and closed.

"Morgan."

"Marsha Walsh." Her sweet smile turned seductive.

"I see you've met Kenny."

"I have."

Kenny's gaze bounced between them both.

"I assume you're here about the bomb."

"Yes."

"This way."

Morgan followed Marsha into a small office where they sat. Marsha was at a desk littered in papers, and Morgan sat in the only chair not covered with papers. She had no idea how Marsha managed to keep everything sane and organized in there or how she managed to find anything. Surely someone would have told her to clean it up already.

"Do you have an update for me?"

Marsha sent her a sly look. "There was one bomb."

"I knew that."

"It was simplistic enough someone could have ordered the items needed to make it or picked it up at the local store. There was a timer on it, kitchen timer. Some of the other materials can be bought pretty cheaply."

"So this isn't someone who has a good amount of money?"

Marsha stared at her directly, her dark eyes close to a void of information. "Perhaps. We found a partial print, but it's not going to get you much. It was very difficult to piece everything back together. Whoever it was must have added something to use as shrapnel in the blast."

"Added what?"

"Haven't figured that out yet, but the materials used for the making of the bomb were pretty much decimated."

"Okay. You have a report for me?"

"It'll be finished within the hour."

Morgan rubbed her palm on her thigh, her canteen still firmly in her other hand. "I look forward to reading it."

Standing up, she made to leave the office, but Marsha's voice caught her attention. "Don't scare the new kid, Stone. He's quite smart, and I'd like to keep him around as long as possible."

"All right." She waved to Kenny on her way out. Morgan had one more stop to make before she'd go back up to her desk and hope someone had sent her a report to read by then.

Morgan stopped at Adena's floor, but she bypassed Adena's desk and found another of the analysts there. As much as she knew she could have asked Adena, she didn't want to annoy the woman to the point that she would renege on their date that evening. She really needed to have a proper roll in the sheets. Adena would no doubt deliver on that.

Jaime Alverez had seen her come through the elevator and watched just about every step she took toward his desk. She beamed at him. "Got a question for you."

"You've already been down here once today."

"Observant." She flirted back. "Have we had anything on BMAP show up recently?"

"How did I know you were going to ask me that? They put you in charge of Operation Time Lord?"

"Jesus, why does everyone think it's called that."

He smirked. "Because it is."

"It is not. I haven't named the case yet, and if I'm in charge, I get to name it."

"You can think that." He stared directly at her. "But to answer your initial question, no. Nothing has come up on BMAP. I no doubt would have found you and told you."

"Fine. You keep an eye on it for me? We're looking for regular run of the mill stuff, nothing fancy."

"Scout's honor." He saluted her.

Morgan rolled her eyes, a flush hitting her cheeks as she turned around and went back to her desk. When she saw Pax coming over from the copy machine, he muttered at her as he sat down. "Have a good walk?"

"Excellent."

Morgan ignored him and focused on typing out her profile and waiting on the reports to come in from all the other departments. She knew they were working as fast as they could, but still, she had hoped she would have more information already. Wexford would no doubt be knocking on her metaphorical door asking for updates and intel as soon as she had to stop avoiding and as soon as it truly came out that Morgan was the FBI portion of the task force.

CHAPTER FOURTEEN

THE FESTIVAL had been the perfect choice. Ian drove up, parking six or seven blocks away. The three of them made a note of where the car was, knowing they were to meet back there in an hour and a half. That meant Ian would have to blend in for that time, so would the others. He would have to pretend like he wanted to be there and was enjoying himself.

"Set it for around twelve," Ian whispered.

"So this timer isn't like the others?" Spencer asked.

Ian shook his head. "No, not a specific time. A countdown. Aim for noon, and then we'll catch them all by surprise when they don't all go off at once."

Spencer grinned. Ian clenched his jaw as he shifted in his seat behind the wheel of the car. Tim looked pale as a ghost. If Ian was going to guess anyone was going to chicken out that time, it was going to be Tim. Their factory attempt at starting a war had failed miserably. The news had covered it only as an accidental explosion, which had meant no one was scared, no one was nervous about going to work or gathering together, no one wanted to leave the country and go back home.

"It has to work this time," Ian muttered. "We have to make an impact."

"We will," Tim whispered and shifted his gaze into the backseat to look at Spencer. "Right?"

"Yeah." Spencer nodded. "We're going to do this right this time."

Ian lit a cigarette and sucked it down, the smoke filling his lungs and calming his jittery nerves. He had no idea why he was nervous. It wasn't the first bomb they had set, and the entire purpose was to begin their defense of their country and take it back. The government could fight wars overseas all they wanted, but unless they kept those dogs off their turf instead of just opening the doors and letting them in, there was never going to be a difference made. Fighting a war overseas was pointless if they were just going to bring them all back here anyway.

Spencer smoked down his own cigarette in the back, but Tim remained stoic, sitting next to them. Ian left his pack of cigarettes in the car, not wanting to leave any trace of himself where he set his bomb, and he knew if he brought them with him he would smoke the entire pack in the meantime while he waited to find the perfect spot.

There were white people and brown people wandering toward the pier, but to him, they were all on the same level. He knew it would be a mix of whoever was there, the festival some sort of religious gathering.

Women walked by them with their husbands and children in tow. He wondered briefly if that was Tim's hesitation, the kids. But those kids would just grow up to be adults with the same viewpoints, the same beliefs, the same goal of taking over their country as the parents who raised them. They were just as much the enemy.

"You ready for this, Tim?" Ian asked.

"Yes." His answer was firm and confident, but he didn't look it.

Ian grabbed one more cigarette and lit it. "We need to defend ourselves. We can't keep letting them in here to take over so we have no control. This country won't be ours if we don't do something about it now. In fact, we have waited far too long to do something about it. We can't trust the government to stand behind us any longer. They're just letting them in here freely to do as they want."

"I know," Tim whispered. "This will be the second step toward making this country the place we want to raise our kids in."

Ian nodded his agreement, staring directly at Tim with hope bursting in his chest. If Tim could understand it, and risk everything for it, then Ian had no doubt others would follow soon. Glancing in the rearview mirror at Spencer, Ian took another long drag from his smoke.

"What say you, Spence?"

"I say we light them up. Let them know who's boss. Show them that we will defend our country with our lives."

Snubbing out his smoke, Ian turned the engine in the car off. Reaching behind the passenger seat, he pulled out a small black backpack and handed one to each of them. Gripping his own firmly, he set his jaw. "Let's do this."

Ian smiled at the people who passed him by, and he started up small talk. He knew exactly where Tim and Spencer were, but they didn't talk to each other. There were brown-skinned folk, black-skinned folk, and white-skinned folk all around the festival. It made his stomach churn. They should not be celebrating some deity who could bring them nothing, who was nothing more than pure fable. Anger pooled in Ian's belly as he wandered around the streets.

Spencer had been right. It was the perfect place to launch their second defense against their way of life. Nothing could be more true than turning such a celebration into what it really should be, a day of reckoning, a day when the reality of who's God was the real God would shatter the glass and allow these people to know truth.

Ian stepped up to a street vendor. He'd been at the festival for a little over an hour. He paid cash for a small meal. He was to drop his bag somewhere in a one block radius. Tim and Spencer were doing the same. The timer set for thirty minutes. It would give them enough time to get away from the explosions, but also to finally see his masterpiece at work.

Clenching his jaw, Ian ate the chicken on a stick slowly while he wandered around to find the best place to leave his bag. He'd have to do it subtly, in a way that no one would suspect. He found a street sign and leaned against it as the parade from the mosque started. Chewing on his food, his stomach settled. He was about to make his stand.

It was the end of Ramadan as Spencer had explained it. He would know. He worked with many of them in his own factory job. Ian took Spencer at his word, listened about what they would be doing that day, all things his co-workers had told him would be happening. They had decided during the parade would be best, that it would make the most impact. But it was hard to judge when it would be by right where they were going to set up their defenses.

Ian settled his bag against the bottom of the street sign as he continued to eat. He nodded to those who walked by him, plastering on a smile to pretend like he was enjoying himself. It was harder than he thought it would be, but he was well-practiced. He'd had to do to it every day at his last job before they shafted him within his ninety-days.

With tense shoulders, Ian looked around. No one was looking at him. He bent down and set the timer for thirty minutes. Ian leaned against the street sign once more, counted to sixty twice over, and then walked away. Their bombs wouldn't go off at the same time, but that would help increase the panic. He knew it would.

It was their most brilliant plan yet. He put his head down and stepped out of the crowds and down the streets to where he left his car. Sliding into the driver's seat, he waited. Tim and Spencer should be joining him any minute. He watched the clock tick down. When he got to twenty-two minutes left, Spencer slid into the back seat.

"Where'd you set it?"

"On the pier."

Ian nodded. "Time?"

Spencer glanced at the clock. "Should be about twenty minutes now."

Ian nodded. His bomb wouldn't be the first to go off. It irked him, but he let it slide. The point wasn't for him to make the most impact but to make a point that they would not let their country be overrun by people who had no claim to it, they would not let their jobs be taken any more, and they would not let their children grow up in a world where they didn't have grand opportunities to thrive.

"Tim?"

"Don't know." Spencer pulled out his phone. "He hasn't called or texted yet."

They waited with bated breath and in silence. Tim finally showed up, seven minutes later. Ian's excitement rose in his belly, the gurgling making him want to get out of the car and walk around. He wanted to see the panic on their faces when they didn't know what was happening, when that first bomb went off and they would be running. He wanted that rush of adrenaline and power.

But he didn't move. He stayed in his car, hands on the steering wheel. They really should leave. They didn't want to be caught in the throng as people ran to get away, but he couldn't help himself. He wanted to see his creation explode.

"We should go," Tim whispered, his leg bouncing off the floor board in the front seat.

"Not yet," Ian muttered.

Tim turned to him with wide eyes full of fear. "Ian—"

"Not yet. Wait until the first one, then we'll go."

"No. That's stupid."

Ian twisted and glared at Tim. "I want to make sure it works this time."

"They'll work. It did last time."

"Barely," he said through clenched teeth.

Tim turned to look in the back seat at Spencer. "Don't you think we should go? That was the plan."

Spencer nodded. "Yeah, but he's the one driving, and I don't think we really get a say."

Ian focused his gaze out the front windshield. They weren't in a busy part. He had specifically parked a good distance off. They wouldn't see anything except the flood of people running from the explosions. But he wanted to see it. Next time, he'd have to work it so that the other two could leave and he could stay—if that was what they really wanted. He wanted to make sure their defense had the best impact it could, and he wanted to see that impact first hand, not through some stupid news media that would no doubt spin it in a different direction because of all the liberal influence.

"How much time on yours, Tim?"

"Uh...twelve minutes."

"It's last."

Tim nodded his understanding. Ian stared down at the clock again. Two minutes to when Spencer's was supposed to go off. Four until his. Tim might be lucky in that his would make the biggest impact since there was so much time in-between, or it would make the smallest since most people would have vacated by then.

"Where'd you set it?"

"Two blocks out from the pier by a bunch of parked cars. I put it underneath a car."

Ian turned to him with appreciation in his gaze. "That was smart."

"I thought so."

Somehow, they had worked it perfectly. Spencer's would go off first, shoveling people toward Ian's bomb, which would go off shortly after. Then they would all run toward Tim's. Perhaps this would be the perfect influence to mount their defense on.

The first shock ricocheted through Ian's chest. Excitement built up as he leaned forward to stare out the windshield and maybe see some of what was happening. They were too far away. He waited impatiently for the second blast to go off, the one that should have been from his or Spencer's bombs, but nothing happened.

It took a full two minutes before the wave of people running toward them started. Tim bounced in the seat next to him. "We should go."

"Not yet."

"We don't want to get stuck."

Ian's breathing was heavy, joy reaching deep within him. "It's working."

"It is," Tim answered. "And if we want a chance to do it again, we need to get out of here."

Just as the first person ran by their car, Ian pulled out of the parking space and headed down the street at a snail's pace. He wanted to see it all. He kept glancing in the rearview mirror, hoping to catch some glimpse of the damage he had done, but there was nothing to bring him that satisfaction other than the scared looks of fear on those running toward them.

Tim's bomb must have gone off because those who were running stopped or picked up their speed. Ian wanted so badly to turn around and see it all, but he'd have to settle for watching on the news. Tim leaned into his chair, closing his eyes and taking deep breaths. Spencer was halfway through the back seats into the front of the car as he looked around.

"Let's go," Spencer whispered.

"Yeah, yeah," Ian answered.

When they got back to Ian's basement, they flicked on the television and turned it to the local news station. Sure enough, the reporters were already there, lining the streets as they interviewed people who were running. The police were barricading things off, dogs running around, ambulances.

Something settled in the pit of Ian's stomach. A sense of calm, ease, and relief. They were making a difference. Finally, on their third try, they were making a difference.

CHAPTER FIFTEEN

MORGAN HAD spent so many hours at the bombing scene that her head hurt. She'd had a late night with Adena, which had gone perfectly, and then had been thrown straight into dissecting another bomb. Fiona had been there, but Morgan had ignored her. However, there was no more avoiding she could do when her phone rang shrilly.

Gritting her teeth, Morgan stared down at the name flashing across the screen. She hadn't answered any of Fiona's calls or texts since the fateful night the week before. But with the not-so-subtle hint that Pax had dropped, Morgan knew she was about to run face first into a demon of her own making.

With the phone to her ear, Morgan answered, "Wexford."

"Morgan." Fiona sounded out of breath.

"That would be me." She could have face-palmed herself for being so obtuse and stupid in how she responded to Fiona, but she needed that distance. Morgan had almost crossed the boundary that she promised herself to never willingly step over.

"You've been avoiding me."

"I've been busy." Morgan stepped on the gas as she drove through the lower west side. "I hear you're heading up the task force from your end."

"Yeah. Morgan, do you think we can talk about the other night?"

"No. We have a meeting in an hour. I'll see you then." Hanging up, Morgan slipped her phone into the cupholder and finished driving toward the bureau. She needed to gather everything for her task force meeting, which she was just so thrilled to have to attend. On one hand, she wanted to be in charge. It was a wonderful and perfect opportunity to have her name on something. She was only hesitant because Fiona was on the other end of it.

When she got to the office, it was a whirlwind. She collected all the files she had and that she knew she would need and shoved them into her briefcase. Checking in with Taylor, she got the okay, and then stared at Pax's empty desk. He was with Dimitri, and it broke her heart that she couldn't be there with him while he went through another round of interviews. She so desperately wanted that case to be one-hundred percent hers, especially since she'd already been working on it for years.

Sighing, she filled her travel mug with coffee and headed to Adena, grabbing what she had heard over the weekend about groups claiming or not claiming the attack. They were going to try and keep it as quiet as possible to not make anyone panic, but by that point, Morgan wasn't sure she would be able to keep it quiet. They would have to be very controlled with what information they had. When she pulled up outside of Fiona's precinct, she gave her another call while she gathered her bag.

"Morgan?"

"What floor am I going to?"

"The third one. Take a left down the hall, go to the third conference room on the right."

"Got it. Be there in a few." Hanging up, Morgan got into the building and followed Fiona's directions. She expected everyone to be there, but there was no one but Fiona. Cocking her head in Fiona's direction, Morgan's lips thinned. "This is the right room, right?"

"Yeah. You're fifteen minutes early."

Glancing down at her watch on her right hand, Morgan nodded. "You're right."

"Can we talk?"

"We can talk about the case." Morgan dropped her bag on the large table and pulled out files and reports, things she had made copies of for everyone who would be there.

"No, not about the case." Fiona moved over to the door and shut it.

When Morgan glanced up, Fiona leaned over the edge of the table, her palms flat on the surface. Her shirt opened slightly at the top, and Morgan wondered just what kind of bra she wore underneath it before she chided herself and focused on the papers in her hand.

"I will talk to you about the case." Morgan sent her a sharp look. "Nothing else. We can talk about the rest some other day, but now is really not the place or the time."

"Morgan..." Fiona came around the table, standing right next to Morgan. Reaching out, Fiona's fingers brushed Morgan's forearm, sending tingles straight up to her shoulder and chest. "I want to talk about it."

"I don't."

"We didn't do anything wrong."

"No, we didn't." Morgan turned, staring straight into Fiona's eyes. "And it won't be something we do again, at least not any time soon. Let's drop it. We have a case to work, and you and I need to do an interview after we're done here."

"Interview?"

Nodding, Morgan set the papers out on the table. "Help me with this, would you?"

Fiona distributed papers around the large conference table and propped open the door but not before getting Morgan's attention again. "You promise, Morgan?"

"Promise what?"

"That we'll talk."

"Yeah, sure."

Fiona's lips thinned into a line, but Morgan ignored it. She knew she was being a bit of a bitch, but she had to protect her own heart at some point. The mixed signals were a bit much, the ones Fiona had and the ones Morgan herself was giving. Fiona was right, they would need to talk at some point.

Once everyone was settled, Morgan sat at the head of the table, Fiona right next to her. "Everyone, we have a case on our hands which we're pretty sure is only going to escalate the longer it goes on. Now, we've had two separate incidents of bombings in the Muslim community. We are unsure how these two incidents are connected because one targeted a specific race while the other targeted a specific religion."

Morgan looked around the room. Some of them seemed surprised but the others didn't. She sent a glance to Fiona, knowing she would pick up the conversation soon.

"Now, we do know these two incidents are connected because of the bombs that were used. If you look at the report from our investigations, the first bomb at the factory matches the materials used in the Eid al-Fitr attack. There were some minor differences, which indicate these bombs were not made at the same time. So that tells us whoever is behind these attacks is most likely not finished."

She was just about to go on another rant when Fiona interrupted. "We have had no one arrested yet in these attacks yet, and no one suspected in these attacks yet."

Morgan nodded at her. "No group has come forward to claim them, either. We have our people watching the terrorism groups and the online chatter. Thus far, which is mostly odd, no one is claiming them."

"So what does that mean?" One of Fiona's officers asked from the back of the room.

"What it means is this is likely an individual rather than a group, and it is much harder to find an individual."

"Agent Stone is going to give us the profile in a minute, but I wanted to say one thing before she does that. This case is very sensitive. There is already a sense of panic amongst the Muslim community, and we don't want to increase that panic, but we do want them to be cautious."

"Wexford is correct. We want to be very careful about what information gets out. Everything we talk about in this room is highly classified. It does not leave this room unless we discuss it and decide it is reasonable information to allow leaked to the media."

Fiona gave Morgan a look she couldn't quite read. There was something heated behind the gaze, but Morgan couldn't be sure what it meant exactly. They had never worked this closely together before. Fiona had only asked Morgan for a second opinion on some of her cases, and the only other time they may have potentially worked together, Morgan had taken over the case. Fiona finally broke the eye contact.

"No one talks to the media except Agent Stone and myself, understood?" Everyone nodded at Wexford's request. "Good, we are going to send out surveillance in the area of the second bombing to see if anyone saw something. We're also going to send out people to the homes of factory workers to properly interview them again, those who were coming in for a shift and leaving a shift that day are the priority."

Morgan let Wexford take the reins for a bit. She knew it would be tossed back to her when they came to who they were looking for. That was her area of expertise, and Wexford wouldn't want to touch that part of the conversation with a six-foot pole if she could avoid it.

"Since the FBI has a...how do I say this delicately...spotty history with the Muslim immigrant community in this area, we are going to pair one and one—one agent to one detective."

Morgan turned up at Wexford then, tightening her lips as she stared at Fiona's dark eyes while she took command. They had not discussed *that* part of the plan previously, and Morgan felt completely thrown under the bus. Although, it would make it easier to hide the fact that she wanted only Wexford to come with her to interview Ray again. They'd have to talk through strategy on that one before they went to find him.

"My agents will meet you there," Morgan added, knowing she was going to have to make a quick phone call. Wexford wasn't wrong. The FBI and Muslim community did have a spotty and distrustful past, though it hadn't been on her. It was part of the history and it would make it much harder for any member of the FBI to do an interview. She'd already run into that with Diric and the others at the factory.

Her phone buzzed in her pocket. When she glanced at it, it was her mom, but she decided to take the opportunity while Fiona was talking to make the other call. She held the phone up so Fiona could see and then walked out of the room.

"Ma, now is not the time. You seriously have the worst timing."

"That's not a very nice way to greet your mother."

"I'm busy in the middle of a conference meeting."

"Why did you answer then?"

Morgan drew in a deep breath. *Why had she answered?* "I'll call you tonight. Promises."

"Don't break your promise, baby, please."

"I won't." Something in her mother's tone set her on edge, but she really didn't have the time to delve any deeper into it. Ending the call with her mom, she immediately called Taylor. "Hey, boss."

"Stone. How's it going?"

She drew in a breath. "Good. We're almost done with the briefing. We'll be setting up grids for interviews soon, but we're wanting to pair one agent and one detective to see if it'll be easier to take statements that way."

He didn't say anything immediately. Morgan worried her fingers together, hoping the way she had phrased it would make him agree because if he knew it was Wexford's idea he probably wouldn't. "Sounds like a plan. I'll inform our agents here."

"Have half of them meet us at the pier in an hour, and the other half at the factory in two hours. We'll split them up from there."

"You've got it."

Hanging up, Morgan slipped back into the conference room to Fiona still talking about what was going to happen. Once she made it to her place at the table, Fiona turned the conversation over to her.

"Right, so we're looking for an individual. He is likely working alone, although he could have roped one or two friends into this plan with him."

"Wait, so is this one person or more people?" the voice at the back of the room caused Morgan to pause.

"That is what we need to find out. We suspect it is more than one person, but there is a ring leader." She passed around a paper she had withheld until that time. "Now, we're looking for a white cis-male, most likely in his late-thirties to early-forties. This person will likely not have an elaborate life. He might not even be employed. He is smart enough to create and build a bomb, but these are not very sophisticated, so he likely found the information through some Internet searches."

The same voice interrupted her again. "Can't you just like...Google who has searched for bomb-making materials?"

Snickers resounded. Morgan flushed. This was why she hated working with task forces that were not from the bureau. But for some reason, Taylor refused to stick Pax on the case, although he would have been a much better option than her.

"Our intelligence unit is looking into recent purchase of the materials used in both bombs and where those materials might have been purchased, but if it was done in smaller quantities it is hard to find those purchases, especially if it was not done all at once or with cash." She felt like she was talking to toddlers.

A snort. "What you're saying is you all have no idea who is behind this and you want us to do your grunt work?"

Morgan clenched her jaw. Something had changed from when she'd left the room to then, and she wasn't sure where she had misstepped. "I'm saying it takes time, and since this second attack, we know a whole lot more information than we do from the first one."

"So we know nothing?"

Morgan was about to retort, but Fiona put a hand on her arm to hold her back. Morgan stopped and stared up at the pitying look in Fiona's eyes. She had to stop so she didn't embarrass herself by losing her temper. She was already on a short fuse, and she needed to reel it back in.

Fiona spoke next. "We have all been thrown a lot of information in the last few hours. It takes time to sift through everything. You all know that. What Special Agent Stone is here to do today is to brief us on the profile of someone we are looking for. We are working together on this case, not against each other."

"They'll take all the credit when we find the guy and arrest him." The disdain in the detective's voice was there.

Morgan was sure he had experienced something similar before, and she definitely wouldn't put it past the FBI to do that. She'd witnessed it, many times. Once again, she was wishing she and Pax could switch spots.

Fiona answered, "We will share credit since we have both put in the time and effort. I will make sure of that."

"As will I," Morgan responded. "But really until we arrest someone who is guilty, then we don't have much to worry about in terms of credit, do we now?" When she got silence as an answer, she continued, "Now, to finish the profile."

"Yes, lets." Fiona sighed as she leaned into her chair.

"This individual is most likely trying to fulfill a deep personal need, some serious self-confidence issues if you will. He likely wants to be seen as something other than who he is readily seen as. He wants to be seen as someone who does something, who is accomplished, who has a purpose. Which tells us that he is likely not seen as that in his every day. This is important, because when it comes to arresting him, if he puts up any kind of fight, that will be necessary to talking him down."

"He's over-compensating." Once again, snickers echoed.

Morgan's frustration rose. She was tired of being in that room with people who just wanted to talk jokes about her profile. She had better things to do with her time, but she pushed through and ignored them. "This is about power for him, about influence over others—perhaps the ones he's convinced to work with him, perhaps over those who he is targeting, or even both. This is about his morality."

"What?"

When Morgan looked to the one who had been cracking the jokes about the FBI, he looked utterly confused. "What are you not understanding?"

"How is this about his morality?"

Morgan dropped the pen she'd been gripping tightly onto the table. "He thinks the rest of us are immoral or unethical. He is taking it upon himself to try and correct that simply because he is not seeing anyone else do it."

"So he thinks we all need to be racist idiots?"

Morgan cocked her head to the side. "He probably would not phrase it like that. He would probably tell us that we don't understand what is happening in our fair city, that we have been brain-washed by the media into thinking nothing is wrong with immigration or with Muslims. He would probably tell us the woes of diversity, that diversity washes away what we know to be true about ourselves and how we stand apart from each other and stay strong. He would probably tell us that we are the only good ones."

She raised an eyebrow at him, knowing that in his likely cis-male and white WASPy world he would never understand what it meant to be a minority and in a lot of ways would fall right in line with the terrorist they were trying to catch and arrest.

"Make sense to you?"

He shrugged.

"Right," Morgan continued, "since this guy likely doesn't have a job, we have no idea where he lives. What we need to do is interview witnesses to see if they saw anyone who they suspected didn't quite fit in with what was going on, especially down by the pier. Our profile tells us he might know how to blend in, but it is rare that someone with his level of intelligence would be able to fit in for long if came push to shove."

"His intelligence?"

"Yes." Morgan drew in a deep breath. "Like I said before, this individual is likely to not be highly educated. He's smart enough to make a bomb but not smart enough to make a really good bomb."

"What do you mean?"

She smirked. "There were three bombs at the pier. Only two went off. He is not smart enough to replicate what he does three times in a row without making a mistake."

At the silence in the room, Morgan felt satisfied. She had successfully put the jerk detective in his place without calling him out directly. They finished up the briefing, and Fiona separated them out into groups, giving them instructions of where to go and when to be there. As soon as the room was empty, Morgan let out a breath she hadn't known she was holding.

"You handled that well."

Morgan lifted one shoulder and dropped it as she gathered the papers left over and the rest of what she had brought with her. "Not my first rodeo."

"This is mine."

Morgan turned to her with surprise. "You first task force?"

"No, not that. My first time being in charge of one, yes. This is a make it or break it case for my career, Morgan. I need this to go well."

Shifting to lean against the table, Morgan nodded at her. "Okay. Let's do this the right way then. You and I can talk about this interview we need to do while we head over to the pier to brief everyone there. Then we'll go to the factory and meet with everyone else, do a couple interviews ourself, and then go see Ray."

"Ray?"

"Yeah." Morgan smirked. "You'll like him."

"Who's Ray?"

"Someone the rest of these idiots don't need to know about for now." Morgan moved her hands across her lips and turned it like it was a lock then threw away the key. "First, coffee. I need more juice in my system."

Fiona's smile warmed her heart, and when Wexford stepped in closer to her, her heart thundered like it had the other night. When Fiona spoke, her voice was hushed so no one else would hear. "Sometimes I think you like coffee more than you like me."

Morgan choked. "Who said I liked you?"

"You did." Fiona's smile was bright and that heated look was back in her eyes. "Last December and a few weeks ago."

"You know how I feel about this."

"I do." Fiona's pinky finger curled around Morgan's. "I do, and don't worry, I'm working on it, but due to some issues, my timeline got delayed."

"Timeline?"

"I'll tell you all about it sometime. Soon, I promise. I hope you'll understand."

"I'll try to, but I'm not a very understanding kind of person." Morgan slung her bag over her shoulder. Everything about that meeting had reminded her how young Wexford truly was compared to her. Wexford still had dreams of promotions. Morgan just wanted to get the job done and the case solved. She wanted to figure out the puzzle of the people she was given to profile. However, the way Wexford had managed to bring everything back around when Morgan had about lost control had been beautifully played.

"Maybe you'll even kiss me again soon."

"What?"

"You heard me."

Morgan clenched her jaw. She wanted to. There was no doubt in her mind that she wanted to.

"Because while you might not be a very understanding kind of person, according to you, I think you very much understand what goes on in someone's head, and I love to watch the way your brain works." Fiona's tones were hushed.

"Uh...right." Morgan glanced toward the door. "Shall we?"

"Absolutely."

With a breath of relief, Morgan stalked for the door to the conference room and headed toward the elevator with Fiona hot on her heels.

Chapter Sixteen

After they had set up the crews at the pier, Morgan drove them down to the factory. They oriented those groups, splitting everyone in pairs. In total, they had about twenty people going on interviews that day to try and get more information. The factory crew had more people to deal with because they would be driving to specific homes unlike those at the pier who would be surveying the immediate area of the bombings.

They would meet the next morning to go over the results of the interviews unless something popped up that warranted a whole lot more attention. Shoving her hands into her pockets, Morgan rocked back on her heels as she stared at Wexford.

"How many do we have on our list?"

"Just three. Why?"

"We've got to talk to Ray today."

Wexford raised on thin eyebrow up in curiosity. "You're really going to have to fill me in on who this Ray is."

"Let's walk." Morgan headed toward the car so they could get on top of their first interview of the day. When they got into the vehicle, Morgan turned the engine. "Where are we going first?"

"Here." Fiona put the address into her phone. "Now, Ray."

"Yes, Ray." Pulling onto the street, Morgan focused on driving. "Do you remember when Pax and I saw you at the precinct early that one morning?"

"Yes." A flush rose in Fiona's cheeks.

Morgan chose to ignore it. "We were there to do an interview on this guy named Ray. He had called in, I think, and then was brought to the station? I don't know. I'm fuzzy on those details. He was there because he claimed he was part of a group and there were some people who were threatening violence. He told the police about it when he was obviously still intoxicated, but he flat out refused to talk to me."

"Were you nice to him?"

Morgan stared directly into Wexford's dark eyes. She couldn't tell if the question had been asked in jest or if she was being serious. "Of course I was nice to him."

"It's just...if you interview people like you were talking today, then I can see why he wouldn't want to talk to you."

"You have no idea how I interview. You've never seen me do it before."

"I saw you the other day."

"What other day?" Morgan stiffened. This was brand new territory for them, and she wasn't sure she liked it at all.

Wexford sighed. "When we were all out here. You were interviewing people from the factory bombing."

Morgan scoffed. "Interviewing a white racist and most likely sexist is vastly different than interviewing a Somali Muslim immigrant who has, unfortunately, quite a bit of reason to be suspicious of the FBI."

"Yeah, about that..."

Morgan shot her a glare. "Let's not."

"No, let's, because that is exactly what has put you into this pickle of having to work with us, hasn't it?"

Gripping the steering wheel tighter than she had anticipated, Morgan took the next turn when the phone told her to. "I was not part of any of those investigations, trust me."

"I wasn't saying you were, but you have to admit that the surveillance your people did on this community has had a vast impact on them."

"Any government surveillance has an impact on a person, whether they are aware of that surveillance or not."

"Touché."

Morgan gritted her teeth. "Which house number?"

"Twenty-three."

Keeping her eyes peeled, Morgan pulled up just down the block from where the small home was. "We need to interview Ray when we're done with these ones. I would like to take another shot at him, but I imagine he won't speak to me at all. He might not even speak to you."

"Why?"

"Because you're a woman."

"We're going to need a strategy."

"Exactly. This interview first. Then strategy."

Morgan turned the engine off and got out of her SUV. Wexford followed her. When they got to the front door, Morgan rapped her knuckles against it and stepped back.

"I'll let you take lead on this, since I don't think they'll be too receptive to me in the long run."

Fiona smirked. "And she finally admits it."
"Shove it." Morgan's tone was harsh, but she was smiling.

It took them until late in the afternoon to get to Ray's house. He didn't live too far from the factory, but it was definitely not in any of the neighborhoods they had been in or where their agents and detectives were. His house was small, a light blue that sat on one level with a basement. Morgan put her hand on Fiona's forearm before they got out of the SUV.
"He's jumpy."
"You said that already. It'll be fine."
"Yeah. I just hope he gives us more than he gave us the first time."
"Which was what?"
"A whole lot of nothing."
Shoving out of the car, Morgan tightened her long jacket around her waist when a chill breeze picked up. The house looked quaint, and honestly, if she wasn't an FBI Agent investigating a hate crime, no one would suspect the house held a family of racists.
"Amazing how they seem to live so normal," Morgan commented.
"They get good at hiding the things people might not like about them. Like the rest of us do on occasion." The look Fiona gave her was full of sadness and pity. They had both hidden from their coworkers and friends for years, for their own reasons, but Morgan had kept her sexuality from Pax for twenty years, and Fiona, well Morgan wasn't quite sure what she was hiding or why she was hiding it, but it was clear she was.
"Yeah."
The front door had some type of big floofy fabric wreath on it with a sports logo, obviously left over from the football season they never gave up on. She'd done her research on him in the last week, checking to see what else Ray had been up to and who exactly he was. She had built his profile rather simply, though it had taken her the better part of a day.
He wasn't a complicated man. Rather, he was one of the easiest profiles she had ever built, and nothing in it told her that he would be prone to violence or had violent tendencies. Morgan knocked on the front door after ringing the doorbell and stepped back to raise an eyebrow at Fiona.
An elderly woman answered, the smile wavering on her face when she saw the serious looks on Morgan's and Fiona's. Morgan asked, "Are you Carla Arnold?"
She nodded.
Morgan opened the weather door and held it with her leg while she grabbed her badge. "I'm Special Agent Stone with the FBI and this is

Detective Wexford with the Chicago Police Department. We're working a joint investigation and were wondering if your husband, Ray, is home."

Carla stepped away from the door. "Yeah, he's in the den."

"Thanks." Morgan moved in first, Fiona following close behind.

The house was neatly kept and dated a few decades at least. It was warm inside. Morgan slipped her jacket off, hanging it over her arm to indicate they were going to be there a while. Fiona, however, did not mimic her move. Morgan, taking the lead, looked up at Carla who hadn't moved an inch.

"Where is Ray?"

"The den."

Morgan couldn't figure out why Carla wasn't leading them that direction, so she decided to guide them through it. "Will you show us where that is?"

Carla led them down the stairs to the basement. She moved slowly, and Morgan had to restrain herself as she followed, knowing it would take time to get to the interview and it would probably take even more time to get anything else out of Ray. Considering he had been so closed-lipped with her during the first interview Morgan had with him, she wasn't hopeful about their second interview.

When they got into the basement, the television was on in the corner to the news station. It was slightly messier down there than it was upstairs, but Morgan could see Carla's imprint had been left on the den even though it was definitely Ray's space.

"Honey, the cops are here," Carla's voice wasn't firm or strong.

Morgan gave her a wan smile as she stepped forward. Ray didn't move. Her heart sank. The niggling feeling in the pit of her stomach reared its ugly head, and she was pretty sure what she was going to find as soon as she walked around to see him. She shot a look to Fiona and nodded at the wife.

"Mr. Arnold, I'm Special Agent Stone with the FBI." She stepped closer to the chair, moving between it and the television.

As soon as she could see him, she stopped. She'd been right. Morgan looked up at Wexford, her voice soft when she spoke but commanding. "Call a bus."

"What?" Wexford said as she stepped forward.

"Mr. Arnold." Morgan leaned down and touched his wrist. "Mr. Arnold."

His skin was cool. He wasn't just dead—he had been dead awhile. Carla put her hand to her lips as she stepped in-between Morgan and Ray.

"Ray!" she screamed. "Ray!"

Wexford took Carla by the arm and turned her to walk back up the stairs. Morgan stayed down with Ray and touched fingers to his neck, finding no heartbeat. She put the back of her hand in front of his nose and lips, hoping there was the faintest of breaths coming out from his mouth. Nothing.

Cursing, she gripped her phone as she heard Wexford upstairs. She texted Taylor, letting him know the witness was dead-on-arrival and they were waiting on medics to arrive. Morgan followed the stairs back up, leaving the dead body behind her. Nothing would happen to him. As soon as she rounded into the living room, Carla's sobs were loud. She sat next to her, pressing a hand to her back and handing her a tissue as tears streamed down her cheeks.

"Mrs. Arnold, take a deep breath."

"He—he's dead."

"Yes, he is." Morgan nodded her head at Fiona. "Call it in, please. I've got her for now."

Fiona stepped into the kitchen with her phone next to her ear as she made the call they hadn't been expecting. Morgan rubbed circles into Carla's back to try and calm her down.

"When was the last time you saw him?"

Carla shook her head. "It's been hours. I...he's normally down there for hours by himself. There's never anything wrong."

Morgan pressed her lips together. "When do you think is the last time you saw him up here or the last time you went down there?"

"I don't know. Early this morning when I brought him some coffee. He normally stays down there until dinner time."

Checking her watch, Morgan glanced up as Wexford came back into the room. "When did you bring him coffee?"

"Nine? Maybe."

"Okay." Letting out a sigh, Morgan continued to rub circles into her back. "Okay. I'm sorry we had to find him like this. Did he have any health issues?"

Carla teared up again. "He had some heart issues and some breathing issues."

Wexford stepped in closer, leaning down to whisper into Morgan's ear. "They should be here in about ten minutes."

"Carla," Morgan started. "The ambulance is going to come and take care of Ray, okay?"

"Yeah. I just...how did I not know?"

Morgan was at a loss for words. This was not her forte at all, but she had to step in and smooth everything over, make sure Carla felt supported because since Ray was gone, Carla was their only connection to what Ray may have known. They would have to interview her as soon as she was through this initial shock.

"It's not abnormal, especially if it was a heart attack, to not know."

"Yeah."

"You'll be okay. Is there anyone we can call for you? A daughter or a son?"

"Uh…yeah." Carla looked up into Morgan's eyes then. "My daughter lives in town."

"Do you have her number?"

"It's by the phone."

Wexford slipped away again, and Morgan could hear her gentle tones in the other room as she made the phone call. When there was a knock on the front door, Morgan got up and opened it, finding two paramedics on the other side. She showed them downstairs and then went back up to sit with Carla.

They spent hours with her and with the daughter as soon as she'd shown up. Morgan hadn't learned too much about their home life, but she'd hoped she'd built a rapport with them to hopefully get further in an interview soon compared to what she'd gotten with Ray. He was taken to the county morgue, and Morgan made sure they were to do an autopsy just in case something else had happened.

She had very little reason to suspect foul play, but if Ray had known something about the bombings, who knew what their suspects were capable of, especially if they thought he was a leak of information. By the time Wexford and she got into the car to leave, it was dusk. They'd had a few texts and phone calls from agents doing interviews but nothing with pertinent information.

As soon as she was behind the wheel, Morgan rubbed the bridge of her nose. "Well, that was a waste."

"Maybe," Wexford said.

"What do you mean maybe? The witness, suspect, whatever, person of interest, is dead."

Fiona gripped Morgan's hand. "Yeah, but you said he wasn't very useful before."

"Doesn't mean he wouldn't have been this time around."

"We'll interview Carla."

"Damn straight, but I have a feeling she's not going to know anything."

"Why?"

Morgan clenched her jaw. "Just a gut feeling. Let's go back and regroup so we can figure out what we're doing tomorrow."

"Sounds like a plan."

CHAPTER SEVENTEEN

LIKE SHE had predicted, door to door had pretty much gotten them nowhere. Morgan sighed and rubbed her temple as the headache threatened to move down the back of her neck and into her shoulders. Ray had indeed had a heart attack, and Wexford had somehow convinced Morgan to wait to interview Carla until after the funeral, which had been that morning.

Pax was still gone, and Morgan had sent Mel a desperate text in hopes she would answer and find a sitter for the twins. She needed someone to just chill with and not think about the disaster her life had become. She walked into the small bar in the basement of the building downtown and knew she was in the right place.

Morgan slipped next to Mel on the bar and pressed a hand to her knee before ordering a beer for herself. "Thanks for coming."

"Any time, you know that."

Mel's smile was genuine, her white teeth bright in the dim room. Morgan let out a sigh. "You talk to Pax?"

"Yes, but I would think you did as well."

Morgan shook her head. "Not today. I was a bit busy with CPD."

"Oh?"

"Joint investigation."

"Is that why he's out there and you're here?"

Morgan shrugged. She wasn't sure she had an answer for Mel, not that she could fully explain everything to her anyway, but at least Mel understood how the FBI worked better than a lot of folk Morgan could talk to. Mel had been married to the FBI for the better part of fifteen years.

Sipping her drink, Morgan ruminated. "Do you think I'm messed up?"

"What?" Mel's dark eyes went wide. "What would make you say that?"

Morgan played with her drink, spinning it in a circle on the bar top. "You've known me for what, sixteen years at this point?"

"Yeah, I'd say so."

"I'm not sure I've ever felt this lost."

"Morgan." Mel leaned in, pressing a hand to Morgan's thigh and lifting her chin so they stared into each other's eyes. "What's brought this on?"

Rolling her eyes, Morgan shook her head. "Last December."

Mel gave her a curious look. "When you were injured?"

"Yeah, there's more to it than that."

"What happened? Pax didn't say anything except that you were hurt."

Morgan debated how much to share and what to share. "The suspect I was following out in Seattle found me—by accident—but she attacked me, so yes, I was injured. Remember, I had that nasty cut on my hand?" Morgan put up her palm and wiggled her fingers, then she pointed to her temple. "But it did a lot up here."

"Oh honey."

Tears threatened to spill over Morgan's cheeks. This had been what she needed, and it had been why she'd avoided Mel for months. She needed the heart to heart. "Yeah."

"Come here." Mel leaned in and pulled Morgan into an awkward hug.

Melting into one of her best friends, Morgan found her center again. She blinked tears from her eyes, wrapped her arms around Mel's middle, and held as tight as she could until Mel pulled away.

"I don't think you're messed up," Mel answered. "I think anyone who has worked for the FBI as long as you and Pax have seen your fair share of the underside of this world. He tries to protect me from it, you know, but I see when it bothers him. He at least has me to rely on."

Morgan snorted. "Yeah, I don't have anyone."

"That's not true." Mel leaned in again. "You've got me. You're one of my oldest friends. I'm always here for you."

Regarding her carefully, Morgan nodded. "That's why I called."

"I knew something was up. It's been far too long."

Morgan shrugged. "Yeah. Blame it on me, it's fine. It's what we do these days."

Mel took a sip of her drink. "What do you mean?"

"Taylor still won't let me leave the jurisdiction. That's why Pax is gone and I'm not. I wasn't allowed to go."

"What? That makes no sense."

"Thank you!" Morgan put her hands out to the side like a prayer had been answered. "Pax thinks I'm crazy and Taylor just wants me on this case, but I know there's something else to it."

Mel rubbed her lips together before she took another sip. "I don't think there's anything else, Mor. You're just imagining things."

"You sure?"

"Yeah."

But the way Mel said it wasn't convincing. Morgan let it drop. She at least had her moment, now maybe she could get past it. It was on the tip of her tongue to talk about Fiona, about the stupid crush she could not get out of her mind no matter how hard she tried. She'd thought after a year of crushing on the young detective would be enough but everything kept pulling her toward Fiona, no matter how much she tried to push the opposite direction, but she and Mel had never really explicitly talked about her dating life, not beyond the few men Morgan had managed to date.

"How are the girls?"

"They're good. Getting ready for middle school. Miss their auntie." Mel sent her a smile and a pointed look at the same time that Morgan knew only a mother could accomplish.

"When's promotion?"

"Sometime in May."

"Make sure to tell me when and I'll be there. You know I will."

Mel nodded. Morgan didn't bring up her work or her dating woes again, but even just sitting with one of her longest running best friends calmed her weary soul. She'd been so off since her stint in Seattle and dealing with the serial killer who had attempted to make Morgan her next victim. She'd have to find a way back to normal soon otherwise she would end up in therapy like her sister, Amya, kept telling her to try.

They ended the night with one more drink, a hug, and cab rides for the both of them. When Morgan got home that night it was the first time she remembered feeling completely relaxed in her own apartment in months. She flopped onto the couch, closed her eyes, and relaxed into the cushions like she didn't have a care in the world. Except she did. Ray was dead, and she needed to know who was behind all the attacks.

When she got to the office the next morning, Morgan felt rejuvenated. Calling Mel had been the exact right choice, and she loved that no matter how much time passed between seeing each other, they were always there and picked up right where they left off. Grabbing herself a cup of coffee, she settled into her desk and searched through her contacts. They needed information on the racist extremist groups in Chicago, and she really couldn't wait any longer.

She had absolutely no undercover operatives in the group Ray had been a part of. It wasn't one that was on their radar as leaning toward violent tendencies, so they hadn't seen the need to plant someone there yet. Besides, to go undercover like that was hard, and they liked to try and limit it. Still didn't mean one of their other contacts didn't know something about them.

She checked out a few of the ones she knew and sent messages to their handlers to let them know she wanted a chat with the operative. Once that was done, Morgan focused in on exactly what would tilt a hate group from their get tabs list to their watch list. What amped them up enough? She knew she could talk to Adena about it, since she was the intelligence analyst who focused on those things, but after their night together, Morgan wasn't completely sure she wanted to broach that if she could do the research on her own. That had been why she tried so hard to keep her distance between relationships and work. Adena had been a slip up, an accidental break down in her rules, more than once.

The deeper Morgan dug into the world of racism in her favorite city to live in thus far, the more she became disgusted. The ability for people to hate so willingly, so voraciously another person weighed heavily on her. It was almost as bad if not worse than the sex trafficking case she had been working.

She read through report after report, skimming for information that may have pertained to her case. All it really told her was people were mad there were immigrants, that there was special preference given to them—at least in their minds. She sighed. It would be near impossible to figure out who it was making and setting the bombs without some type of tip from somewhere and her last hope of that had gone out the window with Ray. Grabbing her phone, Morgan called Wexford.

"Hey," Wexford answered, her breath rushed.

"Hey, got a minute?"

"Always for you."

The perky attitude was odd come from Fiona, but Morgan ignored it. "Has your crew come up with anything?"

Fiona sighed. "Not really. Want to meet over lunch to talk about it?"

"No. Did they find anything else?"

"There have been rumors of people taking action, but nothing has come of it."

Morgan pressed her lips together. She'd found the same. Tapping her fingers against the top of her desk, her mind whirred as she tried to come up with some connection they had missed. "We may need to put out another press release asking for anyone with information to come forward. These cases are hard to break if it's an individual and not a group because there are far fewer connections to be made."

"Yeah, that could work."

"I don't want to create unnecessary panic, though."

"Agreed."

Morgan narrowed her eyes and stared down at her empty coffee mug. Wexford was being decidedly less than helpful that morning. Morgan was going to have to go talk to Adena, whether she wanted to or not. She needed to pull all the possible reports that had come up that she hadn't read yet and see if they matched in any way, and she really needed to read over Ray's initial interview again.

"Shall we visit Carla this afternoon?" Morgan asked.

"Probably."

Morgan rolled her eyes. Everything Fiona was saying that day was hitting a nerve with her, but she couldn't quite figure out why.

"How about one o'clock?"

"Sure."

"Good." Morgan hung up and shoved the phone onto her desk. She needed coffee, and she needed to step away from her work for a moment. Everything about the case was frustrating her. She hadn't wanted to work with Wexford, hadn't wanted to be saddled a new case when she really wanted to be working on the trafficking one, and there she was, stuck doing everything she didn't want to do.

Leaving her phone on the desk, she grabbed her empty mug and went to get some coffee, hoping that would rejuvenate her and perhaps even change her attitude. By the time she got back, her phone was buzzing with a call from Pax.

With the phone pressed between her ear and her shoulder, Morgan answered. "Better have something good for me. I need a pick me up."

He snorted. "Bad day?"

"Bad few weeks. How's Dimitri?"

"He's not halfway bad, actually."

"Well, that's good to hear." Morgan pulled out the information she had on Ray and searched for the report from the initial interview they had done on him and the one CPD had done. "Did he give up any more information?"

"Nothing more than what was in those initial interviews shortly after he admitted he'd seen Mr. Jimmy."

"Nothing at all?"

"No. But he is sticking to his story, so I strongly suspect he is telling the truth."

Morgan sighed, rubbing the bridge of her nose. She grabbed her reading glasses she always tried to avoid wearing and plopped them onto her face. The headache brewing would no doubt only get worse if she didn't wear them. "Will you be interviewing him again before heading back?"

"I'm already back."

"Wh-what?" Morgan looked around the office. "Where are you?"

"Taylor told me to take the rest of the day."

"Why didn't you call to tell me?" Morgan's stomach twisted.

"Thought I'd spend some extra time with the girls if I could."

Morgan clenched her jaw. It was so unlike Pax not to let her know when he got back. Sure they didn't work every case together, but they were best friends for the better part of twenty years, and he usually always kept her in the loop. Even the coffee next to her didn't look very appetizing.

"You do that. I'm going to try and catch me a bomber."

"Any tips come in?"

"Nothing useful so far. Went to interview Ray, remember him?"

"Yeah."

"He's dead."

"What?" Pax's gasp at least sent a shiver of pleasure down Morgan's spine.

She swallowed. "Heart attack. Went to interview him and found him dead in the lazy boy in the den."

"Is this a joke?"

"No joke, Pax. Wexford and I are going to interview his widow this afternoon, see if she knew anything."

"You better get on that."

Morgan narrowed her gaze at her computer. "Plan on it. See you Monday?"

"Yeah. See you then."

"Tell the girls hi for me."

"Will do."

She hung up and headed the one place she wasn't sure she wanted to go. Traipsing down two floors to Adena's desk, Morgan once again slid onto the corner of it. "Get any chatter going on?"

"None."

Morgan pouted. "Can you make sure I'm contacted if there is any chatter, no matter what?"

"Sure." Adena barely looked up from her computer. It seemed they were back to their standard.

"Right. Thanks."

Morgan went back and prepared her interview questions for Carla. After another couple hours, she drove out to Carla's, meeting Fiona there. Together they walked up to the front door, hoping they didn't meet the same fate this time as they did last.

Knocking on the door and ringing the bell, Morgan held her breath as she waited for Carla to answer. Morgan wasn't sure what to say to Fiona. They had barely spoken since they got to the door. Morgan was planning on taking lead, again, but she probably should give strategy to Fiona so they were on the same page.

When the door opened, it was too late. "Mrs. Arnold."

Carla cocked her head at them, shaking it as tears threatened. "What are you doing here?"

"We need to talk to you, may we come in?"

She shook her head again.

"Mrs. Arnold, we can do this down at CPD's office if you'd like, but I'd rather just do it here if you would. We won't be long."

Carla stared at Morgan, flicked her gaze to Wexford, and then opened the storm door wider. Morgan moved in first, Wexford following just like before. They settled into the living room upstairs, Morgan next to Carla and Wexford in a chair across from them.

"Mrs. Arnold, I'm so sorry to have to talk to you about this, but when we came here to talk to Ray...we still need information."

Carla swallowed, her anxiety and fear written all over her.

"Do you have any idea what we are here about?"

"No," Carla answered on a whisper.

Morgan risked a glance to Wexford who was writing Carla's answers down. "Was Ray part of any groups? Did he have any friends he hung out with?"

"Yeah. He was a member of our church. He was a deacon there for years."

"I'm talking more groups that might not have been so upstanding."

"I'm sorry?"

Morgan wasn't quite sure how to word her question without pissing Carla off or offending her. She was pretty sure there was no delicate way to ask if her husband was a secret racist asshole. "Was Ray part of any groups that specifically were opposed to immigration or that believed Christianity to be the true religion of this country?"

"Oh." Carla sighed. "I don't know. He definitely thought those things, but...I don't think he was part of any group."

Morgan spun through the questions in her head. "Was there anyone he routinely hung out with? Maybe some of the guys?"

"There was a group who used to come over every Sunday to watch football in the garage." Carla pointed at the door where Morgan assumed led to the garage. "They didn't do anything more than drink beer and watch football games."

"All right. Do you think you could give us their names?"

Carla shook her head. "So, sorry. I didn't...Ray and I had pretty separate lives. We were married, yes, but that's about it. We haven't...we haven't been a couple for decades."

"What do you mean?" Fiona asked.

Sighing, Carla glanced over at Wexford. "We didn't want to get divorced. We're old. We didn't want to put our adult kids through that, so we stayed married, but we lived separately. I couldn't...Ray believed a lot of things I didn't, and I couldn't condone that anymore."

"Things like what?" Morgan asked.

Carla wrung her hands together. "Things like you were saying."

"What specifically?"

"That we are superior to all other races. That we are better than them. I...I was a school teacher for many years, and I could not put what he said and what I saw on a daily basis together. He was so insulated and never wanted to listen to a different opinion. I moved to the guest room as soon as our daughter moved out and I never went back. After that, we really only spent time together when it involved the kids."

Morgan's heart broke. What a way to live. It probably would have been better if they had just divorced, at least then Carla wouldn't have had to live such a sad existence. "So he did believe in white supremacy?"

"Yes."

"But you don't know if he was part of a group that may have also held those beliefs?"

"I don't know. He might have been, but I have no way of knowing that. Ray was his own man."

"All right. If you were to find anything when you're going through his things, please do not hesitate to let us know. We don't want to tarnish his name in any way, I promise you that, but we do need some answers to our questions."

Carla barely nodded. As soon as they were back at their cars, Morgan let out a grunt and turned to Wexford. "Well, that was mostly useless."

"Kind of, at least we know he was the type of person we are looking for."

"Yes, but we have no idea if he's connected to any of this."

"Then we'll just have to work harder."

Morgan agreed, but she wasn't about to say as much. "See you Monday."

"Monday," Wexford answered with a smile.

With one last look over at Wexford, Morgan realized why she was in such a piss poor mood. Adena had been a nice distraction, but that was it, a distraction. What she wanted, and most likely what she needed, she couldn't have. At least not yet.

CHAPTER EIGHTEEN

IAN LEFT the news on day and night for the first week, and it wasn't until seven days passed that his nerves had calmed enough for him to turn it off and get some sleep. He wanted to know if they were coming, if he needed to speed up his plans to make his stand. What they were planning next was going to be huge, and Ian wanted to make sure they were able to accomplish it.

The bombs he was making were going to be bigger and better than the last ones. He was still sore about the fact one hadn't gone off, which could lead the authorities right to him if he wasn't careful, assuming they had even found it. He wasn't even sure if they had since none of the news channels hadn't said.

What he would give to have an inside source on what was being investigated and what wasn't.

Ian swallowed down a beer as he concentrated on the bombs he was making. These would be bigger and better. These would be perfect. As soon as they set these ones and watched them go off, he didn't care if he was caught. These would do exactly what he intended. Surely, he'd prefer it if he could keep fighting back for what was rightfully his, but this time he knew it would make a difference.

This was the one that would spur others to move with him rather than against him. This would be the time that would allow others to want to join in his cause and realize the faulty ways they had been taught and they had believed for years.

When Tim showed up at his door, Ian was surprised but let him in and led the way down into the basement. Tim didn't hesitate as he grabbed a beer and popped the lid. When he sat on the couch, he let out a groan. Ian watched him carefully, wondering what had set him in such a mood.

"Ray's dead."

"What?" Ian's eyes widened. "What happened?"

"Don't know. Saw his obituary this morning in the newspaper. Service was today."

Ian plopped next to Tim on the couch. "Poor guy."

"Yeah. Never knew a happy day in his life, did he?"

"Nope." Ian cocked his head to the side and took a long swig of beer. "You tell Spence?"

"Yeah. Called him on my way over."

"Fuck. Spence is going to be devastated." Ian knew he would. Ray was very much like a father to Spencer in a lot of ways. Just a young kid lost in what he was supposed to do and how he was supposed to act. Ray had been that steady role for him.

Tim let out a sigh. "It's probably a good thing."

"Why?"

"I was worried he was going to rat."

Ian turned his head slowly toward Tim. He had suspected the same, which had been why he'd shut his trap when they were making plans all those weeks before in Ray's garage. He'd pushed the limits of the conversation to see where Ray fell in the line of his thinking, and it had been just what he'd suspected. Ian downed the rest of his beer.

"We can't wait then."

Tim nodded his agreement. "When?"

"Next week."

"Will we be ready?"

Ian drew in a deep breath. "We'll have to be."

"Spencer?"

"We'll need him. This is going to be it. We may not have another chance after this one."

"Right."

Ian crushed his beer can and set it on the table. He didn't go grab another one. Instead he rubbed his hand over his face and the beard he had forgotten to shave in the past few days.

"Let's hit three places at once." Ian's voice was firm. He'd thought it through already, many times over, and he knew this was how he wanted his last potential stand to be. This was how he wanted it all to end.

Tim's wide eyes told him he was surprised, but before Ian could even explain, Tim was nodding his agreement. "Yes. Let's take the best targets we have figured out so far and run with those. We have to make this one right."

Ian nodded. He knew Tim would understand. Tim always did. "The mosque."

Tim agreed. "We need to hit the apartment this time, scare them where we know it'll hurt."

"The school?"

Tim blanched. Ian knew that was going to be a hard one. Schools always were, but they had looked, they had researched where the schools were that took most of those students. Ian let him mull it over in his mind, saying nothing else. They had done surveillance on it. Tim had largely helped since he could more easily drive by the school without suspicion.

Ian grabbed a blank notebook and drew out a crude map of the mosque. That would be his first target for sure. Tim watched him carefully, eyeing the work but saying nothing. Once Ian had the outside of the building drawn up along with the streets on all the sides, he set it down on the coffee table in front of them.

"Here, here, and here." He pointed to spots right by the doors. "We'll set them for Friday noon. That'll be the first one."

Tim shifted the notebook. "We should add another two here and here if you think you can make them in time."

"We'll have to see how many we want for the rest."

Tim took the pen from Ian's fingers before flipping to an empty page and drawing the apartment complex. "These will need more oomph but if we set them in these four spots, we can take the building down, or at least nearly take it down."

"Friday morning?"

"Yes."

"The school?"

"I don't know, Ian." Tim shook his head and sat back in the couch. "You know how I feel about that one."

They didn't really have a backup that would equal the hitting a school full of their children, and the children were the ones who would grow up exactly like the adults. To Ian they were no better. Ian knew he'd have a battle to make with Tim, an argument to win, but he was prepared for it.

"We need a third place," Ian started.

"Yeah, but the school? There are other kids that go there."

Ian shrugged. "Conspirators."

"No, they don't have a choice, Ian."

Ian clenched her jaw. "Where then?"

"Another mosque? I don't know, but not the school, please."

"I'll do it."

Tim gave him a wary look, still unconvinced. Ian needed to work through a way to convince him. The festival had been great for a warm up. No doubt the filthy animals were already on edge, but they had to make a bigger impact, and what better way than a school?

They fell into another silence. They would have to bring Spencer in on the conversation soon enough in order to complete their plans. They would have to know exactly what they needed. Ian debated whether or not to get another beer, but if he was going to be building even more bombs, he would need to be mostly sober.

"What about the community center?" Tim's question was soft and gentle.

Ian contemplated as he got up and grabbed another can of beer. Popping the top, he mulled it over. It could work. It was similar to the mosque, but it would have the same impact if not an even wider impact since more than just the Somalis used it. "That could work."

Tim's eyes lit up as he grabbed for the notebook and mapped it out. They had done some rudimentary surveillance on that building as one of their options, but had largely discounted it because it wasn't in their specific target group. But it might work. Tim finished his drawing.

"We'll need four."

"You're asking a lot."

"I told you I can help."

"You'll need to." Ian sat on the couch again, spinning the notebook so he could see everything. "So that's how many total?"

"Thirteen," Tim answered. "Maybe we shouldn't do those extra two at the mosque."

Ian raised an eyebrow. "You think?"

Standing, Ian went into his bedroom where he kept all the supplies under lock and key. He sat at the table and got to work making a bomb. Tim joined him after taking a sip of his beer. "You think Ray told anyone?"

"Hope not," Ian answered. "If he did, I'd kill him again."

"He was so nervous that night."

"Which is why he's not here with us now or with us the last two times. He never would have stuck it through."

Tim shifted things around so he could see them better. "We've got to get Spence on board."

"He'll be on board. We've just got to get the timing. None of this has worked out well since the first time we tried. We can't have anything going wrong this time."

"Yeah." Tim wrapped the wires together.

Ian kept glancing at Tim to make sure he was doing everything correctly. He would go back in and triple-check all their work because he didn't want another bomb to fail like the one at the pier had. They needed this to work.

"When are we going to set the community center one?"

"All on Friday."

"Yeah, but morning, noon, night? What?"

Ian shrugged. "We'll need to do some more research on that one I think to figure out what time would be best."

"We can do that this week. You want to aim for this Friday or next?"

"This one. I don't want to wait."

"Worried they'll figure us out?"

Ian nodded. "I know they will. It's just a matter of time, which is not something we have a whole lot of. We need to make these decisions quick."

"Want me to call Spence?"

"Give him the night." Ian finished his bomb that he had started earlier that day and moved on to the next one. Tim's help would be useful, but they would have to make sure that they finished everything. "We should set them Thursday."

"That only gives us five days."

"We can do this in five days."

"You don't think three targets is too many in that amount of time?"

Ian shot Tim a look, wondering not for the first time if Tim was backing out. "No. This may be the last chance we get. We need to make it count."

"Right."

Ian sneered. There was no doubt he was the leader of their little posse, their little rebel riders and fighters, but he had thought many times before that Tim was smarter than he was acting. Perhaps he was too overwhelmed by Ray's death and that was causing him to pull back. Who knew, but it needed to stop. They needed to pull together to make the best impact they could.

"Did you watch the news?" Ian asked, changing the topic slightly. "See all the snowflakes interview the dogs?"

"Yeah." Tim snorted. "Like they were really scared."

"Hmm, some perhaps. Not enough."

"No, not enough. I can't believe they're still here."

Ian pursed his lips. "They just let them walk right through the gates at the airport. There's no stopping them. That's why we're doing this, you know that."

"Yeah, I just figured those asswipes we voted for would do something to make a difference for us, but they seem to not care at all."

Ian couldn't have agreed more. He hadn't voted like Tim because he'd seen the futility in it all, but yes, the government was useless. Everyone was useless, really. No one was fighting back, which was why Ian had to make a stand, had to take all of it into his own hands. Tim and Spencer were just there to help him accomplish what he knew needed to happen.

They worked late into the night, finishing up two more bombs total. Ian pressed them into the bottom of his closet and locked the door just in case his prying brother decided to come down and see what he as up to. Tim went home, and Ian was cast into silence. He could hear his brother and sister-in-law and their two kids running around upstairs starting the bedtime routine, and he knew what he was doing for them. It was all for them, to give those kids a better life than he had been given, more opportunities, and more freedoms.

He was tired of having his own freedoms compromised by people who weren't even born in their country, who didn't uphold the standards and beliefs his country was built upon. They were nothing more than dirty animals if anyone asked him, which of course no one did because they insisted on political correctness.

Growing angrier by the minute, Ian grabbed himself another beer and went to bed. He would get up early in the morning and finalize their plans for everything. He'd double check what Tim had told him about placements, do some more surveillance on the community center and determine the best time of day to take action there.

With his beer done, Ian turned off the lights and closed his eyes. Everything in his chest settled into a feeling of calm and serenity. This may be his last chance, but if it wasn't, he wasn't going to change his goals. He would keep going until he was successful, until they all went back where they came from, until he had what he deserved. Restful and calm, Ian fell into a deep sleep for the first time in a week.

CHAPTER NINETEEN

SIFTING THROUGH information for hours had become Morgan's norm. She'd completely abandoned the trafficking case in an attempt to close out the bombing case so she could get back to the one she wanted to be working on—the one that didn't mean she had to talk to Wexford on the regular.

She was just about to dive into another report when she heard her name in that sweet, pure voice she had been working so hard to avoid. Morgan's stomach tightened as she glanced over the edge of her desk to see none other than Detective Fiona Wexford standing near the hallway, her pristine tan suit with matching blazer, the stark white shirt underneath a contrast. It brought out her dark eyes and the light tones in her hair that Morgan wanted to wrap her fingers in over and over again.

Cursing under her breath, Morgan stood up and regarded Fiona with a very curious look. "What are you doing here?"

"We need a break."

Confusion echoed in Morgan's chest as she tried to flip her mind from personal thoughts to work thoughts and figure out what Wexford was even talking about. It was too early—Pax wasn't even there yet—and she did not have enough coffee in her veins to think straight. The escort who had helped Fiona find Morgan's desk walked away, and Fiona stepped forward.

"In the case," Fiona added.

"Right." Morgan pressed her fingertips into the edge of her desk, wondering just what the fuck they were doing there. She knew they needed to work on the case, but there seemed to be something in their air that said this was more personal. A phone call and Morgan heading to Wexford would have done that, but to have Wexford come to her was too far out of the ordinary.

Pax bumbled in through the elevator. He turned his entire body to the side, his broad shoulders taking up a lot of room, as he passed by Wexford who still stood near the entry into the large room where many agents had their desks. He nodded at Wexford and went straight for his desk, dumping his bag on it.

"You're late," Morgan muttered, not taking her gaze from Wexford's slight form at the door.

"Traffic."

Morgan's lips pressed into a thin line. "Sure. I'll be in the conference room with Wexford most of the day if you need me. Get me that report from Dimitri, though. I want to know what he said."

"Here." Pax handed Morgan a thumb drive, and she glanced down at it, finally breaking eye contact with Fiona. "The video recording for your watching pleasure."

"Hmmph." Morgan tucked it into her pocket and grabbed all the paperwork and reports she had just been going through. Dragging it out of the large room, she stepped down the hallway, saying nothing to Wexford and expecting her to follow. She wasn't disappointed.

Dumping all the papers onto the table in the small conference room, Morgan settled into a chair. Fiona shut the door and sat next to her, but she didn't grab a piece of paper to look at it. Morgan slid one of the reports she hadn't finished reading in front of her and settled in to read. Wexford was right, they did need a break in their case, and she was determined to find on in the sea of paperwork in front of her. All she needed was one little connection.

"I was thinking we should interview Carla again," Fiona stated.

"Why's that?" Morgan didn't even bother to look up at Wexford as she continued to read the papers.

"What if she has more information?"

"I think we'd gain more information by tearing apart that house and finding the connections ourselves than Carla Arnold giving them to us."

Fiona sighed. "Maybe you're right. Can you imagine being married and having nothing to do with your partner?"

Morgan slid her gaze up to Wexford eyes and stared at her like she had two heads. Either Wexford didn't remember her confession about her mother, or she hadn't listened. It had a lot of weight on the reasons why Morgan had zero desire to be in any type of committed relationship, but it was also her experience with her own marriage. She loved Barbie, as a friend, and beyond that they had nothing to do with each other.

"Yes," Morgan stated simply and went back to reading, hoping Fiona would drop the topic.

"I can't."

Morgan tried oh so hard to hold back the snort, but she couldn't manage it. When Wexford still didn't grab a piece of paper, Morgan sighed and looked up at her. "Was there something you wanted to do other than go through these reports?"

"Don't you think we should spread these out a bit with the rest of the task force?"

Morgan cocked an eyebrow at Wexford. "These don't leave the FBI."

Wexford's lips parted, her mouth hanging agape before she snapped it shut. "Did you have enough coffee this morning?"

"No, but that's regardless of the point. These reports are classified, like ninety-percent of my job, and they do *not* leave the bureau."

Fiona drew in a deep breath and held her hands up. "Chill. Just a question."

Morgan kept her mouth shut that time. She had no idea why she was being so antagonistic aside from her own feelings she couldn't figure out how to deal with. When Wexford still didn't have a report in her hand, Morgan grabbed one and slid it in front of her. "Here, read this. Be useful."

"Useful?"

"Well, you're just sitting there. Figured you'd want some reading material to use that insane brain of yours on."

A blush tinted on Fiona's cheeks, which surprised Morgan. It had been compliment, but it hadn't been intentional. Fiona started reading, and Morgan went back to her report. It was from one of the undercover agents in another one of the hate groups. A lot had been redacted, so Morgan knew nothing would be compromising for Fiona to read since she herself wasn't even allowed to be in the know of who the undercover was, but at least she had the report of what was going on.

There wasn't much activity, though their response to the first bombing was interesting. The group had been happy for it, though again, they had not claimed it, no one in the organization had. The undercover suspected there were a couple individuals who could be capable of such a bombing but hadn't given names. Morgan would have to communicate back for them if she really wanted them—which she did.

She made a note in her notebook to get those names. None of the other reports seemed to be relevant to her. When she glanced up at Fiona to see what she was doing, she was surprised to find Fiona staring directly at her.

"All right." Morgan shifted and put her report down. She turned to face Fiona full on. "What is going on? You are not focused, which is not your norm."

"We broke up."

A rush of cold came over Morgan. She glanced to the door of the conference room before standing up to shut it. When she sat back down, she grabbed Fiona's hand and squeezed tightly before letting go and giving her space again. "I'm so sorry."

"I wanted it."

Morgan licked her lips and checked out the glass leading into the hallway, wanting to know who was walking by and who wasn't. "Then why so forlorn?"

"No break up is easy, Morgan."

"True." She knew that from some experiences but others were very easy for her and for the other person. That was why she went into every relationship with clear boundaries from the beginning. She wanted to ask more questions, wanted to open the floor for Fiona to talk, but they were sitting in a conference room in the middle of the bureau. Anyone could walk in at any point, not to mention, they did have actual work that needed to get done.

Fiona brushed her hands over her cheeks. The confidence she had when she came into the bureau that morning was gone, and all Morgan saw was the broken woman who lived underneath. "Let's find something today, please. I'm tired of coming up empty."

"You and me both," Morgan muttered.

They sat in silence for another five minutes before Morgan leaned back into her chair, bringing her knee up to rest on the edge of the table and staring over at Wexford who still had her nose deep in whatever report Morgan had handed her.

"We've been going off the theory these bombings are related to a group, that while they might not be a group doing them, that whoever is setting the bombs and building them is part of some kind of hate and terrorist group."

"Yeah," Wexford answered, finally looking up.

Morgan stared out the window and to the sea that was Chicago before her. "What if they're not?"

"You mean like they just woke up one day and decided to bomb some factory and some pier?"

Shaking her head, Morgan turned back to Wexford. "No, and yes. Whoever this is wouldn't just wake up one day with that in mind. Something would have pushed them to do it, but if they are incredibly introverted or isolated, they may not have sought others with similar viewpoints. They have may just assumed these viewpoints need to be held by the majority and have a louder voice."

Fiona narrowed her gaze. "I'm not sure what you mean."

"They may actually be working entirely on their own, in which case, this is going to be a far more difficult case than we had originally suspected. It means it could end up being another twenty-plus-year case like Kaczynski."

"It won't turn into that," Wexford reassured.

"I don't think it will, but it will be much harder to find our suspect. This suspect is not as smart as Kaczynski, and seems to take a bit more gratification in the bombings themselves. Not to mention, these have all been localized to Chicago. There are no other reports of bombings in the country or in Canada that match the description of these ones."

"Really?"

Morgan cocked her head to the side. "Yes. Didn't you read the memo I emailed you early this morning?"

"I...uh...was a little busy this morning, and then I came straight here."

"Hold on." Morgan stepped out of the conference room and walked down to her desk. She printed out a copy of the memo she had emailed and remembered to grab her reading glasses last minute.

When she got back to the conference room, Wexford was reading a new report. Morgan slid the paper in front of her and leaned over Wexford's form, pressing a hand into the back of the chair and onto the conference table after sliding her glasses onto her nose.

"See? I updated the profile."

Fiona ran her finger along the lines as she read quickly enough.

"I estimate he's smart, but he's no genius. The bombs have been rudimentary at best. They have all been made in a similar fashion, but some of them have had mistakes, including the one that didn't go off at the pier."

Wexford nodded. "What was wrong with it?"

"They missed a wire, of all things. They completely missed putting it in there, not just that it came loose, but like forgot about it."

"Interesting."

Morgan nodded and stared down into Fiona's dark eyes as she turned to look up.

"You're cute with glasses. I don't think I've ever seen you with them."

Morgan shifted to shut the door again and sit down. "Why do you keep doing that?"

"Doing what?"

"Making this personal."

"I thought...I realize we're at work, but I thought we had an understanding."

"Right, we are at work. This is not the appropriate place to have this conversation. You know that. I know that. So why do we keep swinging back around to this?"

Wexford's lips parted in surprise. Morgan's heart sank. She wanted to be that caring person, but she built her life on boundaries and not crossing them as much as she could. While she did want to cross them with Fiona like she occasionally did with Adena, it scared the living shit out of her.

Fiona drew in a deep breath. "Let me get this right, so you can bring up whatever it is between us while at work, but I can't?"

"When have I—"

"Last December. Crime scene."

Morgan flushed, her cheeks heating. She'd known exactly what Fiona was going to say, but she hadn't wanted to remember. She'd felt awful for it two seconds after it happened. "I apologized for that."

"You did." Fiona crossed her arms over her chest. "While at work."

"Fine. You're right. Can we get back to the case now?"

Fiona leaned forward and pressed a hand to Morgan's knee, squeezing lightly before whispering, "Under one condition."

"And what condition is that?" Morgan's heart raced. She wasn't quite sure what was coming over her, but Fiona had never been one to avoid the topic at hand. She was far braver than Morgan in a lot of ways.

Fiona smirked. "Lunch."

"No. I've got a conference call."

"Then dinner."

"I'm not getting out of this, am I?"

"No," Fiona answered with a grin.

"Fine. Case?"

Nodding, Fiona spun around the report she had been reading. It was the report Morgan had been trying to focus on for the better part of the morning. "You have a bomb maker in this group."

Morgan stared down at the paperwork, trying to see what Fiona saw. How she had missed it the first two times through, she had no idea. Right there was a report from her undercover that there had been talk of if there were to be an attack—which the undercover suspected would not happen—it would be done by bombing select targets. No targets were specified, however.

"I'm going to make a phone call." Morgan didn't wait as she grabbed her phone and called the lead on the case. She needed more information than just that, and she needed a direct line to the undercover if at all possible.

When she finished her call with a set up for a meet sometime that afternoon into evening, Morgan focused on Fiona. "You might want to read this."

"What is it?"

"Ray's profile."

Fiona bit her lip as she read through it. "You think he was capable of violence?"

"Yes, but I don't think he was violent. Though, to be fair, I think anyone is capable of violence. I don't think the circumstances were right for Ray to take that final step. I wish he would have talked when we interviewed him. I want to know what he thought he had to share."

"He never told any officers anything other than he knew something was going to happen. Then he just shut up." Wexford grabbed a pen. "Okay, so what do we know?"

"We know there was something that upset Ray. We know there have been at a minimum two attacks."

"Minimum?"

"Well, if one bomb didn't go off at the pier, I wouldn't put it past this guy to have tried and failed before and we just be completely oblivious to it."

"Which, now that I'm reminded, did they ever find a match to those prints on the bomb that didn't go boom?"

Morgan smirked at Wexford's joke. "No, they didn't. But once we do find someone to bring the in at least we have prints to match to them."

"True, but not helpful in the current situation we find ourselves in."

"Nope. We know that the attacks seem to be growing in severity, and rapidly. There doesn't seem to be an easing into bigger and better things. We went from one bomb that did minimal damage to three bombs that did a lot of damage."

Wexford wrote everything down in bullet-point form. "We know this guy is most likely high school educated at the minimum."

"I wouldn't guess more than that."

"Oh?" Fiona raised an eyebrow at her.

"Like I said, small mistakes here and there. There's no game being played. This person isn't out to toy with us, he's out to make a statement, and he doesn't care if he's caught."

"So he's bold."

"Yeah, I guess you could say that. Convicted of his beliefs is more like."

"Okay. What else do we know?" Fiona put the pen to her lips and stared down at the paper.

"What we don't know is if Ray is even connected or if that group he was a part of is connected."

"Hmmm, too bad they don't have some sort of membership list."

Morgan snorted. "That would make life much easier."

"Perhaps too easy."

"We know there is at least one person involved. There could be more. We did find two sets of prints on the bomb that went off, but the second set was obviously only from carrying the backpack. It could be from who placed it and who made the bomb or it could just be the bomber used a used backpack."

Fiona wrote it down. "Were there prints on the others?"

"Only partials that matched the ones on the bomb itself from what we could tell." Morgan glanced at her watch. "I've got my conference call."

"About this case?"

"No...about my other case."

"Your other case?"

Morgan narrowed her gaze. "Yes. So, we can pick this up later, but this call is going to last hours."

Fiona had a slight frown on her lips. "Dinner?"

"Let's focus on this case first, and then we can do dinner. I never said dinner had to be tonight." Morgan stood up and started gathering the files she had brought into the conference room. "I'll call you when I hear back from our undercover about that one report and see what I find in it."

"All right."

Morgan didn't miss the disappointment in Fiona's voice as she sent her on her way. They were going to have to figure out how to continue to work together, but there was a newly niggling hope in the center of Morgan's chest for what they may finally be able to explore. She just wasn't ready to let Fiona in on that fact yet. First they had to talk about Morgan's rules when it came to dating.

CHAPTER TWENTY

MORGAN WAS an hour into the debriefing on the human trafficking case when her phone buzzed in her pocket. She was sure it was her mother calling again at one of the most inconvenient times as was her norm, but when she glanced at the number, she realized it was an internal caller.

Stepping out of the room, Morgan stood right outside the door to the lecture room as she answered, "This is Stone."

"Agent Stone, this is Sean Davis. I've been tracking your requests through BMAP."

"Oh." Excitement rose in Morgan's chest. She glanced at the conference room she had just vacated and stepped farther away from it. She had a piece of paper on the top of her file that she could write something on so long as she could manage to find a pen to write with. "Did you find something?"

"Yes."

Morgan bit her lip, full of anticipation, but it felt as though she was going to have to drag the words from him one at a time. Morgan clenched her jaw and felt up the pockets on her pants and her jacket, trying to find the damn pen she knew she'd brought with her into that conference room, but she was pretty sure it was still sitting on the table.

"And?" she asked impatiently.

"We have some suspicious activity that has been reported to us."

Morgan rolled her eyes. This guy was slow with the uptake on giving her the necessary information. "Do you think you could email me the report? I'm not at my desk right now, so writing things down is going to be tough."

"I can do that. But ma'am..."

Ma'am? When was the last time anyone had called her ma'am? Least of which by a fellow agent at the bureau even if he wasn't a field agent, they still usually called her by her last name. Putting off her unease, Morgan swallowed. "Yes?"

"You should know the information we have hasn't been verified."

"I'll verify it after I look at it. Just send it to me."

"All right."

He hung up without so much as a goodbye. Morgan stared at her phone for a minute before she headed to the floor with her desk on it and slid behind the computer. As soon as she sat down, she woke her screen up and checked her email. Nothing. Grabbing her glasses, she checked it again. Nothing. For a guy who called supposedly with information she needed, he sure was taking his sweet time emailing.

Morgan grabbed her coffee mug and went for a refill, hoping by the time she got back to her desk, the report would be there. Sure enough as she slid into her chair, she saw the email from Sean Davis right at the top of her lists, along with one from Wexford. She ignored Fiona's and read Sean's.

He was right. There was not a whole lot of information and whatever had been bought—if it was to build a bomb—had been a very small amount of material. It wouldn't result in anywhere near the number of bombs that had been created already, although, she did suppose they could do multiple purchases to try and keep the suspicions down, though she wasn't convinced their suspect was quite smart enough to think about that. Or if he was smart enough that he cared enough.

The guy they were looking for had literally done nothing to try and hide his identity. He didn't wipe fingerprints off anything. He put bombs in places that were obvious. There wasn't a whole lot of time between them, and he didn't play games. In some ways, she wondered if he wanted to be caught. If he wanted to be made into a martyr.

Grabbing her cell phone, Morgan called Wexford, but it went straight to voicemail. "Fiona, give me a call asap."

Morgan delved into the financial records for the three individuals who had purchased the materials that were flagged as suspicious. Two had been done by the credit companies themselves and one had been done by a shop owner. She'd start with the shop owner, because that was a far more rare way for someone to be reported to BMAP.

When her phone rang, she had a small thrill go through her chest when she saw Fiona's name flash across the screen. "Wexford."

"You called?"

"I need you to come back up here."

"I—really?"

"You need to come now. We'll debrief everyone when we figure some more out, but we may be making arrests today."

"I'll be there in twenty."

Morgan hung up. In the interim, while she waited for Fiona to arrive, she stared the backgrounds on each of the three individuals, starting with the one who set off her radar. She wanted to know who they were, what they were doing, what group they were a part of, and what exactly they believed. If these people were any way connected to the ones she was hunting for, she wanted to know.

Wexford showed up exactly twenty minutes after the phone call. She waved down Morgan, who called her over to her desk. Morgan didn't hesitate pulling Pax's chair out for Wexford to sit in as they leaned over her desk. Morgan shifted one of the files in front of Wexford, the one she was most interested in.

"Tell me what you see in here."

Fiona read through the file, sighing and making little noises as she went. Morgan skimmed one or two gazes in her direction to check in while she pulled more reports, arrest reports, financial reports, anything she could find on the background for the other two suspects and made files for them. She was about done with the third when Wexford let out a large breath of air and slid the folder onto the table.

"Does the material purchased match the material in the bombs that we know about?"

Morgan's lips thinned. "About a third of it does. The rest? No."

"And this was purchased in Cook County?"

"Yes."

"What do you think?"

"I'm asking you." Morgan pulled her glasses off her nose and plopped them onto her desktop. It was a bit of a test. Fiona had been fascinated with profiling and the type Morgan did for years. That had been how they'd first met, so she wanted to know how Fiona's brain worked and if she was going to make some of the same connections Morgan did.

"I think it's likely he's making bombs. Is it our guy? Not sure on that."

"Why?" Morgan crossed her arms and leaned into her chair.

"Aside from the materials not completely matching up, he's a bit young for our profile. Still within the range, but if we're truly talking about someone with a vendetta and who wants to make a difference, the likelihood that they'll have met some hardships is good. So, I'd presume, they'd be at least about ten years older."

Morgan smirked. "You're good."

A blush rose to Fiona's cheeks. "Why do you say that?"

"This person has a college education." Morgan pointed at the paperwork. "We're likely looking for someone who doesn't."

"So you've said."

Morgan nodded. "Right. Let's look at these other two, and while we may make some arrests today, I doubt it'll be the arrests we want."

It took them two hours to get everyone ready to go and everyone in place. Morgan had insisted she and Wexford be there for the arrest of Nicolas Schohl. Morgan was pretty sure after a few more hours of research and investigation that he was at the very least making bombs. The other two could have been doing anything, she wasn't sure, they would find out during interviews—which she would supervise only.

Morgan strapped her vest over her chest and grabbed her gun in her left hand. They were working with SWAT on this one since Nicolas had priors and there was a strong suspicion he was making bombs. Morgan's heart raced. Once glance to Fiona told her they were both feeling the adrenaline kick in, and they needed to relax.

The grin on Wexford's lips was almost too much for Morgan to bear. They were both going to enjoy this take down. The danger of it, the planning of it, the thrill of catching someone who may be preparing to do something really bad, of getting them before it could get to that point. SWAT went in first like planned.

Morgan and Fiona stayed back, waiting for the go ahead. They were the second wave. They were the ones who would actually bring in the suspect and interview him. As much as Morgan wanted to be in the first wave, as much as she wanted to be on the front line and had trained for it in some regard, working with SWAT meant they took control of the situation and she got to sit back and watch.

In some ways, it was nice. She made sure to observe the excitement in Fiona's face, the lines etched near her eyes and lips that showed her enjoyment of the situation. Fiona never smiled, or barely did, because it wasn't that she was happy to be arresting someone, but she was enjoying the moment, the thrill, the adrenaline, the punch that would take them to the next level of excitement for the day. Morgan understood that viscerally.

When they got the wave from the commanding officer, Morgan barreled out toward the front door to the house. SWAT had already been through everything and cleared it, but she kept her weapon in both hands in case they missed something, not that she didn't trust them, but because it was what she trained for.

She was the only FBI agent there. They had simply provided the information for the local police to do their thing and take over. They would give more information and more resources through Morgan herself should CPD need it, but outside of that, the case was in the hands of CPD and no one else.

Morgan's heart pumped as she walked through the house. It looked like any other house in suburbia. Nice on the inside, well-maintained. There was a bit of mess here and there, clutter where something obviously hadn't gotten cleaned. One officer held a puppy to their chest, a pup that couldn't have been older than four or five months, plastered to this man who looked like he could break its neck with the snap of his fingers.

Nodding at him, Morgan continued through the house. She was ushered into the basement, and then into a bedroom along the back wall. When she opened the room, nothing looked too out of the ordinary except there was a bunch of shit thrown onto the bed where clearly the SWAT team thought they found something.

Morgan shoved her gun into its holster at her side after she'd done another sweep of the room to make sure she was alone and nothing was going to pop out and get her. Wexford came in a few seconds later and also put her gun away. Slipping a glove onto her left hand, Morgan rifled through the bags on the bed. Inside were the materials Nicolas had bought that had been flagged by BMAP. They were all still neatly wrapped up and unopened.

She shoved it toward Fiona and walked around the room. The kid was put into the back of a vehicle and taken down to the station where Morgan and Fiona would interview him. They spent an hour at the house before trekking back to the station. They had discussed repeatedly their strategy for interviewing, but as soon as they entered the room, it all went out the window.

Nicolas sat at the small table, fear written all over his body. He was hunched over, his light blond hair covering his eyes, his broad shoulders pulled together. He didn't even dare to look up at them. Morgan slid Wexford a glance as she sat in the farthest chair from him, letting Wexford take point on this one.

"Nicolas, I'm Detective Fiona Wexford."

He nodded at her, but that was it. Fiona slid a glance to Morgan who nodded in Nicolas' direction, trying to encourage Fiona to get on with the interview. Fiona wanted to learn, and this was a prime time to do it.

"Do you know why we were at your house today?"

Nicolas said nothing.

Wexford bided her time, giving him ample opportunity to speak up, but he just sat there, hands pressed together as he leaned over and stared directly at the floor. Wexford clenched her jaw, the little muscles on the side of her face tensing. Morgan waited.

"Do you remember going into the Hometown Hardware on the corner of twenty-sixth and Apricot?"

Again silence.

"Nicolas," Wexford started, "We can sit here all day if you'd like, but if you're not going to answer any of my questions, it'd be helpful to know that."

He didn't move, not even an inch other than his steady breathing. Morgan wondered if he'd fallen asleep and thought about slapping the top of the desk to see if it'd get a reaction out of him, but Wexford was the one in charge of the interview, not herself.

"Nicolas, do you remember going into the hardware store?"

A very slight, almost imperceptible nod. Morgan couldn't hold back the smirk that lit her lips or the light that was in her eyes as she turned to Wexford to encourage her silently.

"Good, because the owner of that store, Mr. Gary Burnateli remembers seeing you there, too. We just wanted to talk to you today because we were a bit concerned about what you purchased."

"It's not for me." Nicolas' voice was so quiet, Morgan wasn't sure she had heard him correctly.

Wexford, however, didn't miss a beat. "What do you mean it wasn't for you?"

Nicolas' tongue dashed out against his lips, his fingers clenched tightly. "It wasn't for me. My friend needed it and asked me to get it."

"And which friend is this?" Wexford had a pen to paper, ready to write down exactly who Nicolas said. They would have another interview to do that day and perhaps maybe it would lead them down the road they wanted to go.

Nicolas tensed. "He's...he's not really a friend."

"Okay. What is he then?"

"M-more like a boyfriend."

Morgan's heart clenched. This was very unlikely the person they were looking for. Savviness in terms of sexual coercion was not something that would fit the profile of their killer, especially with someone of the same sex.

"Okay, so this guy is your boyfriend?" Wexford asked, her pen still ready to no-doubt write a name down.

"No." Nicolas' head shook, his light blond hair flinging out to the sides.

"You want him to be?"

Nicolas barely nodded.

Wexford let out a breath. "Okay, Nicolas. What is this guy's name?"

"Y-you're not going to talk to him, are you?"

"We're going to have to."

"D-don't mention I said he was my boyfriend."

The tension in Morgan's neck and shoulder increased at the fear in Nicolas' voice, in the fear in his eyes as he stared directly at Wexford. She wanted to speak, but Wexford beat her to it.

"Why would you ask us that?"

"He—he doesn't want anyone to know."

"Okay, but the two of you are in some sort of relationship?"

Nicolas nodded.

"Okay. That's very helpful for us to know, thank you, Nicolas. Can you perhaps tell us his name now?"

"It's Luca Rossi."

Morgan had to clench her jaw to keep from drawing in a hiss of breath. Fiona barely managed to write the name down before she sent Morgan a curious look. Apparently, Morgan's tension hadn't gone unseen.

As soon as they finished the interview, Morgan was on her phone and walking down the hall. She had Taylor on the line. "Hey, boss."

Fiona grabbed Morgan's arm and spun her around. "What the hell is going on?"

Morgan held up a finger. "This isn't related to my case."

Fiona moved in even closer, her body pressing against Morgan's side, and the thrill that went through Morgan's nerves was not because she was about to make a break in another case. Fiona's lips were near her ear without the phone. "Tell me what's going on."

Morgan ignored her. "This kid said he got the stuff for Luca Rossi."

"Bring him."

"Yeah."

Morgan hung up and shoved her phone into the pocket of her gray slacks and turned to Wexford. "I'm taking Nicolas down to the FBI."

"What?" Shock registered in Wexford's case. "You can't...you can't just take another case from me."

"This is...I'm taking Nicolas, Fiona. I can't tell you more than that."

"What the fuck, Morgan?"

The anger lanced straight to Morgan's heart. This was why any relationship between the two of them would be an awful idea. Any time Morgan ended up with information pertaining to a case they were working on, she'd have to come upon this anger, this betrayal, and she wasn't sure she could do it.

"I can't talk about it." Morgan stalked into the interview room. "Nicolas, I need you to stand up."

"What?"

"Stand up." Morgan reached behind her back for her handcuffs and pulled them out.

"Where am I going?"

"I'm Special Agent Morgan Stone with the FBI, and I'm going to take you to a more secure location."

Fiona stood at the door with her arms crossed and a glare on her face. "This isn't right, Morgan."

"It's the only right way to do this. Trust me. You don't know even the surface of it." Morgan took Nicolas by the shoulder and led him toward the elevator. It wasn't long until she had him back at the FBI in a new interview room and the agents on the case proper were preparing to question him.

When Morgan finally made her way to her desk, she had radio silence from Wexford. Her heart raced as she flipped through missed calls from her mom and a few missed texts from her sisters. She'd get back to them all that night—she made a vow to do it. She really needed to focus more on them than whatever was between her and Wexford, because Morgan knew without a doubt it would be a disaster if they were to get involved.

CHAPTER TWENTY-ONE

MORGAN WAS ready to go home. It was late. She'd stayed late on purpose, catching up on the conference call notes that she had missed and finalizing what she could of the report from the arrest she'd made, though that report would never be finished until the other agents figured out what they could for it.

It was nearing eight, and as much as she had promised herself she was going to call her mother back, the energy she'd had to put in to that phone call had diminished to absolutely nothing. Morgan gathered her stuff up and slid her bag over her shoulder. It took her the standard twenty-two minutes it always did for her to get home at that late hour.

When she pulled into the parking garage, she stopped short at the sight of the black SUV sitting in the guest parking near the elevator. Sighing, Morgan debated whether or not to even get out of her vehicle because she was more than sure what was about to happen. Deciding she couldn't wait any longer, she shoved the door open to her car and stepped into the dim light of the underground parking garage.

Wexford was out of her SUV before Morgan had even managed to finger the fob and lock her own vehicle. The exhaustion that she'd felt at the office was very much still present, but she ignored it as she stepped closer to Fiona, knowing where the argument was going before it even started.

"You can't keep taking my cases." Fiona's words cut like a knife.

Morgan sighed. "Can we do this upstairs? I want a whiskey and to sit."

"No."

Morgan clenched her jaw. "Fine. I did not take your case as you so think I did. That boy we arrested today was completely unrelated to our case, and you know it. Was he going to attempt to make a bomb? Perhaps, but that is for my agents to discover, not your detectives."

"It was my case, Stone."

"Oh, so we're here using last names, then. This is just a jurisdiction-pissing match, is it?" Morgan rolled her eyes and started toward the elevator. She really did not want to have the conversation out in the open for the rest of the world to hear. She had done her best to not let her neighbors know she worked for the FBI, and she really wanted to maintain that cover.

Dutifully, Fiona followed her. Morgan refused to talk until they got up to her floor and she unlocked her door. Shutting it behind Fiona, Morgan dropped her keys onto the small kitchen table she kept and dropped her bag onto the chair. Without pretenses, she started to pull off the gear she wore every day. Her jacket slid onto the back of the chair where her bag was, her gun settled onto the table, the holster to follow.

Fiona watched everything she did in silence but with a firm look of anger in her eyes. It wasn't until Morgan slid her shoes off and walked into the kitchen that she finally spoke. "I can't tell you about the case."

"Why the hell not?"

Morgan turned on her then, raising one thin eyebrow and shaking her head slowly before she pointed a finger. "You're talking to a federal agent with the FBI. Like you, we don't talk about cases. Unlike you, there are a fuck ton more consequences if I do leak confidential information."

Fiona drew in a sharp breath. "Fine. I do get it, even if I don't like it. But you cannot keep taking my cases. First Lollie, then this."

At the mention of Lollie's name, Morgan's shoulders tensed. Her fingers wrapping around the neck of the whiskey bottle tightened and her molars ground together. Setting the whiskey back on the table, knowing she really probably shouldn't be drinking anyway, Morgan slowly turned back to Fiona. "I can't help it if you keep stumbling onto cases that are too big for your britches."

Fiona's eyes went wide, and Morgan knew she'd touched a nerve. "I don't even know what to say to that, but you know as well as I do, that either of these cases I could handle on my own."

"Really?" Morgan's eyes narrowed. "This is your first time leading a task force, and a joint one at that. You told me as much yourself. Do you have any idea what you're doing? Because standing here in a pissing match with me is really not the way to get the job done." Grabbing a glass from her cabinet, Morgan filled it with cold water in her fridge and took a long sip. She would be remiss if she offered Fiona anything. She wanted her out of the apartment so Morgan could have the night to herself to sit and mope and wonder and think—but most importantly, sleep.

"Don't talk to me like I don't know what I'm doing." Pain flashed across Fiona's gaze.

Sighing, Morgan set her glass down and stepped in closer. She put a hand on the side of her arm and squeezed. "I'm sorry. You're right. That was mean. Neither of those cases were ones I wanted to take, trust me, I have my own. I don't really want to be working this bombing case either. I want to focus on my trafficking case, and I want to be there when we take the bastard down, but I've been assigned this case. That's coloring my attitude."

Fiona gave the slightest nod. Morgan sighed again.

"Really, I'm sorry."

"Thank you. I'm not some young, green detective, Morgan. I know what I'm doing."

"Yes and no." Morgan bit her lip, trying to look into Fiona's dark eyes that were cast in doubt. "You have experience, but you are still so young. Take it from someone who has been in this world for decades, Fiona. You have years to go still before you become jaded."

"You're not jaded."

Snorting, Morgan rolled her eyes. "Sure, you can think that if you want."

"You're not." Fiona looked up then, their gazes locking.

Morgan knew what was going to happen. Fiona was going to kiss her. Morgan's tongue dashed against her lips, her chest tightening in anticipation. A kiss like they had shared the other week but without alcohol might be too much for her own sensibilities, but God, she wanted it. She'd desperately wanted it for over a year, and now—now Fiona was finally unencumbered with whatever relationship she'd been in.

Fiona stepped in, fingers sliding against Morgan's cheek and cupping the side of her face. Morgan tilted her head into the move, desperately loving the warmth from Fiona's hand against her skin. Her eyes fluttered shut as she waited to see what would happen next.

"I want to kiss you," Fiona whispered, the breath from her mouth brushing against Morgan's nose and lips.

Morgan let out a groan. "We need to talk first."

"We can talk later."

God, she wanted to. She wanted to dive right into whatever the hell had been building and run with it, but Morgan knew Fiona was still angry with her, knew they hadn't cleared the air, knew they had to set up some rules. They couldn't—they shouldn't—do this while still working on a case together.

"No, no, we can't talk later." Opening her eyes, Morgan stared directly into Fiona's. She was so close. She was right there in front of her. Surely one kiss wouldn't hurt anything. They would still be able to work together, figure out whatever. They'd done it before and didn't have a problem working the case. Yet it wasn't the kiss Morgan was afraid of, it was what the kiss might lead to. She moved her hand from Fiona's arm to her shoulder and then down, skimming her breast before settling her fingers against the dip in

Fiona's waist. She wanted so desperately to say fuck it and bring their mouths together. It was a struggle just to tear her gaze from Fiona's and step away—something she had yet to manage to accomplish.

"Morgan..."

"Don't. Just...just give me a second here."

"I want this."

"I know," Morgan whispered. "God, I know. But there's still this case."

"We don't work together," Fiona answered.

"Yet, we do. Isn't that why you're here? Because you're mad I interfered in your work with mine?" Morgan pulled her lip between her teeth and shook her head, trying so desperately to force herself to step away. "We work together, Fiona. Right now we work together a lot. We have to set some boundaries."

"What boundaries?"

Fiona's anger gave Morgan what she needed to retreat into her kitchen again. She grabbed her glass of water and took a very long sip of it before facing down the beautifully angry woman standing near her front door.

"Not tonight, please. I am exhausted after today, and I just need...I need some good sleep and a few days to get my head on straight."

"That's rich." Fiona snorted. "Are you going to even call me in if something goes down with the case?"

Morgan pressed her lips together. "I have shared all the information I can with you, every single piece of it, and I have called you in to work with me more than any other agent would have, so do not think I would hesitate to call you in or rely on your judgement for the rest of the case."

Fiona visibly relaxed, her shoulders dropping and the tension in her face easing. "I'm sorry. You're right. I don't...I don't know why this is so hard."

"Because we happened to shove a bunch of complications into life. Well, we didn't, but there have been, and we have to navigate those. Hence, why we need to talk and set some boundaries."

"Hmm." Fiona cocked her head to the side. "Sure, I'll agree to that, just one thing."

"What?" Morgan turned to stand up straight just as Fiona took three long and quick steps right up to her, cupping both her cheeks and bringing their mouths together.

Morgan gasped, her fingers curling into the soft material of Fiona's blouse just at the tops of her hips as Fiona's tongue pressed against hers. Fiona's body tightly held her to the counter, her back pressing into the edge of it sharply, but most of Morgan's focus was on the woman stealing her breath, shattering her resolve, arousing her body.

Whatever they had done before when drunk—this was so much better. It was worth it. Digging her nails into the soft flesh at Fiona's sides, Morgan dared herself to take the kiss as far as she could without moving beyond a kiss. She pressed a palm flat against the small of Fiona's back and tugged her in closer, their hips grinding together from their closeness.

When Fiona's hand moved from her cheek to her neck, tightening lightly and then loosening as she trailed her fingers down, her thumb brushing Morgan's nipple through the fabric of her shirt and bra. Morgan moaned and jerked away, breaking the kiss.

"Stop." She breathed out the word. "Stop, Fiona."

"I thought you wanted this."

"I do. I do want this." Morgan put her forehead onto Fiona's shoulder and closed her eyes, drawing in a deep breath. "I do want this, trust me, more than you probably know, but not right now, not when you're upset, not before we've talked about things, not when we're still working this case together."

Fiona's chest rose as she drew in a deep breath. "Okay. So what now?"

"Now, you go home. I go to sleep—maybe, if I can after that. Tomorrow, we solve this fucking case."

Chuckling, Fiona drew Morgan's chin up and kissed her hard but brief. "I don't think we're going to solve it tomorrow."

"A girl can hope."

Grinning, Fiona stepped away, giving Morgan the much needed space she wanted and desperately didn't at the same time. Fiona raked her gaze up and down Morgan's body and then laughed lightly. "You're much better at that when you're sober."

"Shut up." Morgan couldn't stop the snort from leaving her nose. "Get out. I'll see you tomorrow."

"Tomorrow."

As soon as the door was shut, Morgan let out a rush of breath. Stepping to the door, she flicked the deadbolt into place. She was going to need an ice bath after that. With thoughts and fantasies rampaging around her brain, Morgan stripped the rest of her clothes and left them in a pile on the floor of her bathroom while she hopped in the shower she refuse to turn on hot. It was going to be a long night.

The next morning, Morgan had barely stepped into the office when she noticed Adena sitting at her desk. The woman, while not the prettiest one out there, certainly knew how to flaunt what she had. She sat on the edge of Morgan's desk, her legs crossed and the pencil skirt above her knee.

Morgan had slept but with dreams of Fiona accompanying every moment of it. Cocking her head to the side, Morgan dropped her bag next to the bottom of her desk and raised an eyebrow at Adena.

"You're late," Adena stated.

"Not really. It's one minute past eight. What's up?"

"There's chatter."

"You're shitting me."

"Nope." Adena handed over a file she'd kept behind her. Morgan flipped it open without hesitation as she read the report. Something had gotten out. "Who?"

"Girlfriend."

"Where is she?"

"Interview."

"Who's in there?"

"Waiting on you."

Morgan's broad grin was perfect. If they weren't standing in an office full of other officers, she may have kissed Adena. Instead, Adena slipped off Morgan's desk and headed for the elevator without another word as was her norm. Without hesitation, Morgan called Fiona and told her to skip going to the police department and head straight for the bureau.

It took Fiona ten minutes to get there, but as soon as she arrived, Morgan was waiting with the file in her hand, the file she had read over at least ten times in that ten minutes. "What's got you so happy?"

"You said we weren't going to solve this case today, and we may very well might."

"What break did you get?"

Morgan handed the file over. "Girlfriend of some guy who said he's been acting funny and asking a lot of really odd questions. Want to go interview?"

"Yes." Fiona's eyes light up with excitement, the same excitement she'd had right before they went to arrest Nicolas Schohl.

As soon as they entered the room, Morgan took lead. This was her place of work, and this was her case. She sat down next to the woman, who clearly looked like she'd been on a binge of some kind of drugs or alcohol. Morgan gave her a small smile.

"I'm Special Agent Stone. You're Cassidy, right?"

"Yeah." Her voice was strong, without a slur, so perhaps she wasn't as intoxicated as Morgan had initially assumed.

"You called into the police early this morning talking about your boyfriend. You want to tell me a little about that?"

Cassidy looked at Wexford. "Who's she?"

"She is Detective Wexford. She works with the Chicago Police Department."

"Why's she here?"

"We're working this case together." Morgan tried to bring as much patience forward as she could. These interviews were all about waiting for the answers they needed and waiting for someone to say something that would click with the case. "Why don't you tell me what you called in about this morning?"

Cassidy sneered. "I don't want to talk to her."

"You're not talking to her. You're talking to me."

"I want immunity."

Morgan slowed her movements at that. "Cassidy, in order to have immunity you need to have done something wrong. Did you do anything wrong?"

Cassidy shook her head.

"Okay, so why don't you tell me what you called in about this morning so we can help you?"

"Nothing to help." Cassidy's voice was low, deep, and without hope. "My boyfriend has been hanging out with these new guys. I don't like them much, but whatever, he's just my bae, right. I don't have much say in that. These guys...they're older than him."

"How much older?"

Cassidy gave Morgan a scathing look but didn't look at Wexford again. "One's as old as you. The other as old as her."

"And he knows these men, how?"

"Don't know. Don't care. But...Spence has been asking a whole lot of questions about the building I work at, weird questions."

"Like what?"

"Like where the cameras are and what doors are locked, that kind of shit."

Morgan swallowed. "And why do you think he's asking that?"

Cassidy's lips thinned, and she slid a look over at Wexford. "These guys he hangs out with, they say some shit I don't agree with."

"Like what?"

"That there's an immigrant problem, that they're taking over this country. Racist shit like that."

Every nerve in Morgan's body was geared to every word Cassidy said. "Do you know these men's names?"

Cassidy shook her head. "Not their last names."

"First names will be enough." Morgan held her breath.

"Tim and Ian."

Morgan wrote the names down and glanced at Wexford. She needed someone to start doing some research quick, but Wexford wouldn't know who to even get hold of. Holding a finger out to pause Cassidy, Morgan nodded her head toward Fiona and handed her the sheet of paper. "Give this to Pax, would you? He'll know what to do."

Fiona's face paled, but she took it and started out of the room. Morgan didn't want to wait until Wexford got back, so she turned to Cassidy again.

"Your boyfriend was asking questions about where you work. What was it that seemed so odd about the question?"

"Look, I'm just housekeeping. I don't want to get anyone in trouble, but I've mentioned to him before how frustrated I get when I find doors unlocked when they shouldn't be. Anyway, he seemed to take a sudden interest in which doors, asking multiple times which ones they were."

"And where do you work?"

"Community Center, the one off Irving Park."

"I know the one," Morgan answered just as Wexford slid back into the room. "What is it that makes you so worried that you would bring it to us? Asking more about his girlfriend's job seems like a thing a good boyfriend would do."

Cassidy shifted her gaze from Morgan to Wexford and back. "It's the things he's been saying."

"What things?"

"Look, Spence is a good guy. I really like him. He's got shit to figure out, but he's not a bad guy."

"We're not saying he is," Morgan reiterated. "But what is it that's got you so worried?"

"These guys he's been hanging out with. They worry me. They do things Spence doesn't normally do."

"Like what?"

"They don't like people who aren't like them."

Morgan narrowed her gaze. "You're going to have to spell this out for me, Cassidy, otherwise I can't do anything about it."

Cassidy leaned forward on the table. "Spence has been talking about bombs, about fixing up things so it's better. I don't know what he means by that. I don't think he knows what he means by that."

Morgan's heart raced. "Bombs, what about bombs?"

"He was freaking out over the bombing at the pier the other week. Like really freaking out. He was saying Ian was so mad at him, but he wouldn't tell me why. As soon as I asked, he clammed up and got so wasted and high he passed out for the night."

"Cassidy, where is Spence now?"

"Work."

"Where does he work?"

"Battery shop."

"Okay, I'm going to be right back. Wexford?" Morgan stood up and dragged Fiona out of the room with her. She nodded at the officer who would watch Cassidy while Morgan made a direct line to Pax and Taylor. She didn't wait as she shoved open Taylor's office door with Fiona hot on her tail. "We've got something."

"What?"

"The holy grail." Morgan grinned as she laid everything out for Taylor. In the span of twenty minutes, they had people going to pick up Spence and others researching who the hell Ian and Tim were, but they would definitely know more as soon as they got Spence into the room with them. Morgan could barely wait for that interview to begin. Fiona had been wrong the night before. They had gotten the break in the case they needed, Morgan knew it.

CHAPTER TWENTY-TWO

THEY WENT to the mosque first, wanting to wait until the middle of the night before going to the housing complex, when there would be least likely people to catch them. That was going to be the most dangerous of the three to set up. Ian had all the bombs in the trunk of his car. He'd dressed in all black so that he would less likely to be seen as they set them.

Tim had everything planned. Ian pulled up a few blocks away. They would grab the bombs from the back of the car, and then they would walk the rest of the way, separately. Spencer would stay in the car and let them know if anyone was coming or showed up, but it was just going to be Tim and Ian on this one.

As Ian swung the bag over his shoulder, he let out a grunt. It was a chill evening, but they had chosen this day for a reason. There would be more people in the mosque on a Friday than on any other day of the week. They wanted to make the biggest impact that they could, scare them out of their wits so they'd leave his city alone.

Ian lit up a cigarette as they walked. The security that they had found at the mosque was rudimentary at best, but they also weren't planning on going inside. They just needed to manage to steer clear of the cameras in the parking lot and by the doors, which should be easy enough.

Ian's cigarette was gone by the time he got to the parking lot. Tim had taken the other route, but he could see Tim's slender figure also dressed in dark clothes with a ball cap covering his head standing across the way. They could do this.

Ian placed his two bombs, making sure they were set and the timer was perfect to go off right in the middle of morning prayers. The impact they were going to make over the next two days was going to be so much better than what they'd attempted at the pier. This time, they would succeed. Ian knew it in his gut. They had planned for this as best they could, and he knew they would see some fallout from it, some type of reaction from the Muslim community. There was no more playing around.

Ian held his breath when the lights of a car shone in his direction. His heart raced as the lights on the top of the white cruiser told him exactly his worst fear. The cops were there, no doubt because of the pier, no doubt doing extra checks just to be sure there was nothing else going on. He stayed as still as possible after shuffling behind a large trashcan and trying to shrink himself into nothing. He could only hope Tim did the same.

Waiting was the worst. The officer shown the spot light against the wall of the building, moving it all around. Ian froze his entire body, making his breaths shallow so as not to move him more than necessary. It took probably only a minute, but it felt like an hour, for the cruiser's spot light to go off and the cruiser to leave the parking lot.

Ian let out a breath of relief and counted to sixty before he dared to move. They had to hurry up. He'd been getting far too cocky in thinking they wouldn't run into any issues, and God had just reminded him he wasn't invincible, and this wasn't without risk. The risk was worth it, but so would be finishing out their plans for the night. Spencer would flip out if they didn't show back up in the forty-five minutes they'd said they'd be gone.

When Ian felt safe enough, he stepped away from the trashcan, his knees groaning at the ache from sitting still and tense for so long. He didn't hesitate as he finished setting the two bombs that were designated his and booked it back toward the car. He met up with Tim a block away and let out a rush of relief.

"You see that cop?" Tim asked.

"Yeah. Don't mention it to Spence, he'll freak out."

"Right. I was about ready to run."

"Glad you didn't. You get it all set up?"

Tim nodded. "I was halfway through the first one when the cop showed up and I had to stop."

Ian's jaw clenched. "Community center next. We need to get this done. They're starting to get suspicious, which means we don't have much time to get our work done."

"You're right."

Ian slid into the driver's seat of the vehicle and rolled his shoulders before lighting up another cigarette. His hand shook as he brought the cig down to the steering wheel to go to their next location. He hoped Tim and Spencer didn't see it.

They stopped, and Spencer and Ian go out of the car. It was Tim's turn to sit and watch the rest of the bombs. It didn't take them too long to get everything set and ready, this time without any interruptions. When they got back to the car, Tim was already in the driver's seat, waiting to go to the housing complex.

Three in the morning had come very quickly. It had taken them less time to set the bombs than Ian anticipated. Waiting by circling the neighborhood until thirty passed the hour, Ian directed Tim to park the car. All three of them were going to get out for this one. Ian carried two bombs while the others carried one.

They stuck to the shadows and hoped they wouldn't be seen. Most of the lights in the building were off, but Ian could see lights here and there that indicated someone was awake, whether it was in a bedroom or living room. The hall lights were on so people who were coming and going could see their way in.

Ian's heart beat rapidly. This may very well be their last chance to make an impact, and he knew he wanted it to be a good one. He had no doubts their voices would be heard, perhaps for the first time ever, truly heard in the sea of what those snowflakes kept forcing everyone to believe and say.

He knew not everyone could agree with them but that the majority of the people actually did, but their voices were quieted by the raging voice of the oppressor. Pushing down his anger, Ian focused on the task at hand. He was the one going inside. The other two would stay outside, setting their bombs on the edge of the building, but Tim had said if they wanted to take it down, they had to do something inside. It was easy enough to get into the building, but walking in the full light of the hallway made Ian's skin crawl.

He stepped as quietly as he could down the hallway toward the stairs, where he went down instead of up and into the basement. From there, he walked to the far end of the laundry area, setting the backpack against the far wall. When he stood back up, he cocked his head at the dryers.

That was an unexpected surprise. The gas line ran to the dryers right next to where he'd set the bomb. He'd thought they'd be electric like in most apartment buildings he'd lived in, but this would add the perfect fodder for the explosion. Ian reached into his back pocket for a pocket knife and sliced the gas line, just nicking it. He didn't want to let it leak too much and alert everyone before it was time.

Walking toward the door, Ian crouched down and set the second bomb he'd carried in next to the stairwell. Destroy that and no one would be able to get out as the fire took hold.

The plan was perfect.

Hurrying himself, Ian made for the outside and the car they had stashed blocks away. He was the last to make it back, which wasn't unexpected. He had more work to do than the others. Tim was driving again and took the most roundabout way back to Ian's house after dropping Spencer off since he had to go to work. Tim said his goodbyes and slipped into his own vehicle, heading home to his wife and kids.

They had been up all night, and Ian sucked down the largest coffee he could manage while he sat in the front seat of his run down car. Tim and Spencer weren't with him, but all they had to do was wait. He hadn't been able to resist the urge of going to see if everything was going to work, if this time, he hadn't messed something up.

The first one to go off was supposed to be the apartment building. He'd wanted to catch them before they left for work in the morning if he could. Ian parked at least six blocks away, waiting for the explosion to rock through the community. The cigarette pack in his front pocket only had two left, and he'd have to get more before he went to wait out the mosque.

Ian drew in a breath as the clock in his vehicle ticked over the eight in the morning. The ground shook. He couldn't see much, but he heard the explosion, the effect of what they had set only hours before. It was perfect. Ian staked out his place, watching as emergency personnel came within minutes of the explosion. Everyone came. It was perfect. They would all be so focused there they wouldn't know where else to go and the mosque and community center would be wide open. It was the perfect distraction.

Ian smoked his way through the pack of cigarettes and finished his coffee. Then he waited another twenty minutes before slowly pulling away from the curb and driving toward the small convenient store he'd tried to bomb the first time that had failed. It was a good thing he had gotten so much better at making the bombs since then.

He paid for a new pack of cigarettes and refilled his coffee. Ian filled the tank of his car with gas and got back in, driving toward the mosque. Noon was going to come quickly. He'd changed the timers on the ones for the community center last minute to go off simultaneously with the mosque. He wouldn't be able to be there for both, and he'd want to go home and watch the news of it all soon enough to see what kind of impact they had made. Surely this was going to be a better and bigger impact than the festival at the pier.

Ian parked a little closer than he had at the apartment complex. There were cars in the parking lot and along the street to the mosque, but he had no way of telling how many people were actually inside the building. They hadn't gone in to set the bombs, so most of the damage wasn't going to be to take the building down but just to make a point. He'd wanted to take down the apartment, to do the most damage to where the animals lived and to their families. That was going to be the best way to get them to leave, and it would open up the most opportunities for him and people like Tim's kids.

The bombs went off almost all together. One after the other. The blast rocked into Ian's chest, and utter glee filled him at seeing his creation explode. With wide eyes he stared as the dust mixed into the air. People around the mosque were running and screaming and crying, but he remained still. He remained fixated on the damage he had done and caused, on the statement they had made.

That had been the purpose of all of it, make a statement, make a difference, let people know what they thought and believed, be the voice for those who wouldn't and couldn't speak. Ian sucked down a cigarette and drove back to his brother's basement.

Pulling up outside the house, he parked his car and went inside. His phone buzzed, and he answered on the third ring when he saw Tim's name. "Hey."

"Hey, do you know where Spence is?"

"Nope. Haven't seen or heard from him since we dropped him off." Ian went inside and climbed down into the basement. "Why?"

"He's not answering my calls. I called the shop, and they said he was there for an hour before he was arrested."

"Arrested?" Ian's spine straightened. "Arrested for what?"

"Well, not arrested. Two guys came in and told him they wanted to talk to him, and they all left. His boss had no idea what happened."

"Fuck," Ian muttered.

"That's what I thought."

The plans Ian had hoped he wouldn't have to put into place burst into the forefront of his mind. He'd have to finish one more bomb before he left his brother's house. But if they had Spencer, it wouldn't be long until they had him. He wanted to make one last impact, one last statement, just so everyone was clear about what he was doing and why he was doing it.

CHAPTER TWENTY-THREE

MORGAN SAT in the middle of an interview room with Wexford off to her side. She had a notebook pressed into the table along with a whole lot of other files, but what she was most interested in was the young man seated across from her—Spencer Garrett. On paper he wasn't much to look at, which was exactly what Morgan had expected.

He hadn't said much of anything, but she had a niggling feeling in the pit of her stomach that young Spencer had a wealth of information she wanted. He'd been brought in an hour before, and for the last twenty minutes, Morgan and Fiona had sat in the tiny room with him trying to get him to talk, but he'd kept his mouth quite shut, much like Ray had.

Morgan decided on a different tact. "Spencer, did you know a fellow named Ray? Raymond Arnold?"

Spencer's eyes lit up, and he stared directly at Morgan before looking back at the table in front of him. She had him there. He at least recognized the name.

"Did you know Ray died about a week ago?"

Spencer nodded his head. Morgan smirked and glanced over at Wexford. They were making progress. She just had to keep her patience in check, use a boat load of it and then maybe they would know about what all had been planned.

"He died of a heart attack, but not before talking to the Chicago Police, which is why Detective Wexford is here." It wasn't too much a lie. A stretch of the truth, perhaps, but it would fly if it got them the information they needed.

Spencer's jaw clenched.

"How did you know Ray? He would have probably been closer in age to a father or a grandfather for you."

She still didn't get a response.

"Did he perhaps play that role for you? I know your own father died when you were very young." She rifled through some papers she had in front of her. "Did Ray take over that role a bit for you? Teach you some things about being a man."

Spencer's lips pressed hard together, and he nodded.

"Good, what did he teach you Spencer?"

The door to the small interview room slammed open. Morgan jumped and turned to see Pax standing with his hand on the doorknob, glaring at Wexford. "We need to talk."

"I'm in the middle—"

"Now." He didn't wait as he walked away, leaving the door wide open and no room for discussion.

Morgan gathered her papers and stepped out of the room, Wexford with her. They shared a look of confusion before following Pax down the small hallway and into the main room where their desks were. On the television screens in the corner of the room was a breaking news story.

"We don't know the cause as of yet, but the building housed Somali Muslim immigrants primarily. There was discussion about whether to build a mosque in one of the buildings on the property for the residents."

"What kind of explosion?" Morgan turned on Pax.

He raised an eyebrow at her. "Don't know yet, but likely a bomb."

Morgan dropped all her papers on her desk and stalked straight back to the interview room. Wexford followed, grabbing her arm and spinning her into the wall.

"You can't go in there like that, Morgan."

"Watch me. I've been in there with him over an hour, and he could have prevented this."

"Yes, he could have. You...you could not." Wexford's lips were mighty close to Morgan.

Drawing in a deep breath, she let it out slowly and nodded. "You're right."

They both stepped toward the edge of the room, listening in on the plans for the fallout. There were crews already on their way to determine what kind of explosive device was used, if there was one, if there were any leftover that didn't go off, and see if it was a match for the bombs that had been set on the pier. Morgan waved Pax down, and he came over to them.

"You update me as soon as something comes in," she stated.

"Where are you going?"

"I'm going to finish my interview."

Pax held her arm, staring over her at Wexford. "You sure that's a good idea?"

"Yes." Morgan gawked at him. "Why the hell wouldn't it be? Kid clearly knows something."

"He's not told you anything."

"Doesn't mean he won't."

"Let me do it."

Morgan snorted. "Why are you suddenly so interested in my bombing case, the one you have tried to avoid this entire time I've had it?"

Pax moved his gaze from Wexford down to Morgan. "No reason."

Tension filled Morgan's chest as she turned and looked from Pax to Wexford. Cursing, she clenched her jaw. She would deal with that later. "I'm going to finish my interview. Let me know what they say about the bomb."

"Yeah, sure."

"No, Pax. No hedging. You do it." She stuck a pointed finger into his chest to make herself clear. "No more games."

"Fine."

Morgan stalked straight past Wexford without looking at her. She was done with it all. She had been absolutely right to stop them the night before, especially now. Pax and Fiona—now it made complete sense. How Fiona had known things she shouldn't have about what was going on with Lollie's case, how she'd known Morgan had been injured in Seattle. That look they'd shared the morning Morgan and Pax had been down interviewing Ray. Everything clicked into place.

Disgusted with Fiona and far more than a little angry at Pax, Morgan spun into the interview room, waiting for Wexford to follow her and shut the door. She'd have to turn that energy onto Spencer and get everything out of him that she could until they could prevent another bombing.

"Spencer, do you know what time is it?"

He shook his head.

Morgan glanced at the watch on her right hand as she sat down. "It's about eight thirty in the morning. You've been here that long."

"Oh."

Snorting, Morgan shifted in the chair and glanced at Wexford. "Detective, what would you say would be the prime time to bomb an apartment building with people who go to work, assuming you are from a white collar community?"

Wexford smiled. "I'd say between eight and nine. School kids gone, but enough adults home that they'll be just leaving for work."

"Right." Morgan glanced at Spencer who had lost all the color in his pale cheeks. "But the problem, Spencer, is that the targeted building isn't full of white collar workers, now is it?"

He shook his head and froze. Morgan grinned. She had him right where she wanted him. Morgan leaned over the table, keeping her gaze on him.

"Spencer, here's what I'm not understanding. If the target was that apartment complex, why would someone think eight to nine was the perfect time for an attack? Hmmm?"

"T-they wouldn't."

Satisfied to finally get an answer from Spencer, Morgan tried to keep her composure. "Right, so who would? Surely someone who didn't know better, who wasn't raised that way, someone who was...perhaps...white."

Spencer nodded.

"Want to tell me what happened?"

Spencer tensed, flicking his gaze to Morgan then to the table. "He wanted to hit where it hurt."

Morgan's eyes narrowed. "Who?"

"Ian."

The name raised the hair on the back of Morgan's neck. She knew someone was watching the interview, so surely someone would be tracking down Pax to let him know Ian's name had come up again. Morgan leaned into her chair, trying to exude a sense of calm. "Who is Ian?"

Spencer shrugged. "Some guy I know."

"How do you know him?"

"Through a group a friends."

"Which friends? Through Ray?"

Spencer shrugged his answer.

"All right, let's go back a bit, what do you mean hit where it hurt?"

Swallowing, Spencer fisted his hand and then relaxed it. "Cassidy works at the community center."

"She does." Morgan tried to keep track of where Spencer was going with the conversation.

"Sh-she left for work this morning. I tried to convince her to call in sick so we could get drunk and high." He cringed at the last statement.

Morgan eyed him carefully. "Why would you not want her to go to work?"

Spencer's pink tongue against his lips and the multiple times he swallowed told Morgan he had fear coursing through his veins but that he was on the verge of telling her what was going on. She almost had him.

"B-because something's going to happen."

"What's going to happen?" Morgan waited with bated breath. She knew Wexford was on the edge of her seat, waiting for the confession. They were so close.

Spencer glanced from Morgan to Wexford and back. "B-because we put bombs there."

"We?"

"Ian. Ian put bombs there."

Morgan knew there was about to be a flurry of movement outside of the small tiny room they were stuck in, but she wasn't going to move. She had Spencer right where she needed him, she had him right where he was going to spill everything to her, tell her everything. She reached over and gripped his hand lightly, squeezing.

"Okay, we'll get someone down there to get everyone out and make sure they're safe. Can you tell me when they were set to go off?"

"Noon."

Morgan nodded and let out a breath. "Thank you, Spencer. You just saved a bunch of lives right now. You're a hero."

Wexford shifted in her chair as Morgan relaxed. "How many bombs are there?"

"Four."

"Do you know where Ian put them?"

Spencer nodded, and Morgan shifted a blank sheet of paper Wexford gave her over with a pen.

"Mind drawing a picture?"

While Spencer worked on that, Morgan took a moment to look at Wexford. They had them. Had anyone asked the night before, she never would have suspected they would have gotten their big break in the case that day. She was about to smile at Wexford when she remembered she was mad at her, that she was disgusted with her. Caught between the two emotions, Morgan turned back to Spencer.

"Thank you, Spencer. I'll be right back, okay?"

They stepped outside the room again. Morgan walked directly to Taylor and handed him the piece of paper, explaining what was on it. He handed it off to someone else and came back to her.

"We've got a bomb crew out there already, working with CPD to block off the area of the community center and evacuate it."

"Good." Morgan let out a breath, her hands planted in fists on her hips. "I'm glad we got that from him so far."

"He's being forthcoming now?"

"Yeah."

Taylor looked beyond Morgan and at Wexford. "You two are doing good. Keep it going. See if we can get full names for the other two. We're having some struggle connecting them all and figuring out who they are exactly."

"Pull Spencer's phone?"

"Waiting on the provider to get back to us."

Morgan nodded. That could take far too long, but since there was an imminent threat, Morgan hoped they could get it sooner rather than later and that someone would be able to look at it immediately. That would be the best way to figure out who this Tim and Ian were, although Morgan strongly suspected Ian was the ring leader of the group.

Stepping away from Taylor and back to her desk, Morgan rifled through the papers until she came upon the profile she'd written out for their suspect. "Fuck."

"What?" Wexford asked.

"This profile is entirely based on an individual. It still fits, for the most part, but if this person is working with others as Spencer is saying, some things change."

"Things like what?"

"Volatility level, but it also means that unless we get all of them, then we're not sure if the threat has been completely eliminated and in order to do that, we really need to find this Ian guy."

"What about the other one?"

Morgan glanced up into Wexford's curious and young eyes. "Pretty sure Ian is the ring leader."

"Why?"

"Feeling. But let's go find out. Let's ask Spencer."

"Sure. Morgan..." Fiona's voice quieted to barely above a whisper. "Are you okay?"

"I'm fine." Morgan ground her teeth.

"You sure."

"Yes. Let's finish this out. I don't want another bomb to go off in this city today. Let's make sure it was just the two targets." Morgan stood up and started toward the interview room.

"Are we going to tell him about Cassidy?"

Freezing, Morgan turned on Wexford. "Not any time soon."

"Okay. Is there something else?"

"I'm fine, Fiona. Drop it."

Pushing past Wexford, Morgan went back to the interview room. They had to finish out the interview, and Morgan knew they were going to spend the better part of the day in the tiny room, wringing information from Spencer as they went. She grabbed a bottle of water from the mini fridge in the kitchenette, wanting to make Spencer as at ease as she possibly could.

When they got to the door, Morgan put a hand on Wexford's arm. "I may want you to do some of the questions, but right now I think I've got a good rapport going with him."

"I agree."

"But, I may piss him off and then you may need to swing in as the good cop."

Wexford raised an eyebrow and cocked her head in Morgan's direction. "Piss off how?"

"By asking some really pointed questions about his home and family life. I'll need you to swoop in and play that nurturing mother role."

"I can do that."

"Good. Because we're going to get everything we can out of him before he decides to stop talking."

"Agreed."

Morgan drew in a breath and let it out slowly. "Let's get this done."

Spencer hadn't moved from his spot, not that Morgan had expected him to. She slid the water in front of him as she sat down. "Spencer, I wanted to let you know that we're evacuating the community center as we speak, so no one will be hurt."

"Cassidy?"

"She's safe and sound."

"Thank God." Spencer lifted his hands to his face and brushed his cheeks and then his hair. "I told her not to go in to work today, but she said we had to pay rent somehow."

"Is your income not enough to help with that?" Morgan asked nonchalantly. "You work at the battery store, right?"

"Yeah, part-time. Hard to get good work nowadays."

Morgan thought the phrase he used odd coming from a kid who was barely into his twenties, but she didn't call him out on it directly. "Have you had trouble finding work?"

"Yeah. No one wants to hire me."

"Why do you think that is?"

"Don't meet certain diversity requirements."

Morgan made eye contact with him. His racism was coming out nice and bright, although she was pretty sure Spencer had no idea it was happening. "I'm sorry. It's so hard to be unemployed. At least you have a part-time job."

"Yeah," he muttered.

"Can you maybe tell me a little more about Ian?"

Spencer shrugged. "What about him?"

"Well, you said he was the one who set the bombs at the community center. Did he also set them at the apartment complex?"

Spencer's shoulders tightened, his eyes scrunched in the slightest, telling Morgan he was massively uncomfortable with the turn of the conversation. "Ian's a friend."

"Is he? What do you do together?"

"Drink. Watch football."

"Is that what you did with Ray?"

Spencer paled again. Morgan wasn't sure why, but for some reason talking about Ray hit far more of a nerve than talking about Ian. It would be a trail she would follow for sure. With her notes in front of her, she checked them.

"Spencer?"

"Yeah. I watched the game and had drinks with Ray."

"At Ray's house? At your apartment?"

"Ray's house. We had to stay in the garage so his old lady didn't get mad."

Morgan glanced up at Spencer. "Did you ever meet Carla?"

Spencer shrugged. "Couple times. She'd make us snacks for the game."

Inwardly groaning, Morgan made a note of what he said. She hadn't thought Carla and Ray were as estranged as Carla made it out to be, but this pretty much confirmed it. She should have gone far deeper down that rabbit hole than she had.

"How did you meet Ray?"

"He used to come into my shop a lot."

"The battery shop?"

Spencer nodded. "Yeah, he was always tinkering with shit at his house. Carla hated it."

Morgan forced a smile onto her lips. "He invited you to watch the games then and introduced you to Ian?"

"Yeah."

"How long ago was that?"

"About a year ago."

Morgan wrote it down on her notebook. "How did you and Ian get along?"

"Well enough. He's a bit of an ass."

Morgan smirked. "Some people are just like that, aren't they?"

"Yeah. He was really mad when he lost his job again and had to move in with his brother."

"He lives with his brother?"

"Yeah, in the basement." Morgan glanced at Wexford. Everything about the profile was falling into place. She loved it when that happened. "Where does his brother live?"

"Bensonville."

"What's his brother's name?"

"No idea." Spencer shifted in his chair and crossed his arms. Then he stared at the camera in the corner of the room. "Ian's going to be so mad."

"Why's that?"

"He wanted to make a big statement, make an impact or something like that. I kind of fucked that up."

Morgan put her pen down to look right at Spencer. "How did you mess that up?"

"I told you about the community center."

"You did." Morgan nodded her agreement. "But you saved a whole lot of lives in the process."

"Not lives worth saving. None except Cassidy's."

And there she had it. Spencer was truly indoctrinated into the world that Ian and the others had been, into the world of racism and extremism. He wasn't just some lost kid who had grown up mostly on his own, he was someone who truly thought what he believed was right. It was going to take a lot to crack him and even more to rewrite the part of his brain that wanted to believe racism was right, that he was superior because of his whiteness. Morgan prepared herself for a long interview and an endless day of work as she figured out the next question to ask.

They spent hours with Spencer. Morgan and Wexford went back and forth with asking him questions, and she learned a whole slew of information about him that she didn't really want to know, but once Spencer got talking, he didn't shut up. Once again the door slammed open and Pax stood on the other side of it.

"Out. Now."

Morgan grabbed her papers and found herself and Wexford out in the hall with a pissed off and uncomfortable Pax. She thought he deserved the discomfort though. He'd certainly put himself into that situation.

"What now?"

"Kid didn't share everything."

"What happened?"

"We cleared four bombs from the community center right where he said they'd be. What he didn't tell us is they also set bombs at a mosque."

"Fuck."

Pax glared at her. "They went off just after the noon hour."

"When prayers—"

"Just after they'd started."

Groaning, Morgan turned to Fiona, tears in her eyes. "How many?"

"Don't know yet."

Morgan bolstered herself for war. She was not going to let another person die on her watch if she could help it. She was going to find Ian and Tim, and she was going to take them down.

CHAPTER TWENTY-FOUR

MORGAN HAD been in and out of the interview room so many times, she'd lost count. Wexford had followed behind just about every time. Fiona was getting a front row seat to the calm, organized panic in the FBI as they responded to a crisis. People moved in and out with a purpose. Reports where handed and given. Somehow, Morgan ended up in charge of almost everything. Taylor had handed her the reins.

Stepping into a large conference room, she leaned against the table. The death toll was still coming in from the apartment complex, but adding in the mosque to it was almost too much to bear. Wexford sat right next to her, the official liaison on the case now as it had changed for being mostly CPD led to being headed by the FBI with help from CPD.

"Listen up, everyone. We know we are looking for two more men who are suspects in this case. The first is Ian Ballard. The second is Timothy Berry. Both are wanted on suspicion of domestic terrorism."

The silence in the room was strong. Morgan pressed her palms into the cool tabletop to center herself. "We were able to disarm the bombs that were set at the community center. Our suspect in custody, Spencer Garrett, tells us it was only those three locations that they had planned for today. We are still checking to make sure that is the case and he is telling us the truth."

"Do we have reason to suspect he's lying?"

Morgan shook her head. "No. He's been mostly forthcoming and honest."

Silence settled over the room. "We are going to formulate the plans to arrest Ian and Tim tomorrow. Agents are seeking them out now to surveil them to make sure we don't have any runners."

"I want two teams. I want you to come up with a plan of action for arrest for each suspect you are assigned and bring it back to me in two hours." Morgan glanced at her watch to double-check the time. "Then we'll go through it to make sure that the plans are solid."

Morgan divided the room into two teams. She wanted to make sure they had every outcome possible under control. She and Wexford milled around the room, listening in on conversation here and there. When her phone rang, she almost didn't answer, but guilt ate away at her for not calling back the night before.

Stepping out of the room, Morgan pressed the phone to her ear. "Ma, now is really not the—"

"Are you okay?" Worry etched every word.

"Yeah, Ma, I'm fine. Why?"

"I heard about the bombs."

Cursing under her breath, Morgan glanced to the room she had just left. "Yeah. I'm fine, Ma. I wasn't anywhere near the bombs."

"Are you investigating them?"

"Yeah, I am, which is why now is not a great time to talk."

"You're not going to throw yourself into a building with a bomb, are you?"

Clenching her teeth, Morgan tried to reach for all that patience she'd had with Spencer in the interview room, but for some reason, it was unattainable whenever it concerned her mother. "I'm not going to run into a bomb infested building. Look, I really have to get back—"

"Did you know it was going to happen?"

"No."

"Are you lying to me?"

"I'm not lying, Ma. Really, I have to go." She hung up and shoved her phone into her pocket and then brought two fingers up to rub her left temple. Her mother always gave her a headache.

Before she even made it back into the room, she had a text from Amya. It was simple, that she was praying for her and for all the victims. Leave it to her police chaplain sister to have the perfect response.

As soon as Morgan stepped into the conference room again, she made eye contact with Wexford who gave her a curious look. Morgan shook her head, trying to silently tell Wexford that everything was fine and the call wasn't related to the case at all.

Morgan hadn't even been in the room more than two minutes when Wexford grabbed her by the arm and took her to the side, whispering, "Everything okay?"

"Mom called. She saw the news, and she's flipping out as all good mothers do."

Fiona smirked. "Well, she's not the worst mother to have."

"No, that's true. Not sure I'd call her good or the best either. What are they coming up with so far?"

Wexford shrugged. "Not a whole lot from what I can tell, but I'm not exactly sure if this is how you all normally do it or not."

Morgan chuckled. "Oh yeah. We just splat plans out and then sift through the good ones and the bad ones go in the trash. This is brainstorming before we get to the nitty gritty of details."

"All right, then I think it's going well." Wexford let out a sigh. "Do you think we should talk to Spencer again, maybe see if he knows what the others might be planning in terms of arrest?"

"Yeah, wouldn't be a bad idea. You lead that one. I'll listen."

The two of them walked out of the room and down to the interview room where Spencer was munching on a bag of chips from the vending machine.

"Hey, Spencer," Fiona started, her voice far more bubbly than Morgan had ever heard it. "How are you doing?"

He shrugged.

"We wanted to ask you some follow up questions about Ian and Tim."

"What about them?"

Wexford slid into the chair across from Spencer while Morgan took the chair to the side that Wexford had sat in most of the day. She tried to focus on the interview, but her mind strayed multiple times to the conversation they had yet to have. Now she knew why Fiona had been so hesitant to talk about her relationship, why nothing was defined.

"Did they have any other plans beyond today?"

"For what?"

Wexford lifted one shoulder and dropped it. "Like if today were going to be the last, like if today we figured out who they were."

Spencer shook his head, not picking out another chip from the small bag in front of him. "No."

"Did they think they would get caught today?"

"No. Ian always talked about it happening, but he never knew when. He was kind of shocked after every one that it didn't happen, actually."

Wexford relaxed in her chair, obviously trying to play on her age versus Morgan's age and attempting to create some type of relaxed environment where Spencer would feel comfortable talk to her. "What other plans did they have?"

"For what?"

"To make an impact."

Morgan stiffened at Fiona's use of Spencer's phrasing. It was the best way to connect with him, but still, she didn't like to hear it come out of Wexford's mouth.

Spencer slowed each of his movements. He glanced between the two of them like he was debating something where the entire world rested on his shoulders, which Morgan supposed it did. His entire world.

"No."

"What were they going to do if we didn't catch them today?"

"Find a new target I suppose."

"Where else were they looking?"

Spencer hesitated to answer. He hadn't given up the mosque or the apartment complex. Morgan had to keep reminding herself that. While he had willingly told them about the community center, he'd kept the other two quiet and those two had seen fatalities.

"Don't know," Spencer answered.

Morgan waited to see if Wexford's tactic worked better than her own. She'd been harsh with him, tough with him. Perhaps it wasn't the best way to reach him.

Wexford clucked her tongue. "I'm not sure I believe that, Spence."

His head jerked up at that name. "What?"

"I don't believe you. I think you knew about the other two bombings today, and I think you know where they wanted to try to make an impact next."

Spencer didn't answer, his mouth staying locked shut.

Morgan wanted desperately to step in and ask some questions, but she wanted Wexford to have point on this part of the interview, give her some experience, some encouragement as she went along with it all.

"Now, Spence. Where would you want to make an impact next if it was just you?"

Shaking his head, Spencer finally answered. "I wouldn't."

"You wouldn't?"

"No."

"Did you want to do any of these?"

"N-no."

Intrigued, Morgan stayed as still as possible, not wanting to ruin the momentum Wexford had found herself in.

"So why did you help Ian and Tim then?"

"Ian said we needed to because no one else was."

"No one else was doing what?"

"Standing up for what we know is right."

"And what is right? What is it that needs to be fixed, Spence? Help me understand this."

Morgan swallowed and prepared herself for what Spencer was about to say because she knew it was going to be a punch to her gut.

Spencer leaned back into his chair and crossed his arms, staring directly at Wexford. "First that women have their place in the homes, and they definitely shouldn't be working in jobs with guns."

Morgan couldn't hold back her snort, and Wexford shot her a sharp look. Shrugging her apology, Morgan crossed an ankle over her knee and waited for the rest of the drama to come out.

"The next is that our government keeps letting these leeches in and they keep taking all the jobs. That's why I can't find anything other than the battery store, it's why Ian can't get a job. We don't want Tim's kids to have the same problem. They need to be stopped. The bleeding of this country's resources needs to stop. We need to take care of our own before we try to take care of others."

Wexford nodded slowly. "I can understand that. Do you understand it?" Wexford turned on Morgan.

"Uh..."

"She's not very smart," Wexford said as she turned back to Spencer. "She doesn't understand these things."

"I can see that."

"So where would you want to hit next? I mean you've targeted just about every place I can think of that would hit where it would hurt."

"Not every place."

"Oh yeah?" Fiona leaned forward on the table, like she was ready to have a secret shared with her. "Where am I missing?"

"The schools."

Morgan's heart thumped. It was Friday. If they were going to the hit the schools, it would have to be that day. They wouldn't do it on the weekend. It took another couple minutes for Morgan and Wexford to escape the room. When they got back to the conference room with the two teams, they added the school curve ball into the equation.

"Keep in mind, the one we think is making the bombs is Ian. He is most likely to be the dangerous one. Tim has a wife and family. He is connected to the community in ways that Ian is not. Ian is the wild card."

The others nodded and went back to work. Wexford scooted in closer to Morgan. "When we get to the point of arrest, who will we be with?"

"Hopefully both," Morgan answered. "I'd like to be, anyway. We'll have to see what they come up with in terms of plans."

Wexford nodded. "What we still don't know is if these three men, or four if you want to include Ray, are part of a larger organization or if they're doing this all on their own."

Morgan crossed her arms as she slid into the free chair next to where she'd been standing. Wexford mimicked her move and sat across from her. "We know they are part of a larger organization. Ray told us that. It was how he met Ian and Tim. They were part of National Freedom Party."

"But we don't think that group is masterminding the attacks?"

Shaking her head, Morgan gave Fiona a hard stare. "No. It's a very nonviolent group, mostly just angry people who rarely if ever make it to the action stage. Like I said before, Ian is the wild card. I'd love to get some more background on him because I'd be willing to bet he's part of more than one group and there's something in his psyche that would push him to this level of violence, and from what we've seen, once he was pushed to that level, he ran with it."

"Agreed," Wexford muttered. "Three massive attacks in such a short period of time."

Morgan paused. She stared at Wexford with wide eyes. "You're right."

"What?"

"These were two massive attacks. He doesn't fit the bill as someone who would jump from nothing to huge. There was the factory bombing in there, but even then that's big enough to attract attention."

"You think there was another bombing."

Morgan raised an eyebrow and cocked her head. "I do."

"Spencer?"

"Yup."

The two of them went straight back to the room with Spencer. Morgan didn't bother sitting. She stood by the door, her feet planted as if for battle as she stared down the young man in front of her. He was so young, so lost, and he really could not have been in the more perfect state for her question.

"Tell me about the first bombing."

"What bombing?"

"The first one." She was vague for a reason, and she wanted to see which way Spencer ran with it.

"It didn't work."

"What do you mean it didn't work?" Morgan wanted to add more to the question, but she restrained herself. The more open-ended questions the better it seemed to work with Spencer, and she didn't want to assume the factory was the first bombing.

Spencer shrugged. "It didn't work."

"The bomb didn't go off?"

His chin went up and down.

"Where were you trying to bomb?"

"Convenient store."

Morgan turned a look on Wexford that said she was pissed she hadn't thought of it before. "Which one?"

"It's a few blocks from the apartment building."

Morgan would have to get video footage from there, but she bet Ian likely frequented the shop and knew that it was filled with people he would want to attack. "Tell me about it. When was it?"

"Month or so ago. Ian put it in the trash can outside the door, but it never went off."

Biting the inside of her cheek, Morgan inwardly cursed. She should have seen the factory bombing wasn't the first one. She should have known better. "Tell me what the plan was."

"Ian was doing it all. He's the one who made the plan. Tim and I just kept a lookout so no one would see him, but then, I don't know, something went wrong and it didn't work."

"Was Ian mad?"

"Really mad." Spencer shuddered. "He...he gets really mad sometimes."

"Mad about what?"

"When things don't go right."

Morgan pressed her hands together, folding her fingers, and then straightening again. "What happens when Ian gets mad?"

"He yells."

"Is he violent?"

Spencer shrugged. Morgan risked a glance to Wexford who looked just as rapt as she was. This would absolutely be helpful when they were bringing Ian in and it lent to what they might be facing when they went to go get him. It solidified the fact that Morgan would be present when Ian was arrested.

Her phone buzzed in her pocket again, and she ignored it. "Is he violent, Spencer?"

"Yes."

"Violent how?"

"He throws shit. It's hard to tell with him."

"Okay." Morgan drew in a breath and stepped out of the room. She checked her phone that was still buzzing. "Carrie, what's wrong?"

"Nothing's wrong here. I just heard about there. Are you all right?"

Morgan sighed. "I'm fine. You don't need to call. I'm rather busy."

Carrie scoffed. "You're my big sister, and I just heard there were bombs going off all over Chicago. Don't tell me not to worry."

Morgan slid a glance to Fiona and shook her head in shock. "I'm fine. I have work to do though if you want me to solve this."

"How did you not know it was going to happen? I mean...you're the best profiler according to you, so how did you not know? Is the FBI just inept?"

"Now you sound like Mom, and I'm hanging up. Have a good day, Carrie." Ending the call, Morgan reoriented her brain as best she could.

"Sister?" Wexford asked.

"Who else?"

"Well, your mom—"

"Oh, no, she called earlier. Be glad you only have one brother to worry about. I expect the rest, Amya excluded and perhaps Clyde, will call in the next few hours. If I didn't need to keep my phone on me for work things, I'd just leave it at my desk."

"Don't answer."

Morgan snorted. "That'll just make it worse."

"Have one of them play communicator."

Morgan nearly choked. While it was an idea in theory, she'd tried that several times through the years and it never worked in the long run. "Been there, done that."

The smile playing at Fiona's lips tugged at something in Morgan's chest, but she wasn't going to play into it. She was still pissed about what she'd figured out.

"Come on, let's finish this case."

"Couldn't agree more."

CHAPTER TWENTY-FIVE

THE SUN wasn't even up when Ian pulled up outside of Tim's house. Tim sat on the front steps of the whitewashed porch, a cigar between his lips and a glass with a brown amber liquid in it between his fingers. Ian parked and stepped out, moving to sit next to Tim on the porch.

"Pretty sure they have Spence."

Tim snorted. "Yeah. They got him first. I feel bad for the poor kid. Who knows what he's going through in there."

Ian shrugged. "What are you doing out here?"

Sliding his gaze from the sidewalk in front of him to Ian, Tim sighed. "You know what I'm doing. I don't want to scare the kids."

"You going to kill yourself?"

"No." Tim finished his drink and set the cup to the side before refilling it with the bottle Ian hadn't seen before. The bottle only had a quarter of it left.

Ian held his hand out. "Do you mind?"

Tim hesitated, but he did hand the liquor bottle over. Ian stared down at it, snorting when he saw the logo on it and drank straight from the bottle. It burned as it went down his throat, but the alcohol he had drank earlier that night already warmed his belly.

They sat there in silence for another ten minutes, drinking and smoking. Ian wasn't sure he had ever seen Tim smoke anything before, but it didn't surprise him to see the cigar between his fingers. If Tim was going to smoke anything it would be that. Ian knew that unless Tim went with him that morning they wouldn't ever see each other again. Ian had a plan, and he was going to stick with it.

The dew on the wood they sat on was almost too much. It wetted the back of Ian's pants so the fabric stuck to his skin. Shifting slightly, Ian let out a sigh. He enjoyed the time they had together, refilling Tim's cup several times as they sipped.

"When do you think they'll come?" Tim asked.

Ian shrugged. "Not planning to wait and find out."

Tim took the last drag of his cigar before he snuffed it out into the wood next to him. The sun started to rise over the city. They couldn't see the ball of fire, but it was just the light peeking through the buildings and houses. Tim lived in one of the nicer neighborhoods compared to where Spencer lived and where Ian had lived before he'd moved into his brother's basement.

There wasn't much they could do to avoid the inevitable. Ian had always know Spencer was the weakest link in their chain. If he was captured, surely they would be after Tim and him shortly. That was why he'd made his plans. That was why he'd figured one last impact he could make into everything. He wasn't going out without standing fully for what he believed and what he knew to be truth.

"How are the kids?" Ian asked, not quite sure why he was making small talk, but they were at the end of the line, there was no reason to not.

"They're good. TJ is excited about going to high school next year. AnneMarie is boy crazy as ever."

Ian snorted. He hadn't spent nearly as much time with Tim's family as he had thought he would. The kids were always running all over the place here and there, but Tim's wife took care of most of that. With another drag from the tequila, Ian handed it over to Tim.

"You should come with me," Ian started.

Tim shook his head. "No."

"You can't stay here."

Tim turned to Ian, his eyes wide but clear when he spoke next. "I won't have my kids watching me be arrested on the news, Ian, and I won't have them be traumatized by what they'll do to me."

"I can understand that." Ian stole the booze back and chugged the last of the bottle. "See you."

Standing up, Ian walked to the end of the yard and his car. The tequila sat in his belly, warming him. It took him two tries to get the key into the ignition, but he finally started the engine. Ian sat in the car, staring at the sunrise as the rays warmed the cold dew he'd just been sitting in.

Staring at the sky, Ian bolstered himself. This was going to be his last stand, his last chance to make an impact, and his last moment to show people what they needed to see. He had to burst the bubble of political correctness, and this time, he was on his own for it all.

Ian glanced once more over at Tim, who still sat on his front steps like he was waiting for them to come and take him away. Tim was resigned. He was empty. He had no more fight left to give, but Ian had every fight left and every reason to carry on the war.

Leaning into the passenger seat, Ian pulled out one last backpack. He checked everything inside. This one was different than all the rest. There was no timer. There was no clock. This time, he had a button. He was going to go when he wanted to, when it was the perfect timing and he was in the perfect position.

Ian settled the kill switch he'd hooked up into his lap, and he pulled away from the curb after lighting another cigarette. Smoke filled the cab as he drove out of the neighborhood. It took his full concentration to make it to the main road leading in to where Tim lived.

Ian's eyes widened in surprise as he saw the SWAT cars moving in. His heart ramped up as he tracked their movements. Tim wasn't wrong. They were there. He was going to be arrested. At least Tim would get exactly what he wanted and his kids wouldn't hopefully be witness to it.

Police cars followed from a distance. Ian watched a few pass him going the direction he had just come from, but he stepped on the gas and very carefully coaxed his car away from what was about to happen. If they were there, then there was no way Ian could go back to his brother's. Not that he had planned on it.

His chest rose and fell as he focused everything he could on driving and not letting all the officers in the area think he was drunk or involved. He kept his head down. Ian drove forward until he came to the stoplight. Waiting for it to turn green, he lifted his chin and stared out his side window at a black SUV, no doubt part of the police brigade about to take down Tim.

Inside were two women, both brunettes. The one with shorter hair, cut close to her head was driving, and the other one stared directly at him. Ian swallowed. He couldn't break their eye contact as much as he wanted to. He clenched his jaw, watching as the other one turned the corner to follow the other cops to Tim's house.

Ian's heart swelled in panic when the driver turned her chin up and looked right at him. He was had. He knew it. He shouldn't have gone out to see Tim, shouldn't have stayed so long, drinking. But it had felt so good just to sit with Tim, without the worries, with the resignation they both felt for what was going to happen.

The light turned green. Ian stepped on the gas and went straight through it to the next street. He tried not to look in his rearview mirror, but he needed to know if they had turned around. With his breath held tightly and the tension in his shoulders, Ian looked up and into his rearview mirror.

The dark SUV headed to the end of the block and then pulled a U-turn.

"Fuck," Ian muttered.

He didn't wait. Stepping on the gas, Ian took the next righthand turn to try and get rid of them before they caught up. Ian slid his old beat up car in between the large buildings and into an alley. He waited, driving to the end to see if the SUV drove passed or followed him. He needed to be able to make it to one last place where he could make his stand. He just had to get there.

He made it all the way to the end of the alley and was just about to pull out onto the next road when he saw them. They turned to follow him. Cursing, Ian slapped his palm against the steering wheel.

With his foot to the pedal, he slammed it down. There was no way to get out of it now. Pulling out into the street, Ian drove like he wasn't being followed. He didn't want them to think he suspected anything, although the alley stunt may have given him away, he hoped it didn't. He didn't want to alert them too soon before he got to the community center. Spencer had fucked up that target, but Ian was determined to take it down with him, one last statement.

The weight of the trigger in his lap was heavy even though Ian knew that was impossible. He felt the responsibility on his shoulders. They already had Spencer, then they got to Tim. So it was him left, that was it. He was the holdout on the line, and he had to do the work for all of them.

Ian turned onto the highway, driving from Tim's neighborhood back toward the community center. He knew he couldn't do as much damage as they had originally intended, but he would make the statement and that was far more important. He needed to take someone out with him, take someone who would mean something.

In some ways, Ian wondered if he had failed. In others, he knew he had succeeded. He'd brought notice to his line of thinking. He'd brought light onto the subject and the problems that rampant immigration was having on their community. He was the one who had made people aware of the problems the next generation were going to have if they didn't do something about it right then and there.

Still, there was so much more work to do, but it was going to have to be carried on without him. Perhaps Tim could help wherever he ended up, Spencer too, although their roles would look far different than they did the past few months.

Ian watched the SUV follow him and wondered briefly when the next cop car would turn around and join in the chase. He snorted at the thought. It was a chase. They had no idea where he was going, what he was doing, or that he even had a bomb in the vehicle with him. But they were still following him—two bitches in a car. He shook his head at the thought. He wouldn't let two lady-cops bring him down. No, he would be brought in properly by men who deserved the position and title.

If he was going to be brought in at all.

Ian carefully wove in and out of traffic, keeping to the main roads as much as he could. He wanted to wait until it was time for morning prayers, and he had two hours before that would happen. Luckily, he had a full tank of gas that he'd filled up with the last of the credit on his card. His hand shook as he tried to get the end lit to a cigarette. As soon as he set his lighter in the cup holder, he inhaled the smoke to help relax.

Two hours. He could do that. He could drive around, let them waste their own gas and resources until it was time for him to head to the community center and make his last stand. The SUV that was following him, the one with the two women, stayed decently close by far enough. If he hadn't seen them when he was leaving Tim's neighborhood, he likely could have missed them following him the entire time.

No other vehicle seemed to follow in the chase—at least not yet.

Ian's drunkenness floated into a buzz, and he became more and more aware of the danger he was in of losing out on his last chance to make an impact. He needed to let the world know everything he knew. He needed to let Chicago know that people like him weren't going to keep quiet any longer, that they weren't going to just shut up and suffer in silence. They needed to know the repercussions of the decisions they made and of the people they put into office.

His tongue dashed out to wet his lips as he took another turn. He knew those streets like the back of his hand. He'd driven them so many times between his various jobs here and there, between his various moves as he was evicted and then as he found a new home until the next job dried up. It had been his life for the last fifteen years, never anything good enough to keep him because he didn't have the right skin color to make them have to keep him.

Anger surged through Ian's chest, and instead of driving slowly, he sped up and cut off the driver in front of him. The SUV followed without a beat. He couldn't wait any longer. Screw the community center. He'd just take out the dumb bitches behind him. They'd be enough. They'd have to be.

CHAPTER TWENTY-SIX

MORGAN HAD barely slept the night before. She'd gotten enough rest to feel like she could join in the arrest of Timothy Berry, but when she drove with Wexford sitting right next to her, she wished they had taken separate vehicles. She was still pissed, and she hadn't had a moment to confront Fiona, or Pax for that matter.

With her vest strapped to her chest, Morgan followed the path that was predetermined for her to take to get to Timothy Berry's house. They'd decided he would be the easier of the two to arrest so would go for him first so he wouldn't alert Ian Ballard to the fact they were on to them.

Spencer had been moved the night before to a cell at the jail, but they still had two more to catch and arrest. They had stakeouts going at both men's houses, which should tell them if either of them moved. Spinning the steering wheel between her fingers, Morgan grabbed the coffee sitting in the cup holder and took a sip.

"How much of that do you think you drink a day?"

"What?" Morgan eyed Wexford suspiciously. "What does it matter?"

"Just curious. I think yesterday was the first time I've seen you go without coffee for hours."

Morgan snorted. "Must be why I feel like I'm going through withdrawal this morning. I'll have to make up for it."

She pulled up to a light and pressed her brake to stop before taking a right hand turn straight into the neighborhood. SWAT was going to be doing the initial arrest again, which had been Wexford's idea since they didn't know how armed and dangerous these men were. Morgan had agreed, because it was a better plan, but she still didn't like the fact that she wouldn't be out there doing the arrest herself.

"Is that...?"

"Is that what?" Morgan set her coffee down as she made the turn, skimming the old beat up silver sedan in the far turning lane as she drove. Her heart clenched.

"Is that Ian Ballard?" Wexford muttered.

Morgan's gaze shot up. The car was a dead match, but she had missed the plate because of how their vehicles were facing. Wexford leaned forward and then back to get a better view as Morgan steered the SUV.

"It's him."

"You're shitting me."

"I'm not."

"Why is no one tailing him?"

"Fuck if I know," Fiona muttered. She was nearly halfway out of her seat as she spun around to keep her gaze on him. "Turn around."

"Already on it." Morgan made it to the end of the block and flipped her car around so she could follow him. "Where the hell is the tail?"

"Got me, but that was him, I know it."

"You're sure?" Morgan pressed down on the gas to speed up. She wanted a license plate confirmation.

"Positive."

"Call it in."

Wexford's fingers fumbled on the radio that sat next to Morgan's coffee. "This is Detective Wexford, we have a sighting of our second suspect at the corner of Maple and Underwood. We are following at a distance."

"10-4."

Morgan's heart rate ramped up as she stepped on the gas. The small silver beat up sedan vanished. "Where the fuck did it go?"

"Hold on." Fiona's hand came down to Morgan's arm as Morgan drove along the street, watching carefully for any sign of the vehicle. Her skin burned where Wexford touched it, and she wanted to shake it off, but she couldn't.

She had to focus. Ian was nearby, and then she needed to ream someone's ass about why they weren't watching Tim and Ian to begin with. If Ian was at Tim's, they should have known about it before they rolled up. It totally fucked their plans and put all of them in danger.

"There!" Wexford shouted.

Morgan turned the car down the alley. Sure enough, Ian's car sat at the end like it was waiting for them. He spun out onto the street with a good amount of speed, but slowed down to match the rest of the vehicles around them. Morgan held back, tailing him with at least two to three cars between them while Wexford relayed updates as to where they were to other officers and agents in the vicinity.

Ian wasn't doing anything, which was odd, but when Morgan finally realized he was spinning circles and staying fairly close to where the community center was, she knew what he was planning. She spoke quickly, "Have them evacuate the community center, now."

"I don't think anyone is there."

"Send someone there to be sure. I'm betting he still wants to take that target out, and I'm betting his car is loaded in order to make it happen. He's being way too careful for someone who has killed dozens of people in the last month."

Wexford spoke into the radio, making sure the community center was going to be evacuated. It took thirty minutes, but they got the all-clear that the center was abandoned. Morgan's chest rose and fell in a steady rhythm as Ian finally pulled off the main road and drove exactly where Morgan expected him to go.

When he pulled into the angled parking along the side of the building, facing the wrong direction, Morgan was glad her gut had been right. She shoved her car into park and grabbed her weapon as she pushed her door open. Wexford mimicked every move she made.

Together, they stood at the doors of the vehicle with their weapons drawn and aimed in the direction of Ian's vehicle. Cop cruisers pulled up on the far ends of the street, evacuating as much of the area as they could and maintaining their own distance. Since they didn't know if Ian had any bombs on his car or not, they had to be careful.

Morgan raised her voice, making sure she could be heard from the distance they were at. "Ian Ballard! Come out of the vehicle with your hands raised."

He didn't move to get out. She could see his head swivel side to side as he no doubt looked around and realized just how caught he was. Morgan feared the worst, that this was his suicide by cop, but more importantly that he was going to be taking out as many of them as possible.

Sirens blared in the neighborhood as more and more officers showed up. Morgan couldn't be sure how to count them all, but she heard the radio in her vehicle go off as more arrived on the scene to help.

Once again, she raised her voice. "Ian Ballard! Come out of the vehicle with your hands in the air."

This time he did move. He opened the car door. Morgan held her breath tightly in her chest before she reminded herself to breathe. The car door swung open, the creaking from the older vehicle so loud that even with the rush of her own breath in her ears, she could hear it.

Ian stepped out. The mother fucker was on the younger end of what she'd suspected, far closer to Spencer's age than she'd originally thought. He could barely be much over thirty. He looked a mess, though. His eyes were wide, his steps were uncertain as he stumbled to the trunk of his car, holding on to it to keep himself upright.

"He's drunk off his ass at least," Morgan muttered to Wexford.

"Let's hope that's all it is."

Snorting, Morgan stepped around the safety of her vehicle when she noticed his hands empty. Ian moved to the trunk of his car and leaned against it before putting his hands out to the sides.

"Hands up, Ian," Morgan said, her voice carrying over to him. She crossed in front of her vehicle, her weapon still raised. "On the ground."

He shook his head. "Do you know how hard I worked for this?"

"I don't." Not that she really cared either. She thought what he was doing was disgusting and far too the extreme of what any sane person would do—not that she'd tell him that, ever.

Wexford whispered something behind her, but Morgan ignored her. She had to talk him down so he didn't blow anything else up. She had to get him on the ground and make sure he didn't have anything on him, like a bomb.

"Morgan!"

She didn't turn.

"He's not been cleared."

Morgan knew what Wexford meant, and it had just been what she was thinking, but someone had to go up to him and cuff him. If it was going to be anyone, it would be her. She had nothing to lose—no family, no spouse, nothing tying her there.

"Ian, do you have any bombs on you?" Morgan asked as she inched closer to Wexford's side of the vehicle. The only thing between her and Wexford was the door to her SUV, but she knew Wexford had her back.

He shook his head. "No. I don't have anything on me."

"Good." Morgan didn't see any of the normal signs of lies. He didn't shake his head or tense up at her question. She still didn't want to trust him, wasn't sure she could. If he was far more psychopathic than she'd originally thought then it would be easy for him to lie about something like that. "Then I need you to get on the ground, face down."

Ian laughed. His blond hair that hung to his shoulders but looked so raggedy flung out around him as he moved. He nearly fell off the end of the car with the force of his laughter.

"Ian, what's so funny?"

"I'm not giving up that easily."

He moved far more swiftly than Morgan had thought he could for a man drunk off his ass. He reached into the pocket of his jeans and pulled something out. Morgan's heart thumped hard as she twisted and turned back to the car door she knew was just behind her. Her feet were sure against the broken asphalt of the parking area as she ran around the edge of the door, grabbing Wexford and covering her body against the back door of the SUV when the explosion hit them.

All the air rushed from Morgan's lungs as she was smooshed against the hard metal vehicle. She closed her eyes tight as the pressure in her head increased to a point nearly unbearable. Heat radiated down her neck and the backs of her legs and arms. Morgan couldn't hear anything.

When she dared to open her eyes, Fiona stared at her with eyes wide and concern written all over her face. Morgan turned to look out at the car she'd just been standing and facing down. It was gone. The door Wexford had been hiding behind was gone. Pieces of road, building, and glass, rained around them.

Morgan swallowed and pressed a hand to Wexford's chest, feeling the thick vest she wore and a sigh of relief. They were fine. They were both fine. She couldn't hear a damn thing other than the ringing in her ears, but they were both fine. People moved around them, coming from nowhere it seemed. Chicago police officers, FBI agents—people moved in on the car with guns drawn just like they should.

As soon as they reached her and Wexford, Morgan was pulled away and dragged toward the back of the line of they were holding to protect the rest of the public as much as they could. Morgan's eyes stung as she glanced around, trying to see where the damage had been done, if Ian had managed to do what he'd set out to accomplish.

But the community center still stood. The wall looked scorched like it hadn't before. It'd lost some windows. But it stood. Ian's car was near obliterated, but when Morgan stepped away from Fiona, she saw Ian's still alive form on the ground ten feet from them. Guns were drawn on him as he struggled to breathe.

He must not have had as much explosive material in his car as she'd originally. He'd been flung toward her from the blast, and Morgan was pretty sure the only reason she and Fiona were as un-maimed as they were was because she'd managed to get them behind the door to the SUV.

"You okay?" she asked Fiona, sure her voice made a sound even though she couldn't hear it.

Wexford reached up and brushed her fingers across Morgan's cheek before dropping her hand and nodding. Morgan nodded herself. Pax was there in an instant, moving Morgan away from the center of the incident. Someone else grabbed Wexford.

They were taken to waiting ambulances. Someone had the foresight to call them in. She hadn't. Morgan was seated in the back of one as she watched paramedics wait to be allowed in to the scene to work on Ian. Morgan couldn't believe the idiot was still breathing, although if they didn't get to him soon it wasn't likely to be for long, but they did have to clear the scene and make sure there were no other bombs in the area that he could have planted—though, Morgan doubted there were. This was not as planned as the other attacks. This was done out of desperation.

Everything sounded like she was in a vacuum, and Morgan wondered when she'd get her hearing back. Her head throbbed. When she glanced down at her hands and her body when the paramedics gave her a break, she saw the dirt, the dust, the blood. Curious, she lifted her hands and checked them, trying to figure out where the blood was coming from, but she couldn't make it out.

Her vest had protected what was important, for sure, but where else was she cut. Surely she wouldn't have made it out of that without getting sliced by some kind of shrapnel, either whatever Ian had put in the bomb like he had with the rest of them or just from the explosion itself.

When the paramedic came back, Morgan flagged him down and pointed to the blood on her pants, giving him a questioning look. She had to trust her voice worked even if she couldn't hear it. "Where am I bleeding?"

He shook his head at her and pointed at the other ambulance she'd seen them shove Wexford into. He pointed to his leg and made the okay symbol. Morgan sighed relief. Wexford had been injured, somehow, but it wasn't bad. Still, Morgan knew she had cuts of her own to contend with, and her hearing—that was going to be hell if it didn't catch up soon enough.

Pax moved into the ambulance with her and handed his phone over. Morgan glanced at it and found he'd typed a message to her. Sighing, she read it and shook her head.

"Check on Fiona."

With wide eyes, Pax turned to look out the back of the ambulance, his shoulders completely tense. How Morgan had missed his affair for the better part of who knew how long, she had no idea, but she was pissed at herself for not seeing it earlier. She put a hand on his arm.

"Check on Fiona. For me. You and I can talk about her later. Not today."

Pax gritted his teeth and left the ambulance. It was finally out in the open. He knew that she knew and vice versa. It was going to be a long few months, and she could only hope Mel was strong enough to do exactly what she needed. Hell, Morgan hoped she was strong enough to do the same.

Pax came and went twice more before the ambulance took her to the local hospital. Fiona's ride left well before hers, but Morgan supposed that was because she was the less injured of the two. Pax gave her updates every now and then, including the one about Ian still being alive and heading straight for surgery so they could try to save his life. Tim had been arrested easily. He'd given himself up at the house.

Morgan laid on the stretcher and closed her eyes. It had been a week from hell, not only on her body and her work, but on her emotions. She'd gone from thinking maybe Fiona could be someone who could take a relationship to the next level, someone where Morgan didn't want to stop after a month to realizing she'd never get on that boat.

As the doctors came in and out of the room, Morgan wished she could hear what they were saying. She refused to let them call any of her family, but she also knew her phone was going off the hook already. She texted Amya, knowing she would at least call the rest of them and update them on what she could. She left out the fact she was in the hospital, knowing she'd be out soon enough.

With a sigh, Morgan relaxed. She'd solved her case. They'd closed it. She was supposed to feel good about that, about getting three extremists off the streets, saving lives even though she'd failed so many more. So why did she feel so empty?

CHAPTER TWENTY-SEVEN

ONE WEEK to the day from the bombing, Morgan found herself knocking on Fiona's apartment door. She leaned against the door frame with her forearm and listened for any noise. She knew Fiona was home. They'd arranged the time to meet. It had been a whole week since they'd seen each other, and it felt like months since the last time they'd dined together at the pizzeria and worked Frankie into a tizzy.

She relaxed as the locks clicked and the doorknob turned. Morgan didn't bother to straighten up. She wasn't there for a formal talk about work and what had happened She was there to talk about the catastrophe that was whatever relationship they'd attempted and to put an end to whatever relationship might be between them. She couldn't fathom why Fiona would think that she'd understand.

"Hey," Fiona said, her voice almost a whisper.

Morgan looked over her arm inside Fiona's apartment. She'd been there only once before and it was briefly when she picked Fiona up for a lunch they'd done. Swallowing, Morgan stared nervously into those dark eyes that drew her in every time. No matter what she did, she couldn't quell that lust she felt every time she saw this woman.

"Coming in?" Fiona asked, the words rough as they left her lips.

"Uh...yeah." Morgan straightened and followed Fiona inside.

Fiona immediately locked up the door again, leaning against it with her hands behind her back. Biting her lip, Fiona's gaze raked up and down Morgan's body with a heated look to her eyes. Morgan shuddered. She knew Fiona likely thought she was there for an entirely different reason.

"How are you?" Morgan asked, breaking the silence and trying to figure out what to do with her hands. She put them on her hips, then crossed her arms, then shoved them into her pockets as she stood awkwardly.

"I'm good. Back to duty the end of next week."

Morgan nodded. "Good, good."

Turning on her toes, Morgan looked around to the couch and nodded her head toward it.

"Mind if we sit?"

"By all means." Fiona moved her hand out in front of her to show Morgan to lead the way.

Morgan nervously walked from the door to the couch and sat on the edge of it, nerves ricocheting through every part of her body, and they would *not* calm down. Fiona sat next to her, their thighs brushing and heat coiled deep inside Morgan's stomach. She was going to have to watch herself.

"How are you?" Fiona asked, her fingers snaking onto Morgan's thigh and squeezing.

Morgan nodded and reached for Fiona's hand with the intention of removing it. Instead, she gripped it, entwining their fingers.

"I'm good. Sore as hell, but good." She grinned at the last part of the comment. Morgan sighed. "I think we need to talk."

"Perhaps. We're not working together any longer."

Morgan tensed. "We're not. We'll still see each other in court for this, I'm sure, but that's neither here nor there."

Fiona's tongue dashed out against her lips, and Morgan wanted desperately to lean forward and taste. Clearing her throat, Morgan shifted to put some space between them, but she still couldn't make her hand give up Fiona's fingers.

"You know how I feel about certain things."

"About what things?" Fiona's tone was low, dangerously low for Morgan's sake. She wanted so much to know that tone in an entirely different situation.

"You know how I feel about cheating."

"I didn't cheat." Fiona's entire body language changed. She went from the seductress at ease to defensive in two seconds flat, which Morgan hadn't wanted to do but she knew there was no way to avoid that unless she avoided the entire conversation.

"You didn't, but you were knowingly in a relationship with someone who is married."

"How did you even—"

Morgan snorted. "I'm a profiler, Fiona. I'm an observer by nature. I think the only reason you were able to pull it over me for so long is because I had other things on my mind, especially these last few months when you and I really started to get to know each other. I didn't *want* to see it. I didn't want to believe it."

Fiona's lips thinned. "I'm so sorry."

"You're not. Pax has been my best friend for the better part of twenty years. He knows how I feel about this. He knows how the conversation I'm going to have with him is going to go. I won't hold back with him."

"And you are with me?"

Morgan sighed. "No. But I'm not as angry with you as I am with him."

"You should be," Fiona muttered.

Morgan turned sharply at that. "Why would you say that?"

Once again, Fiona's tongue was at her lips, but this time, Morgan didn't feel the same desire licking at her. "Because I'm just as guilty as him."

"You're not."

"How can you say that?" Fiona's timbre rose. "I knew what I was doing just as much as he did. I knew he was married."

"Yeah, you did. But you're not married. You weren't breaking any vows. You didn't share classified information with a romantic partner."

Fiona froze at that. "He didn't."

"He did." Morgan raised an eyebrow at her. "I know he did because of the things you asked me and told me. I should have seen it before. I always wondered how you knew something. It was never anything major, nothing that's too bad, but God, Fiona, he put his family on the line but he also put his job on the line. He could lose his job over this."

"Taylor knew."

"What?"

"Taylor knew. Pax told him."

Anger surged into Morgan's limbs. She pushed up from the couch, her hands fisted on her hips as she spun around and faced Fiona. "What do you mean *he knew?*"

"That's why you were assigned to work with me on this task force instead of Pax. Because I couldn't work with him."

"Fuck this." Morgan clenched her jaw as she shoved a hand wildly through her hair. "I can't do this."

"Do what?"

"Be with you." Morgan's eyes were wide as she stared down Fiona. "I can't be with you."

The tension in the room was palpable. Morgan wasn't sure what she should say or do, but she knew she had to get out of there as soon as she could. She had to protect herself.

"I introduced Mel to Pax. I knew her first. I am their kids' godmother for Christ's sake, and you've been...you've been fucking him all the while he's played the perfect husband."

"He's not the perfect husband."

"No, well, obviously not." Once again Morgan's hand found its way into her hair, and she tugged and the short brown strands. "He needs to be, and

I cannot do this with you."

Fiona stood up and came over to Morgan, grabbing her free hand and twining their fingers together. Fiona reached up and cupped Morgan's cheek. "Answer me this."

"What?"

"Is it because it's Pax or is it because I was the other woman?"

Morgan hissed. She really wasn't sure if she would be less pissed or annoyed if it wasn't Pax. Her heart raced as she stared into Fiona's eyes, the answer on the tip of her tongue, but she wasn't sure she wanted to say it, wasn't sure she could trust her gut.

Fiona's thumb brushed along her cheek, and Morgan turned into the touch. "Answer my question."

"Because it's Pax." Tears stung at Morgan's eyes as she closed them, not daring herself to look at Fiona. She couldn't. She wouldn't. "He's my best friend."

Fiona's lips touched Morgan's briefly in a tender and sweet kiss, a kiss that didn't entice but comforted. Morgan's heart raced. Her muscles ached. Her body felt like she'd been to hell and back a dozen times in the past week, and she realized just how old she was in the scheme of things and how young and adventurous Fiona was.

"He's my best friend, Fiona."

"Yeah, yeah, he is, and I suspect he and Mel are going to need you around as soon as he talks to her."

"He's going to tell her?"

"He told me he would." Fiona looked up into Morgan's eyes. "But you know him better than I do."

"I feel like I don't know him at all, anymore."

"I can understand that, but Morgan, you know him probably better than anyone, and you may just understand why he did it. I just happened to be in that place and time for him as he was for me."

Morgan jerked her head up at that. "What do you mean?"

"Sit down with me."

Reluctantly, Morgan moved to sit on the couch with Fiona again, this time with a little more distance between the two of them. Fiona drew in a deep breath and let it out slowly. She curled one leg under her body as she turned to face Morgan fully, grabbing her hand again.

"I told you that I was engaged."

Morgan nodded.

"Right, so I was engaged to a man, and we'd been together for six years. Everything had really gone to plan. Dating, moving in, ring, wedding planning." Tears brimmed in Fiona's eyes, and Morgan had to resist the urge to brush them away to make Fiona stop talking so she wouldn't have to relive the pain of whatever she was feeling. "Well, it ended, rather abruptly.

And I threw myself into work. That's why I ended up attending your lecture about profiling, and it's ultimately what led me to meeting Pax at that same conference."

Morgan desperately wanted to ask what happened, she wanted to know why the engagement was broken, but she couldn't bring herself to say the words, to pry even deeper into something she didn't feel was hers to know, but she knew it wasn't because Fiona was a cop. Not after six years of being together.

"I never thought he would leave Mel for me. I never wanted him to. I always knew it would end, and it did. You know that. I didn't lie about that."

"I didn't think you did," Morgan whispered.

"Good." Fiona smiled. "You'll have to talk to Pax to find out why he did it, that's not something I can answer for him."

Morgan had planned on talking to him next. Better to get both tough conversations out of the way in one day than let them linger and drag on. She wanted to yell and scream at him though, but she was pretty sure it was going to end up in some ways very similar to the conversation she was having with Fiona.

Fiona's fingers skimmed against Morgan's cheek, causing Morgan to look her in the eye again. "I plan on talking to him."

"Good. I would hate for your partnership and friendship to be in jeopardy."

Morgan smirked at that. "I can't imagine having to find a new partner."

Chuckling, Fiona gripped Morgan's hands and brought her fingers to her lips, kissing them lightly. "I do hope we can see where whatever we're feeling goes, but I can understand if you want nothing to do with me."

Morgan groaned. She wanted so desperately to walk out Fiona's door and never look back, but the months of building a friendship, getting to know her, toying with the idea of whatever relationship they might have become tortured her. She couldn't just walk away from everything.

"I don't do relationships."

Fiona's fingers rubbed circles on the back of Morgan's hand. "I didn't say I was looking for one, though should one begin, I wouldn't be opposed to it."

"I don't do them."

"Why is that, Morgan? Scared you might find out that love isn't as scary as you think it is?"

Freezing, Morgan eyed Fiona warily. "No."

Fiona laughed lightly as she leaned in, her lips brushing Morgan's ear as she spoke. "Then you have nothing to worry about, do you?"

It would be so easy for Morgan to turn and capture Fiona's lips, to take the kiss, to give the kiss. She wanted to—desperately. They'd kissed before and Morgan could sparsely put words to it, but she wanted it again. Fiona was so close. It wouldn't take much to find herself down that rabbit hole.

"Fuck it." Morgan grabbed the back of Fiona's head and brought their mouths together.

She had planned to not do this. She had specifically talked herself up to not do this, but God, she couldn't resist what was right in front of her, wanton, sexy, desiring her just as much. Their lips moved against each other. Morgan's hand touching Fiona's waist as she brought her in closer until Fiona was nearly on top of her on the couch.

Leaning into the couch, Morgan groaned under the weight of Fiona's body, the heat from her skin, the pressure of Fiona's breasts against hers. Morgan held tight, her hand tangled in Fiona's hair as her other hand skimmed up Fiona's back and then down, toying with the edge of her shirt and debating whether or not she wanted to reach up and touch the heat of her bare flesh—something they had yet to do.

Fiona's tongue pressed between her lips, and Morgan's hips bucked up. Every nerve in her body hummed. She wanted more, so much more, but she knew she was going to have to stop them before they went too far, but she couldn't. She wasn't ready for it, Fiona might be, but she wasn't.

Twisting, Morgan pushed Fiona until she was underneath. Their hips pressed into each other, and Morgan moved her mouth from Fiona's down her neck, nipping at the tops of her breasts through the thin cotton fabric of her T-shirt. Morgan didn't want to stop. As much as she did, she didn't. Conflicted, Morgan desperately tried to get a grip on herself, tried to rein her brain back into place where logic and reason would rule.

Moving back up, Morgan swirled her tongue in circles against the hot and salty skin right at the nape of Fiona's neck. Fiona's nails dug into Morgan's sides, and she was reminded, starkly, just how sore each of her muscles were. Kissing Fiona again, Morgan eased away and breathed heavily as she tried to center herself.

"I want a date," Fiona stated, her voice clear and firm.

"What?"

"A date. I want you to take me on a date."

"I—"

"You said you don't do relationships. You didn't say you didn't date."

"I date." Morgan swallowed. "I date a lot. I just...really? A date?"

"Yes." Fiona's fingers cupped both of Morgan's cheeks and drew her in for a kiss. "I want a date before we go any further, and I want you to be sure of what you want from this."

Stunned, Morgan nodded her agreement. "Okay."

"Good. We can set it up."

"Yeah." Morgan shifted to sit up straight. She glanced at the clock on the wall and knew she only had another twenty minutes before she'd have to leave to go meet with Pax. She'd set up the times like that on purpose. Running her hands through her hair, Morgan let out a breath. "Yeah, we can go on a date."

"Good." Fiona smiled and sat up, leaning into Morgan's side and pressing her lips to Morgan's cheek loudly with a satisfied smirk.

Fiona curved her hand around Morgan's cheek and drew her back in for a heated kiss, although it didn't last as long as the last one or have quite the same burn to it.

"When are we going out?"

"Huh?"

"When are we going out?" Fiona asked again.

"Uh...tomorrow? Neither one of us are cleared yet, so we both have the time."

"Good." Fiona kissed Morgan again. "I suppose you need to go talk to Pax."

"Yeah. I'm supposed to meet with him at Frankie's in twenty minutes."

Fiona hummed and kissed Morgan again. "I like kissing you."

That brought a smile to Morgan. "I will admit that I like kissing you as well."

"Just like you like me?"

Morgan tensed, remembering their conversation last December when Morgan had been flying back from Wyoming and capturing a serial killer. "Yes, just like I like you."

"Good." Fiona kissed Morgan again. "Now, you better get going before I take you to my bedroom and you're late meeting up with Pax, because I really think he needs his best friend, Morgan."

Tensing again, Morgan nodded. "We'll see. I'm still pissed."

"You need to look past your personal experiences and look at what he might be going through. It might surprise you."

"Like I said, we'll see."

With one last lingering kiss, Morgan found herself leaving Fiona behind with a date to figure out for the next day. She left Fiona's and went straight to the pizzeria. As soon as Morgan parked, she gave herself the same pep talk that she'd given before she'd walked up to Fiona's third floor apartment.

Frankie was behind the counter, but he didn't have his normal pep in him when he greeted her. Instead, he knocked his head toward Morgan's normal seat. "He's in there."

"That bad?" she asked.

"Probably worse than what you're thinking."

"Great." Morgan stepped around the side and toward the back booth that was her favorite. Pax had even saved her favorite spot to sit in. Siding into the booth, Morgan put her hands on the top of the table, knowing Frankie would bring her coffee and her standard order soon enough. She started, "Hey."

"Hey," Pax answered.

"Been awhile since we've talked."

He didn't dare look her in the eye. "Yeah."

"So talk, Pax. Tell me all about it."

"You know?"

Morgan sighed. "She didn't tell me, if that's what you're worried about. I figured it out. Though I wish you had talked to me before it even started."

Pax nodded. "Yeah. I probably should have."

"So tell me now. I've got the damn time." Chuckling, Morgan grabbed the coffee from Frankie as he brought it over and thanked him. Focusing on Pax, she took a sip of her coffee and stared him down. "Come on, Pax. Tell me what happened. You're not the cheating type."

"Apparently, I am."

"We'll figure it out. Promises."

"You're not going to request a new partner?"

"I've kept shit from you and you didn't. We can work through this."

Just her saying those words relieved him. Morgan sipped at her coffee and settled in for a long conversation. Surely they would be able to find some balance and trust again. A twenty-year partnership and friendship wasn't something she wanted to give up so cavalierly. Fiona had been right. They could and would work through it.

ABOUT THE AUTHOR

Adrian J. Smith has been publishing since 2013 but has been writing nearly her entire life. With a focus on women loving women fiction, AJ jumps genres from action-packed police procedurals to the seedier life of vampires and witches to sweet romances with a May-December twist. She loves writing and reading about women in the midst of the ordinariness of life. Two of her novels, *For by Grace* and *Memoir in the Making*, received honorable mentions with the Rainbow Awards.

AJ currently lives in Cheyenne, WY, although she moves often and has lived all over the United States. She loves to travel to different countries and places. She currently plays the roles of author, wife, and mother to two rambunctious toddlers, occasional handy-woman. Connect with her on Facebook, Twitter, or her blog.